THE TRIP IS ON HITCHCOCK—

and those along for the ride include:

—Poor Harvey Fenster, who is in for the shock of his life in *Dream of a Murder*.

—Neal Potter, who comes close to producing the perfect alibi, until Sheriff Denton discovers he was only spinning his wheels in *The Missing Miles*.

—Rita, who is all heart, until she loses her head in *An Estimate of Rita*.

—Karen Iser, who, to her eternal regret, trusted a corpse to lie down and stay dead in *The Case of the Helpless Man*.

—Bradley, who discovered that luck can be lethal in *The Noncomformist*.

BUT THE JOURNEY'S ONE-WAY IN...
A HEARSE OF A DIFFERENT COLOR

A HEARSE OF A DIFFERENT COLOR

ALFRED HITCHCOCK

A DELL BOOK

Published by
Dell Publishing Co., Inc.
1 Dag Hammarskjold Plaza
New York, New York 10017

Copyright © 1972 H. S. D. Publications, Inc.

DREAM OF A MURDER by C. B. Gilford. Copyright © 1965 by H. S. D. Publications, Inc. Reprinted by permission of the author and the author's agents, Scott Meredith Literary Agency, Inc.

THE MISSING MILES by Arthur Porges. Copyright © 1965 by H. S. D. Publications, Inc. Reprinted by permission of the author and the author's agents, Scott Meredith Literary Agency, Inc.

ADVENTURE OF THE HAUNTED LIBRARY by August Derleth. Copyright © 1963 by H. S. D. Publications, Inc. Reprinted by permission of the author and the author's agents, Scott Meredith Literary Agency, Inc.

AN ESTIMATE OF RITA by Ed Lacy. Copyright © 1961 by H. S. D. Publications, Inc. Reprinted by permission of the author's agent, Howard Moorepark.

THE FULL TREATMENT by Rog Phillips. Copyright © 1961 by H. S. D. Publications, Inc. Reprinted by permission of the author and the author's agents, Scott Meredith Literary Agency, Inc.

ANOTHER DAY, ANOTHER MURDER by Lawrence Treat. Copyright © 1961 by H. S. D. Publications, Inc. Reprinted by permission of the author and the author's agents, Scott Meredith Literary Agency, Inc.

THE LIVING DOLL by Richard O. Lewis. Copyright © 1967 by H. S. D. Publications, Inc. Reprinted by permission of the author and the author's agents, Scott Meredith Literary Agency, Inc.

THE FLAT MALE by Frank Sisk. Copyright © 1965 by H. S. D. Publications, Inc. Reprinted by permission of the author and the author's agents, Scott Meredith Literary Agency, Inc.

CHAVISKI'S CHRISTMAS by Edwin P. Hicks. Copyright © 1969 by H. S. D. Publications, Inc. Reprinted by permission of the author and the author's agent, Scott Meredith Literary Agency, Inc.

THE CASE OF THE HELPLESS MAN by Douglas Farr. Copyright © 1960 by H. S. D. Publications, Inc. Reprinted by permission of the author and the author's agents, Scott Meredith Literary Agency, Inc.

FAT JOW AND THE SUNG TUSK by Robert Alan Blair. Copyright © 1970 by H. S. D. Publications, Inc. Reprinted by permission of the author and the author's agents, Scott Meredith Literary Agency, Inc.

ECHO OF A SAVAGE by Robert Edmond Alter. Copyright © 1964 by H. S. D. Publications, Inc. Reprinted by permission of Larry Sternig Agency and Scott Meredith Literary Agency, Inc.

THE NONCONFORMIST by William R. Coons. Copyright © 1961 by H. S. D. Publications, Inc. Reprinted by permission of the author and the author's agent, Scott Meredith Literary Agency, Inc.

THE SAPPHIRE THAT DISAPPEARED by James Holding. Copyright © 1961 by H. S. D. Publications, Inc. Reprinted by permission of the author and the author's agents, Scott Meredith Literary Agency, Inc.

All rights reserved. No part of this book may be reproduced in any form or by any means without the prior written permission of the Publisher, excepting brief quotes used in connection with reviews written specifically for inclusion in a magazine or newspaper.
Dell ® TM 681510, Dell Publishing Co., Inc.

ISBN: 0-440-13550-8

Printed in the United States of America
Previous Dell editions:
First printing—November 1972
Second printing—December 1974
New Dell edition:
First printing—August 1980

CONTENTS

Introduction by Alfred Hitchcock 8

Dream of a Murder by C. B. Gilford 11

The Missing Miles by Arthur Porges 22

Adventure of the Haunted Library
by August Derleth (novelette) 36

An Estimate of Rita by Ed Lacy 59

The Full Treatment by Rog Phillips 67

Another Day, Another Murder by Lawrence Treat 82

The Living Doll by Richard O. Lewis 98

The Flat Male by Frank Sisk 112

Chaviski's Christmas by Edwin P. Hicks 122

The Case of the Helpless Man by Douglas Farr 139

Fat Jow and the Sung Tusk by Robert Alan Blair (novelette) 151

Echo of a Savage by Robert Edmond Alter 176

The Nonconformist by William R. Coons 189

The Sapphire That Disappeared by James Holding 195

INTRODUCTION

A state of honor exists between myself and thieves, and contrary to what many people believe about no honor among thieves, it is my firm conviction that there is definitely honor among thieves. These statements are not uttered lightly nor without good cause.

At the risk of sounding immodest, may I also say that many of these miscreants know of my reputation as an authority on crime. As a result thieves are often eager to disclose their exploits in glowing boastful terms, trusting me to remain silent, and since I consider their trust a privilege, it is what I've always done.

This brings to mind a man I shall hereinafter refer to as Louis D. Obviously the name is false. However, I can assure you that if his true identity were revealed, you would recognize him immediately.

Several weeks ago Louis D. called and said in a mysterious tone that he had something to show me that would blow my mind and would also knock me flat on my back.

The thought of either prospect wasn't appealing. Having my mind blown conjured up a mental picture of an airhose placed against my right ear, or possibly the left, depending upon which direction I was facing, of course, and then having a blast of air eject my brain from my head. Equally uninviting was getting knocked flat on my back, which suggested a bout with the flu or being struck sharply by an irate pugilist.

When I asked him what it was, he declined to tell me and insisted that I had to see it.

I refused, explaining that I was having a terribly busy

evening. However, he persisted, saying, "Come on, willya, if I say you'll like it, you'll like it. You'll flip when you see what it is. I'm sending a guy down with transportation for you." Confronted with his bubbling enthusiasm and my own curiosity, I accepted.

Louis D. suggested that I walk east after I left my building and the man who was going to pick me up would identify himself.

"Why the intrigue?" I asked.

"Look, do I ask you how you do business?" Louis D. countered.

Faced with this irrefutable logic, I left immediately. Outside I hadn't walked for long when a closed van pulled over to the curb and an ominous chap behind the wheel said, "All right, Hitchcock, let's go."

I hadn't expected to be driven in a truck and to add insult to injury the driver insisted that I ride in back. "For what reason, my good man?" I asked.

"So you can't see where you're going, my good man," he replied. "Anybody goes out to see the boss has got to ride in back. It's a rule he's got."

We drove for an hour on good roads and then I was bounced violently for fifteen minutes over roads or fields so rutted they threatened to break the truck's springs. In the middle of the night I stepped from the van onto a moonlit field and walked to a dark ominous farmhouse.

Inside Louis D. in a finely tailored suit and with a Scotch in one hand, greeted me and shook my hand warmly. He apologized for the mode of travel and told me that only last week his wife of twenty-five years had come out to see him and she had also traveled in the same manner. "Anybody who comes out to see me doesn't know where he is going or where he's been. It's a rule I follow that helps keep me alive."

His explanation left something to be explained. I said, "But what about the driver?"

Louis D. smiled thinly. "I don't worry about him. I know things about him. If anything happens to me, certain information finds its way to the D.A. and he's sent up for three hundred and fifty-six years."

He led me to a darkened room and switched on the lights. With a kingly flourish Louis D. asked, "Well, what do you think?"

There on the walls were paintings by Claude Monet, Degas, Georges Rouault, Paul Cézanne, Soutine, Picasso, and Dufy.

"Originals, of course," I said.

"Would I have copies?" Louis D. asked scornfully. "What do you think of them?"

"Beautiful," I replied, as indeed they were. I spent the next fifteen minutes viewing an exhibition that was truly extraordinary. I assumed that the paintings were stolen and knowing Louis D. and his reputation, this was the part that surprised me. I was sure he knew that when an important art theft occurs, all major law enforcement agencies are notified through Interpol, which distributes photographs of the stolen paintings. It makes disposal of the paintings extremely difficult. Nevertheless, I was certain that Louis D. had stolen the paintings because of the overwhelming motive of money. When I asked him what he was going to do with the paintings, he regarded me uncomprehendingly for a moment. Then he said, "I do what I always do. I look at them, I admire them, and I get pleasure from them. Don't laugh, I've got a consuming passion for art."

Truly these were the sentiments of knowing collectors.

He then announced with a playful glint in his eye that he had heisted the entire collection from the thief who had stolen them for profit in the first place.

I was immediately reassured and heartened when Louis D. informed me that he fully intended to have the collection returned on his death, proving once and for all that there is honor among thieves.

Fortunately, those of you who are Hitchcock cognoscenti won't have to await a demise to enjoy the treasures this book holds.

ALFRED HITCHCOCK

DREAM OF A MURDER
C. B. Gilford

Harvey Fenster had committed murder, plain and simple. The crime hadn't been detected. His wife, Beryl, was dead and in the ground, and they'd called it an accident. The police weren't bothering him. Nobody blamed him. In fact, what few acquaintances he had sympathized with him. Poor old Harvey. An accident. And now he was all alone. Plain and simple. That was the kind of murder it had been. And that was why it had succeeded.

The only trouble was, Harvey Fenster dreamed.

The first dream started with the murder. It was so clear, so detailed, and so accurate, that it was just like committing the crime all over again. Once had been bad enough.

"Harvey, I've just got to have a new washing machine." It was a whine of complaint, like everything she said.

He let his newspaper fall to his lap and glanced up at his wife. She was standing there, wringing her hands as usual, her pale face sad, wisps of gray hair falling over her forehead; scarcely forty and already looking like an old woman.

"What's the matter with the washing machine?" he asked her, and he didn't try to make the question sound friendly.

"Take a look at it, will you, Harvey? I got another shock from it today. Honestly, I'm going to be electrocuted some time for sure."

He went down to the basement unwillingly. The washing machine loomed out of the dim light, high and huge, like an old Model T. There were more places where the paint had chipped off, he noticed. Obviously Beryl hadn't taken proper care of it. He squatted down to take a preliminary look and he saw what the trouble was right away. The wire was worn, just where it went under the machine to the motor. The insulation had dried and cracked, that was all.

What should he do? Replace the cord? No, just some electrician's tape. He went to the tool chest and rummaged around. No tape. He remembered now. He'd asked for some at the hardware store, and when the clerk told him it cost seventy-nine cents for that skimpy little roll, he'd refused to buy it and walked out. He wondered now if it were worth even seventy-nine cents to keep Beryl from getting electrocuted.

And then he knew the answer to that question.

She was only an expense. If he tried to divorce her, he'd have to pay alimony. And he was tired of the nagging, the complaints: fix this, buy me that, this is so old, that's worn out. He wanted silence, blessed silence.

His preparations for murder were simple and straightforward. The machine was unplugged, so he could work with the wire in safety. He bent it back and forth dozens of times at the place of wear, then scraped it patiently on the bottom rim of the machine, till the copper strands gleamed bright and bare. Then he wedged it up under the rim so that the wire would be in contact with the metal of the machine itself. Finally he plugged it in. Now the whole washer was "hot," waiting. Last of all, he doused water on the concrete floor. The "ground" was waiting too.

Near the bottom of the steps was the pair of old shoes his wife always wore while washing in the basement where she might get her feet wet. He picked up the shoes, examined the soles. Both, he saw, were almost worn through. Calmly, carefully, he dug at the thin, crumbling leather with a fingernail. He kept at it till there was a clear hole the size of a nickel.

After that, it was only a matter of getting her downstairs to try the machine. She was difficult, as she often was.

"I think I've fixed it and I want you to try it," he called up to her.

"I wasn't planning to do a washing tonight. . . ."

"Well, I want you to try it anyway. If it doesn't act right, then we'll think about replacing it."

The promise, vague as it was, lured her. She came obediently down the stairs. Her legs, he noted, were bare. Automatically she changed into her work shoes. With her mind on the washing machine, she seemed unaware that the skin of the sole of her foot was in direct contact with the floor. At least, she didn't wince.

"How'd everything get so wet?" she asked him.

"I was testing," he assured her.

He knew his plan wasn't a certain thing. Electrical shorts are tricky, unpredictable. She mightn't be killed, only injured, or possibly not harmed at all. But he felt lucky, somehow, and about time!

He watched her. She approached the machine gingerly, as if doubtful or even afraid. Her feet were in the film of water that clung to the floor around the drain. She reached out to touch the machine with both hands, like a child exploring a new toy. He waited in an agony of suspense, the moment elongating into a near eternity.

And then her hands were gripping the rim of the metal tub, gripping it and could not let go. Shudders and spasms racked her body. What sounds did he hear? Did he actually hear the crackling of the electric current? And what sounds came from Beryl? A scream or a moan? Or did she make any sound at all? Was it his own voice instead, uttering an inarticulate cry of triumph? On and on. . . .

Until another sound interrupted it, louder and more insistent, a buzz like a terribly swift jackhammer, clamoring right in his ear. He reached out a hand, partially to ward off this sound, partially to stifle it. Finally, he did the latter. His groping hand found the alarm clock on the bedside table, his numb fingers reached the button and pressed it.

By that time he was fully awake, wide-eyed and shaking and sweating, with the clock in his lap, pulled to the full length of its cord. Tremblingly he replaced the thing on the table, then wiped his perspiring face with a pajama sleeve.

But it was a time before he fully recovered from the experience. Afraid of getting a chill, he burrowed back under the blanket, and stayed there until his quivering body was still. This was the way he had reacted when he saw Beryl die, he remembered now. His body had jerked and shuddered just as hers had, the two almost in tune.

It had been only a dream, hadn't it? But how could a dream of a murder, real as it might have seemed, affect him more deeply than the actual murder itself? Anyway, the thing was over with now. Done. Finished. He was safe again in the waking world. He smiled.

Harvey Fenster's day was busy, ordinary, untroubled, work-filled. In the evening he watched television, which was more pleasurable now that he didn't have to argue with Beryl over the selection of programs, and went, at last, to bed.

He wasn't expecting to dream.

But it happened. A dream. . . .

"Harvey, I've just got to have a new washing machine" . . . till Beryl's body shuddered in the grip of the electric current. Her cry—or his.

What then? Yes, he had gone upstairs. And he was going now. In a voice broken by grief and terror, he called a doctor, an ambulance, and the police.

The last arrived first, two uniformed officers in a patrol car who acted with the efficiency and compassion of men who had seen things like this happen before. It was one of them who told him that his wife was dead.

The policemen handled everything. Harvey stood dumbly by the front door and watched the sheeted corpse being carried out on a stretcher. He answered a few questions automatically, stunned.

In all the time between the death and the funeral, the only one who seemed unkind was a plainclothes police officer named Godney. Joe Godney had a sharp face, thick brows, and under them, black piercing eyes.

Godney hinted that Harvey Fenster should have known about the condition of the washing machine, and Harvey kept answering that he certainly would have attended to it had Beryl ever mentioned the matter. Then an accusation finally came out in words. "You know, Mr. Fenster, I'd call it almost criminal negligence on your part."

He didn't crack. He didn't even start guiltily. "Don't you think I haven't thought about it myself? Don't you think I've blamed myself? That washer was pretty old. I should have checked it over once in a while. But it never gave any trouble...."

"Okay. Okay, Mr. Fenster. I'm not trying to make a case out of it." Godney's face looked very sharp, honed like an axeblade, his eyes glittered malevolently, and he added a strange remark. "Not that I wouldn't like to."

What was ringing? The phone? Or the doorbell? Harvey tried to rise from his chair, anything to escape from Godney's accusing stare. His hands reached, to clutch something to help him....

And he was wrestling with the alarm clock again, pulling at it, almost pulling it out of the wall. But now, as he awakened, he knew enough to press the button to shut off that persistent ringing.

Shaking in every extremity, sweating profusely, he sought refuge like an animal in its lair and dove under the blankets. But in the warm dark it was a long time before the shaking stopped and his sweat dried.

"Criminal negligence." What was it anyway? Maybe something you accuse a homicidal driver of, or maybe a doctor who was careless during an operation. But him, Harvey Fenster, for harboring a beat-up washing machine? He laughed.

But at the bank that day, he made a mistake that took him hours to locate. And in the evening he watched television grimly, until the last late-late show was finished, until the final weather report, until the screen went blank. Then he stared at the blankness for a while.

He succumbed finally, however. Weariness forced his

surrender. He staggered into bed, letting his eyes close, hoping he wouldn't dream.

"Harvey, I've just got to have a new washing machine. . . . Your wife is dead, Mr. Fenster. . . . Criminal negligence. . . . I'm not trying to make a case . . . not that I wouldn't like to."

A knock at the door. It had happened before. . . . A dream? He didn't know who was knocking. Too late to run. The house was surrounded.

"Hello, Mr. Fenster. Sit down, Mr. Fenster." Godney smiled when he opened the door. Two other plainclothesmen came in and disappeared somewhere on mysterious errands. Harvey sat down, but he sat on the edge of his chair, fearfully. Godney sat in Harvey's easy chair, made himself comfortable, and took a long time in lighting a curved-stem pipe.

"I've just remembered something, Mr. Fenster, a circumstance of your wife's death. I know the memory is accurate because I checked with several other people who were on the scene. It's been bothering me all this time, but just today it started to make sense. A funny thing. Very funny."

"What's funny? What. . . ."

"When we found your wife, the cement floor of the basement was all wet. Do you know what was funny about that? Just this. Your wife hadn't been in the middle of doing a washing. No wet clothes. The inside of the tub wasn't wet either. Only one thing was wet. The floor."

Why hadn't he thought of that?

"Can you explain that, Mr. Fenster?"

He tried to speak, but had no voice. But even if he had, what was he to say?

One of the other plainclothesmen entered from the bedroom. He was carrying Beryl's old shoe, and he handed it to Godney.

"I remember looking at your wife's corpse," Godney went on. "On the sole of her right foot there was a deep burn, about the size of a nickel. Yes, this was the shoe she'd been wearing." Godney turned the shoe over and was staring at the bottom of it. The hole was there, about the size of a nickel. "A very curious hole this. Looks like it's been picked at. Looks like somebody was trying to enlarge it. This hole was manufactured, Mr. Fenster. It's perfectly obvious."

Harvey mouthed words, silent, voiceless, futile words.

Godney tossed the shoe to the man who'd brought it in. "Label that 'Exhibit A.'"

Now the second plainclothesman appeared, coming from the basement. "I've checked the washing machine, Joe."

"And what did you find?"

"Fenster's fingerprints all over it."

Godney chewed happily at his pipe stem.

"Not only that, but Fenster's prints are on the frayed wire too."

"Yes? Yes? Yes!"

"And there's been some funny business with that wire, Joe."

"I think that should be enough," Godney said. "More than enough. Label that washing machine 'Exhibit B.' What do you say now, Mr. Fenster? Ready to confess?"

"No!" His own scream burst inside his skull. Did anyone else hear it?

Harvey leaped out of the chair and tried to run. But quickly strong arms seized him from either side. The front door opened, uniformed cops flooded in. A great mass of hostile bodies bore him to the floor by their very weight.

He reached out, groping, searching. He had it, wrestling with it in his bed as if it were a live thing, until his eyes were fully open and he realized, with a vast sense of relief, that he was awake again. He was awake and the clock was ringing. Fumbling, he found the button, pressed it.

But he didn't let go of the clock. This little box was his savior. Its cord going into the wall was his lifeline. He cuddled the little clock like he would an infant. And he waited there, fondling it, waiting for the awful fear to subside a little, for reality, the undream world, to establish itself once again.

What a frightening difference between this dream and those preceding it! The first two dreams had repeated events which had actually occurred. But this last dream was a fiction, an imagining. These things hadn't happened.

Godney hadn't connected the wet floor with the lack of wet clothes yet, but he might think of it in the future. If he did, he might come to look at the shoe and the washing machine. Warning . . . Well, I'll do something about that!

Gleefully he hopped out of bed, replaced the alarm clock, got dressed quickly, ran down the basement stairs. Yes, there were the shoes.

It wasn't until then that he realized how fortunate he was. The shoes hadn't been carted away with the body. They had somehow dropped off, and then just lain here. He stuffed them into his pockets.

The washing machine wasn't so easily handled. Wrestling it into the car trunk took a lot of doing, for Harvey wasn't a big man. But he managed it because he had to. The trunk lid closed down far enough to conceal the contents, and he tied the lid handle to the bumper. Then he backed the car out and started driving.

He knew of only one sure place, the old quarry beyond town. The pit had filled with water, which people said was thirty or forty feet deep. Harvey drove there and found the place abandoned. No one witnessed his strange actions, he was certain, as he lifted the machine out of the car trunk and pushed it over the cliff. It made a tremendous splash and sank reassuringly. He tossed the shoes in after it.

He was late in arriving at the bank that morning, but nobody questioned him. He worked so cheerfully and diligently that day he didn't fall behind in his job.

He was cheerful because he felt safe. All day.

"Harvey, I've just got to have a new washing machine." Her face, Beryl's face, leering accusingly down at him; her voice, not whining, but shrieking vindictively. . . .

"I'm innocent!" he shrieked in return.

But the white-haired judge, Lieutenant Godney in black robes, only sneered down at him from his high bench. And the twelve stern men in the jury box shook their heads in disbelief.

"Was this your wife's shoe?"

The lawyer—he was Godney too—shoved the incriminating object in front of his face. Attached to it was a large tag, "Exhibit A." There was no sole to the shoe at all, no sole and no heel.

And then came the washing machine, carried into the courtroom by two men wearing diving helmets. The machine was rusted and still dripping with weeds and slime. Affixed to it was a clean, fresh tag saying, "Exhibit B."

"Mr. Fenster," Godney said, "your fingerprints were all over it, and on the wire where the insulation was scraped off."

"Impossible!" he shouted at them all. "This is a frameup!"

But the twelve men didn't listen. Like a chorus they stood up together, and like a chorus, speaking with one voice, they announced their verdict, "Guilty!"

The judge beckoned Harvey to the bench. He hadn't the strength to move, but the police dragged him, inert, like a gunnysack of straw. Judge Godney extended a long arm, and the forefinger wagged in Harvey's face. "I sentence you . . . to death . . . in the electric chair. . . ."

But there was a bell somewhere, very distant, ringing, weakly, forlornly. Harvey reached for it . . . the alarm clock . . . more with his desperate mind than with his helpless body; he leaped. . . .

. . . And got it. Somehow . . . a little metal cube with rounded edges that had an insistent buzz inside it.

"I love you . . . I love you. . . ." He was saying it to the clock, and covering the cold metal with wet grateful kisses. And he didn't want to press the button to silence the thing. The sound was too precious, too beautiful, too reassuring.

The bell will wear out! No . . . no. . . . Reluctantly, almost fearfully, he did, at last, press the button . . . and then trembled in the dreadful silence that followed.

A dream, that's all it was, Harvey Fenster, you imbecile, you idiot. Don't you know the difference between waking and sleeping? Between dreams and reality? This is the real world, the real thing, right now, right here. You're in bed, alone. Beryl's dead, but they didn't find you out. They didn't, really. The shoes are gone and the washing machine is gone, just like Beryl, gone. They can't come back. . . .

The electric chair! Now they were going to get even with him and kill him with electricity.

Who was going to do that? Who was they? The police? The police couldn't touch him. No evidence. The shoe, the washing machine, the fingerprints. . . . And they'd convicted him! They were going to send him to the electric chair! Would their electric chair be real?

It would only seem real. After all, it was a dream. . . .

Which was the dream?

He didn't know!

"Harvey, I've just got to have a new washing machine."

He looked around for somewhere to run. Anywhere to escape that shrill, nagging voice.

"Harvey, I've just got to have a new washing machine."

When he tried to run, he was stopped by the bars. No, not bars—cords, electric cords—a maze of electric cords enclosing him like a fly in a spiderweb.

"Take it easy, fella, you don't have very long to wait now."

"Let me out!"

"There's only one way out of here, fella. For you, that is. Through that door. Just five more minutes. Can't you wait? What's your hurry? Why can't you wait?"

They came for him. Two huge guards. He screamed and cringed into the farthest corner. But they dragged him out of it, yelling and writhing. The door opened, and it was a basement door, the door to his own basement. And there was the chair . . . somehow like a chair . . .

but really . . . a washing machine!

"No!"

"Relax, fella. That's all you have to do. The electricity will do the rest. As long as you stand in this water on the floor. . . ."

"I'm innocent!"

"Strap too tight, fella? It's just to keep you here till the juice comes on. Don't worry about it. It doesn't last too long."

"Beryl," he shrieked, "does it last long?"

But she didn't answer. She was already dead. Dead and gone.

"Left arm okay. Now let's have the other arm."

No, don't give them that other arm. Reach out! Reach hard! Reach far!

"Come on, fella. . . . Boy, that right arm of his is strong. What's he trying to reach for? What's he trying to hang onto? Trying to pull the cord out of the wall? Come on, fella, give up."

"No! No! Give me my alarm clock!"

"Give it to him, boys."

It's just a dream. That's all it is—a dream. This is my alarm clock, my own. . . .

Lieutenant Joe Godney looked down at the twisted, contorted body, and then stooped to untangle it. From the very middle of the tightly wrapped ball, and after prying away the rigid grip of the fingers, he drew an electric alarm clock. While the others looked on, he patiently examined the thing.

"Worn wire right at the terminal," he explained, showing them.

"Looks as if," said another plainclothesman, "he didn't let go as you ought to when you get a shock. He was holding on for dear life. You wouldn't call it suicide, would you, Joe?"

"Accidental death," was the judgment of Godney.

THE MISSING MILES
Arthur Porges

Sidney Pine was just settling down to a frugal lunch in his secluded weekend cabin before trying his luck with the fish, when to his surprise his partner, Neal Potter, appeared at the door.

"What the devil are you doing here?" Pine asked gruffly. Their relationship had always been a cool one, and for many months they had been quarreling bitterly, so that now it was a case of intense mutual detestation. The cause of their present battle, one of several in recent years, was Pine's desire to sell the business and retire. He was only fifty-eight, but not too well. Being a bachelor, he could easily live on his half of the proceeds. Golden State Electronics, a big outfit, had made them a reasonable offer; at least, Pine thought so, and since he held a slight edge in stock, he could have his way.

Potter was against the whole idea. He felt that the components they were beginning to make could send their profits zooming in the next few years. He was too young to retire, but too old for a fresh start. Golden State had made it clear they were not interested in keeping him on in any executive capacity. Any day now Pine would stop listening to his partner's objections, and accept the offer. The only reason he hadn't done so already, Potter knew, was that by pointing to him as an obstacle, Pine hoped to squeeze a little more out of the buyer.

"I drove thirty miles to see you," Potter said in answer to Pine's rasping question. "That's sixty miles round trip; ninety minutes on these roads."

"What's that supposed to mean?" Pine growled, gulping

some coffee. He didn't offer Potter any. "That you came all this way out of love for me? I should live so long!"

"Matter of business," Neal said, his heart beginning to race. "Got something you'd better see—a new patent that infringes on our top seller."

"Wha-a-t!" Pine exclaimed. "Lemme see that. Give it to me."

Potter spread a paper on the table; Pine bent his head down for a look, and then the bigger man, putting his muscular right shoulder into the blow, struck his partner on the back of the neck with his clubbed fist. Pine collapsed over the plates of food, grotesquely smearing his face. He was out cold.

Potter looked at his watch: ten-forty. Had to keep a tight schedule; that was vital if he were to get away with this. Now came the messy part; too bad the punch hadn't been fatal, but it wasn't so easy to kill a man with one blow of your fist, no matter what the fiction writers dished out on the subject.

He got Pine's pillow from the bunk, returned to the table, raised the smaller man's soiled face, and clamped the soft cushion over nose and mouth. When he removed it, minutes later, Pine was unmistakably dead. It was now ten forty-five.

The next step was to waste time; the job done here had to be the sort that would take any man at least fifty minutes. Potter set about wrecking the cabin; he worked hard and fast, but kept at it for fifty-three minutes. He was big and strong; the dumbest cop would know that this job had taken a man nearly an hour. And it was now eleven thirty-eight.

Potter went back to his car parked a few yards from the cabin and started back to his "zero point." Thirty miles to go, and then the next phase. Pine was dead; according to their partnership papers, the business would now be completely Potter's. Besides doubling his wealth, he was now free to carry on without selling. That is, he told himself grimly, if I get away with this small matter of a cold-blooded murder.

THE MISSING MILES

Back at his zero point, where he had ostensibly stopped to do some photography, Potter made a last mental check before beginning an irreversible sequence that was supposed to end up with his proved innocence of any crime, but that might, if he bungled, end up with him in the gas chamber.

He looked at the mileage meter. When he'd picked the car up at the agency at ten in the morning, after its thousand-mile check, the meter had shown exactly 1048; now it had increased to 1112, showing that he had gone sixty-four miles since then. It was a figure that could kill him. He had made sure the mechanics had noted the morning's reading. All the cops would need was a peek at the gauge now. It was a sixty-mile round trip to the murdered man's cabin: your car shows just such a trip; you had a motive; ergo, come along with us to the Death House.

Well, it wasn't going to be like that; he would fox them good.

Potter got out, crawled under the car, and with a suitable wrench drained all the oil from the crankcase into an old can brought for that purpose. He carried the oil several hundred feet away, and poured it into an old brushy gully. He covered the pool with dirt and leaves, and returned to the car. Then he started the engine, and with the gears in neutral, gave it plenty of gas for about ten minutes, at which time, naturally, the abused mechanism, with a shriek of overstressed dry metal, froze tightly. Nobody could say he'd driven another foot in this car.

Now came a critical step, the first of two. Potter hung a rag carelessly over the dashboard until it covered the mileage gauge. This was tricky, but even the most nosy cop would have no reason—now—to examine the reading. And a cop there must be: one of those nice cleancut highway patrol boys to act as his witness and alibi.

Potter went half a mile to the highway and after fifteen minutes flagged down a cruiser. The patrolman wasn't young, but he was vigorous and alert, which was all that mattered.

"My car's conked out," Potter told him apologetically. "I don't know a thing about motors. D'you suppose you could have a look?"

He knew how to make a pitch: just the right amount of helpless pleading without appearing too sissy about it. The cop was willing, if not exactly enthusiastic. He made a cryptic report over his radio, left the car, and followed Potter to the scene. It took him only thirty seconds to diagnose the obvious.

"This engine's froze solid," he said in disgust. "You've been driving without oil. How come?"

When Potter looked blank, the officer, pursing his lips, moved gingerly under the car, careful of his immaculate uniform. "Drain plugs out," he called. "No wonder she froze."

"Those jokers at the agency," Potter said. "They must've forgot to tighten it."

The patrolman stood up, brushed himself, and said, "You're not going anywhere in that baby, I'll guarantee you that. Want a lift to town?"

Potter shook his head. "I'd just as soon stay here and do some photography as I planned. But if you'll call the Ace-High Garage and tell 'em that Mr. Potter's out here and wants a tow, I'd be much obliged."

"Suit yourself," the officer said brusquely. "It'll take a couple of hours, I'd say."

"Well, it's only twelve-eighteen—or is my watch out, too?"

The patrolman looked at his own.

"That's right," he said. "Twelve eighteen, about."

Potter could have hugged himself. No interest in the mileage gauge and the time firmly fixed; things were going like clockwork.

The officer left. It would be at least ninety minutes before Sam Corrigan came with the towtruck. That was the second critical period. This was a good spot; it was a million to one against anybody seeing him at his shenanigans. Just give him about sixty or seventy minutes alone, and after that the cops could grill him brown; he'd be in the clear. Potter unlocked the trunk and got busy.

Ordinarily, Sheriff Pete Denton spoke very little, but was in no way unfriendly, allowing his eyes and warm smile to communicate his obvious good will. But when he was working on a difficult case, the sheriff became oddly garrulous, using one of his two deputies as a sounding board for one fleeting notion after another. If neither deputy was available, Denton was not above talking to a comic figurine he kept hidden at the back of a file drawer.

At present, however, both deputies were on hand, and, by command of their boss, all ears. Not that they minded; even if they did all the legwork, it was Denton's guidance and experience that so often led to cracking the case.

"As things look now," the sheriff was saying, "the best, and only, suspect seems to be in the clear."

"Seems, nothing," Bill Alvarez said. He was small, dark, good-looking, and cheerful, in contrast to Fred Hicks, blond and mournful of mien, not because he was actually gloomy, but merely because a melancholy expression is easy on the facial muscles and interesting to women.

"If ever a guy had a solid alibi, it's Potter," Alvarez continued. Even if he hadn't thought so, he knew it was his business to challenge anything Denton said. The old boy wanted it that way: it helped him to clear a path to the solution. "When he left the agency, he had ten hundred and forty-eight miles on the car; the garage vouches for that. All right; when picked up for questioning, the gauge showed a hundred and fifteen more—at least two hours' driving. We figure the killer had to spend almost an hour in Pine's cabin in order to tear up the place the way he did. So are you going to tell me that Potter drove over a hundred miles in about an hour—on our roads!"

"I agree with Bill," Hicks said. "Stirling Moss couldn't do it."

"You seem to forget," Denton said mildly. "Those gauges can be doctored."

"Not without leaving traces; this was practically a new car, and the gauge is sealed tight. Nobody messed with it.

I know cars and I stake my life on it. The garage backs me up."

"Suppose he jacked 'er up and ran the engine to add miles without moving the car at all?" the sheriff suggested.

Alvarez whistled softly. "Sa-ay—" he began, but Hicks interrupted him. He spotted the twinkle in Denton's eyes.

"Oh no you don't, Sheriff!" he said. "Foul—foul! It would take just as long that way as actually running on a road, or close enough, anyhow. When did Potter have the time?"

"Not so fast," Alvarez came back again. "What about after the highway patrol left, when Potter was doing his camera work and waiting for a tow. He jacked it up then, and this knocks out his alibi, right?"

"How about that, Fred?" Denton asked, smiling at Hicks.

For a moment the deputy looked blank, then he shook his head firmly.

"You forget, or think I do, that when the patrolman left, Potter's engine was done for: frozen solid. He could jack up the rear end all day, but he'd have no engine to spin the wheels."

"By hand?" Bill suggested halfheartedly.

"Come off it!" Hicks said. "Run off sixty miles by hand? Ever try turning the rear wheels of a big car, or any car, that way? Ten miles would ruin a football pro in good condition."

"Still," the sheriff said softly, "it comes to this. The only reason we can't nail Potter for the murder is a small matter of sixty miles on that gauge. On every other count he's our boy for sure. Motive, everything else is there."

"Sure," Hicks agreed. "But there's only one way to put mileage on the gauge—by running the car. He has the cop to prove that at twelve-eighteen, two hours and eighteen minutes after leaving the garage with ten hundred and forty-eight miles on the car, no more driving was possible. Since the gauge shows roughly one hundred and twenty more miles, Potter simply couldn't have had time to ransack the cabin and tear it up that way."

"You absolutely *sure* not by hand—in neutral, remember?" Alvarez persisted.

"Impossible," Hicks snapped. "He wasn't dirty and exhausted when the towtruck came, either. But let me try the sliderule." Looking rather sheepish, he took it out of his desk, along with a pencil and paper. "Let's see how many turns, okay? I'll simplify by calling the diameter of the tire two feet; all we need is an idea. Then the circumference is about—" he worked the slide rule quickly, "six point three feet. Turns per mile, five thousand two hundred eighty divided by six point three, about eight hundred and forty. For sixty miles, over fifty thousand." He grinned at them. "Can you see old Potter spinning those wheels fifty thousand times, and coming up looking fresh as a daisy?"

Alvarez groaned.

"He's got us, Sheriff."

"Got you," Denton said, his lips twitching. "I never said anything about how they were turned, now did I?"

"He had almost two hours before the truck came," Bill said.

"If he had six, it would still be one helluva job," Hicks replied. "His hands would be a mess; he'd be soaked in sweat. I just don't think you can turn heavy tires that many times by hand. You'd cramp up in no time, neutral or not. You'd have to keep pushing, even if they spun pretty well for each shove."

"Well," the sheriff said quietly, "if he didn't do it by hand, then he fooled us some other way. Better go over all the figures again, both of you. I'll do the same and we'll talk about it again tomorrow."

The next morning Sheriff Denton was in the full tide of his occasional garrulity. Seated across from his two deputies, feet on his desk, he talked in a seemingly aimless manner.

"Can we put Potter in that cabin?" he asked. "Sure we can, but it's his partner's, and both men were there before, so that's no help. If we could put him there the day of the killing, that would do it."

He crossed his ankles the other way, cleared his throat, and continued.

"Where does he claim he spent those two hours plus? Driving around looking for something to take pictures of, he says. We can't find anybody who saw him, though; but that's not much help either; it's a quiet section up there. And he's got pictures, but he could've taken those days before."

"Maybe we can tell they weren't taken that day, by the sun or something."

"If he took 'em that week, the difference'd be pretty slight," Alvarez pointed out, and Denton nodded agreement.

"Too tricky-technical," the sheriff said. "No jury's gonna convict a man just on that. If we had that, and more, lots more, then maybe."

"What if somebody else drove the car, while he did the killing?" Hicks asked.

"Not likely," the sheriff replied. "Potter's separated from his wife; has no kids. A man would need a mighty close friend to make him an accessory and put both of 'em in reach of the gas chamber. Remember, the other guy would have little to gain. Potter isn't likely to have that kind of friend. He's a pretty cold fish, I'd say."

"Another thing," Denton added. "Why was that cabin taken apart? Anybody would know a man doesn't take a lot of money to a weekend fishing cabin. What was the killer looking for? Any ideas?"

"Something to do with the business, some paper that incriminated Potter?" Alvarez suggested.

"Maybe. Maybe," the sheriff said moodily. "I think it was done to kill time, to show that Potter couldn't drive sixty miles more than the round trip to the cabin and do all that damage.

"And that frozen motor, such a good proof that he didn't jack up the car and spin the wheels while waiting for the towtruck; it's too durned handy. The garage doesn't like the idea that one of their men forgot to tighten the drainplug. They say that's an important thing even the greenest mechanic watches for. It ruins an engine completely; too expensive a goof to permit."

"You still think he turned those wheels himself," Hicks said. "How can I convince you?"

"I'm convinced it wasn't by hand; he'd have to do more than one turn a second for most of the two hours." He smiled his warmest, eyes twinkling. "I can figure a little, too." Then, more seriously, "You noticed that he lied to the highway patrol."

Both deputies looked doubtful and exchanged glances.

"He said he didn't know from beans about cars. Why? We see the man's technically trained, partner in an electronics manufacturing business. People at the garage say he knows more than most about engines; not like a pro mechanic, of course, but no dunderhead like he made out." He took his feet off the desk and, sighing, stretched them out to the edge of Alvarez's chair. "Circulation ain't what it used to be," he grumbled. "Once I could keep 'em up there all day." He paused, eyed each of them critically, and asked, "What about that dry engine? Doesn't that car have an oil pressure gauge?"

"It's a warning light," Hicks said. "Flickers when the pressure drops too far."

"Thought so," Denton said complacently. "And Potter just ignored it, a man with his background; drove right along until he messed up the engine. Well, if he did, it was deliberate."

"Why are you so all-fired certain he's guilty?" Alvarez asked, his face wooden.

"All too neat: car breaking down to give him an alibi; his fights with Pine about selling; all those lies. Pity the ground was baked so hard at the cabin; we might have got his tiretracks where he pulled off the highway."

"If he pulled off," Hicks said. Then, as Denton scowled at him, he added quickly, "Too bad yesterday's rain didn't come earlier."

"It'll be too bad if Potter does get away with this," the sheriff said. "And the way things are going, he will. Fred," he said briskly, "I want you to go to that spot where his car broke down. Make a thorough search."

"For what?"

"How would you make an engine freeze that way, right when and where you wanted it to?" Denton countered with another question.

"Drain out the oil and just run her dry for a spell."

"Right. And you'd dump the oil somewhere—not too close."

"Guess I would."

"And what about the plug? You'd claim it fell out, remember."

"Hmm," Hicks said thoughtfully. "I'd fling that into the brush; or maybe carry it home in my pocket, to hide later."

"It would be hard to find," the sheriff said. "But the oil—that's a chance. Be a couple quarts, maybe, and messy stuff. You look for it."

"Gonna be muddy out there."

"Too bad," Denton said with genuine sympathy. "But we can't overlook any bets, can we?"

"Guess *we* can't," was the reply, delivered dryly. "See you later." And Hicks sauntered out.

Alvarez squirmed in his seat, wondering what the old boy had in mind for him. Nothing good.

"Bill, you go out to Potter's place and snoop. Don't ask me what for, but just get a peek into his garage and his house, too; but nothing illegal, mind."

"Practically anything I do is illegal without a warrant; you know that."

"Sure, I know it," Denton said blandly, "but officially I don't know what you're going to do when you get there. My orders are to stay strictly within the law," he added, one eyelid drooping.

"I'm on the way," Alvarez said, grinning. "If they lift my badge, you can write me a letter of recommendation."

"Know just the words," the sheriff said pleasantly. "'This young man enjoys a good appetite and a good opinion of himself. Sincerely yours—'" They exchanged broader smiles, and Bill left.

Alone, Denton mused for a while, but to no effect.

Then, redfaced, he brought out the comic figurine and set it on the edge of his desk. "Hilda," he said gravely, "those boys are on the wildest goose chase since Widow Pointer's gander ate the grain with brandy spilled on it. But if one of 'em gets lucky, we might still nail this guy. Not that Pine was any great shakes, a sourball; but murder just isn't nice, is it, Hilda girl?"

He rambled on, rehashing the case, for almost an hour, but without any fresh insight. If Potter had made those wheels spin to add sixty miles to the gauge, his method was still too much for the sheriff and both deputies; and the knowledge rankled. Finally, his mind like a drained reservoir, Denton put the doll away and, feet on desk, dozed.

When Hicks returned several hours later, however, the old man was busy with paperwork, which he detested. The deputy was happy to see this; ordinarily the chore would have been his, but the sheriff was compensating for the mud.

"Well?" Denton asked without marked enthusiasm. He hadn't really hoped for anything.

"Got lucky," Hicks said, to his surprise. "He could have dumped that oil anywhere in ten scrubby acres full of nettles, but I spotted rainbow colors by a gully."

"Hah!" the sheriff said gustily.

"Hah is right; oilslick colors. Traced 'em back and found a pool of oil, or what was left of one after the rain washed through it."

"Without that rain, there wouldn't have been any colors in the open."

"Don't I know it? That's why I said 'lucky.' "

"Well," the sheriff said with satisfaction, "we can be pretty sure now that he did it, and damaged the car, but we still don't have enough for a jury."

"Unless Bill comes up with his own luck," Hicks said.

"Bill doesn't," Alvarez said from the doorway. "I didn't find anything suspicious at his house. Here's a list of what's there, and in the garage, too." He tossed his notebook to the sheriff.

"I'll plough through this," Denton said. "You boys might as well call it a day."

"I don't believe it!" Hicks said. "He's freeing us at four-fifty-two, a whole eight minutes early!"

"Let's get out of here," Alvarez said, "before he changes his mind."

With exaggerated haste, they went out on tiptoes. Chuckling, the sheriff began to study the notebook.

After fifteen minutes he came to an item that made him stiffen in his chair. Could this be the gimmick? Certainly there was a possibility in that appliance. But he'd have to know more about it. One of the deputies could get the information tomorrow. Potter wasn't likely to dispose of the thing; that would be a bad mistake. He'd just let it stand there so innocently in his garage. Almost every householder had one.

"Bill," Denton asked Alvarez the next morning, "what about this power mower in the garage? Gas or electric?"

"Gee, I'm not sure. Wait, it was gas: no cord."

"Hah!"

"Holy smoke!" Hicks exclaimed. "You don't think—?"

"Why not?" the sheriff asked. "He could have had it in the trunk. Now, don't the wheels of some such mowers turn along with the blades?"

"Sure, but much slower; they just amble over the grass, as fast as a man walks."

"Lazy generation," the old man said reprovingly. "I mowed a million acres as a kid, for about a dime a section!"

"Those wheels could be changed," Alvarez said. "Once you have a good gas engine, it isn't hard to fiddle with the gearing. And it isn't like asking for a lot of horsepower, just turning loose car wheels. The Boss could be right."

"Pick up that mower," Denton ordered them. "Go over it bolt by bolt and see if it's been fooled with. You know, the motor pulled out of the frame recently, or the gear ratios changed. Even if he put everything back, things will be scratched or loose or too bright." He peered owlishly at Hicks. "You get a sample of the oil out there?"

"Of course. You think I'm an idiot? Figured you'd want some."

"Only with women," the sheriff replied evenly. "Well, it can be matched with some from the car; there must be traces left, even after draining. No matter, I suppose, if it's burnt or gooey."

"With a spectroscope," Hicks said rather pompously, "you can match any damned thing to nine decimal places."

"And that oil wasn't on any road, I take it."

"Heck, no," the deputy assured him. "In a gully where not even a jeep or Land Rover could go."

"I still don't see how he did it," Alvarez muttered.

"Do you?" Denton asked Hicks.

"More or less. He'd jack up the car and use just friction—let the tire press against a mower wheel. He'd have the mower up on something; a simple wooden frame would do, with a wheel against the rubber tight enough to take hold. He'd have the mower geared up to turn faster; that wouldn't be hard. Or take power directly off the shaft, since the load would be very light once the car wheels got moving. Either method would work."

"If anybody came along, he'd be dead," Alvarez said darkly.

"He picked a safe spot," Hicks reminded him. "Pretty isolated; it wasn't much of a risk; not compared with the rest of the deal, anyhow."

"All right," the sheriff said. "I think we've got Mr. Potter. If you boys can show a court how that mower's engine can spin a car's wheels fifty thousand times in a couple of hours, and the oil matches, he won't be able to wriggle out."

"It was a mighty slick idea," Alvarez said. "Gotta give the guy credit."

Denton's feet were back on the desk. He closed his eyes. "You both know what to do," he said, yawning cavernously. "Get at it."

At the door, the two deputies looked back. The sheriff was breathing heavily.

"Asleep?" Alvarez murmured. "Or just faking?"

"How do I know?" Fred grinned. "Am I a detective?" They left.

ADVENTURE OF THE HAUNTED LIBRARY
August Derleth

When I opened the door of our lodgings one summer day during the third year of our joint tenancy of No. 7B Praed Street, I found my friend Solar Pons standing with one arm on the mantel, waiting with a thin edge of impatience upon either my arrival or that of someone else, and ready to go out, for his deerstalker lay close by.

"You're just in time, Parker," he said, "—if the inclination moves you—to join me in another of my little inquiries. This time, evidently, into the supernatural."

"The supernatural!" I exclaimed, depositing my bag.

"So it would seem." He pointed to a letter thrown carelessly upon the table.

I picked it up and was immediately aware of the fine quality of the paper and the embossed name: Mrs. Margaret Ashcroft. Her communication was brief.

> Dear Mr. Pons,
> I should be extremely obliged if you could see your way clear to call upon me sometime later today or tomorrow, at your convenience, to investigate a troublesome matter which hardly seems to be within the jurisdiction of the Metropolitan Police. I do believe the library is haunted. Mr. Carnacki says it is not, but I can hardly doubt the evidence of my own senses.

Her signature was followed by a Sydenham address.

"I've sent for a cab," said Pons.

"Who is Mr. Carnacki?" I asked.

"A self-styled psychic investigator. He lives in Chelsea and has had some considerable success, I am told."

"A charlatan!"

"If he were, he would hardly have turned down our client. What do you make of it, Parker? You know my methods."

I studied the letter which I still held, while Pons waited to hear how much I had learned from his spontaneous and frequent lectures in ratiocination. "If the quality of the paper is any indication, the lady is not without means," I said.

"Capital!"

"Unless she is an heiress, she is probably of middle age or over."

"Go on," urged Pons, smiling.

"She is upset because, though she begins well, she rapidly becomes very unclear."

"And provocative," said Pons. "Who could resist a ghost in a library, eh?"

"But what do you make of it?" I pressed him.

"Well, much the same as you," he said generously. "But I rather think the lady is not a young heiress. She would hardly be living in Sydenham if she were. No, I think we shall find that she recently acquired a house there and has not been in residence very long. Something is wrong with the library."

"Pons, you don't seriously think it's haunted?"

"Do you believe in ghosts, Parker?"

"Certainly not!"

"Do I detect the slightest hesitation in your answer?" He chuckled. "Ought we not to say, rather, we believe there are certain phenomena which science as yet has not correctly explained or interpreted?" He raised his head suddenly, listening. "I believe that is our cab drawing to the curb."

A moment later the sound of a horn from below verified Pons's deduction.

Pons clapped his deerstalker to his head and we were off.

38 ADVENTURE OF THE HAUNTED LIBRARY

Our client's house was built of brick, two and a half stories in height, with dormers on the gable floor. It was large and spreading and built on a knoll, partly into the slope of the earth, though it seemed at first glance to crown the rise there. It was plainly of late Victorian construction, and while it was not shabby, it just escaped looking quite genteel. Adjacent houses were not quite far enough away from it to give the lawn and garden the kind of spaciousness required to set the house off to its best advantage in a neighborhood which was slowly declining from its former status.

Our client received us in the library. Mrs. Ashcroft was a slender diminutive woman with flashing blue eyes and whitening hair. She wore an air of fixed determination which her smile at sight of Pons did not diminish.

"Mr. Pons, I was confident that you would come," she greeted us.

She acknowledged Pons's introduction of me courteously and went on, "This is the haunted room."

"Let us just hear your account of what has happened from the beginning, Mrs. Ashcroft," suggested Pons.

"Very well." She sat for a moment, trying to decide where to begin her narrative. "I suppose, Mr. Pons, it began about a month ago. Mrs. Jenkins, a housekeeper I had hired, was cleaning late in the library when she heard someone singing. It seemed to come, she said, 'from the books.' Something about a 'dead man.' It faded away. Two nights later she woke after a dream and went downstairs to get a sedative from the medicine cabinet. She heard something in the library. She thought perhaps I was indisposed and went to the library. But the library, of course, was dark. However, there was a shaft of moonlight in the room—it was bright outside, and therefore a kind of illumination was in the library, too—and in that shaft, Mr. Pons, Mrs. Jenkins believed she saw the bearded face of an old man that seemed to glare fiercely at her. It was only for a moment. Then Mrs. Jenkins found the switch and turned up the light. Of course, there was no one in the library but herself. It was enough for her; she was so sure that she had seen a ghost that next morning, after all the windows and doors were found locked and bolted, she gave notice. I was not entirely sorry to see them go—her husband worked as caretaker of the grounds—because I suspected Jenkins of taking food from the cellars and the refrigerator for their married daughter. That is not an uncommon problem with servants in England, I am told."

"I should have thought you a native, Mrs. Ashcroft," said Pons. "You've been in the Colonies?"

"Kenya, yes. But I was born here. It was for reasons of sentiment that I took this house. I should have taken a better location. But I was little more than a street waif in Sydenham as a child, and somehow the houses here represented the epitome of splendor. When the agent notified me that this one was to be let, I couldn't resist taking it. But the tables turned—the houses have come down in the world and I have come up, and there are so many things I miss—the hawkers and the carts, for which cars are no substitute, the rumble of the underground since the Nunhead-Crystal Palace Line has been discontinued, and all in all I fear my sentiments have led me to make an ill-advised choice. The ghost, of course, is only the crowning touch."

"You believe in him, then, Mrs. Ashcroft?"

"I've seen him, Mr. Pons." She spoke as matter-of-factly as if she were speaking of some casual natural phenomenon. "It was a week ago. I wasn't entirely satisfied that Mrs. Jenkins had not seen something. It could have been an hallucination. If she had started awake from a dream and fancied she saw something in their room, why, yes, I could easily have believed it a transitory hallucination, which might occur commonly enough after a dream. But Mrs. Jenkins had been awake enough to walk downstairs, take a sedative, and start back up when she heard something in the library. So the dream had had time enough in which to wear off. I am myself not easily frightened. My late husband and I lived in border country in Kenya, and some of the Kikuyu are unfriendly.

"Mr. Pons, I examined the library carefully. As you

see, shelving covers most of the walls. I had very few personal books to add—the rest were here. I bought the house fully furnished, as the former owner had died and there were no near heirs. That is, there was a brother, I understand, but he was in Rhodesia and had no intention of returning to England. He put the house up for sale, and my agents, Messrs. Harwell and Chamberlain, in Lordship Lane, secured it for me. The books are therefore the property of the former owner, a Mr. Howard Brensham, who appears to have been very widely read, for there are collections ranging from early British poetry to crime and detective fiction. But that is hardly pertinent. My own books occupy scarcely two shelves over there—all but a few are jacketed, as you see, Mr. Pons. Well, my examination of the library indicated that the position of these books as I had placed them had been altered. It seemed to me that they had been handled, perhaps even read. They are not of any great consequence—recent novels, some works by Monsieur Proust and Monsieur Mauriac in French editions, an account of Kenya, and the like. It was possible that one of the servants had become interested in them; I did not inquire. Nevertheless, I became very sensitive and alert about the library. One night last week—Thursday, I believe—while I lay reading, late, in my room, I distinctly heard a book or some such object fall in this room.

"I got out of bed, took my flashlight, and crept down the stairs in the dark. Mr. Pons, I sensed someone's or something's moving about below. I could feel the disturbance of the air at the foot of the stairs where something had passed. I went directly to the library and from the threshold of that door over there I turned my flashlight into the room and put on its light. Mr. Pons, I saw a horrifying thing. I saw the face of an old man, matted with beard, with wild unkempt hair raying outward from his head; it glared fiercely, menacingly at me. I admit that I faltered and fell back; the flashlight almost fell from my hands. Nevertheless, I summoned enough courage to snap on the overhead light. Mr. Pons—there was no one in the room beside myself. I stood in the doorway. No one had passed me. Yet, I swear it, I had seen precisely the same apparition that Mrs. Jenkins had described! It was there for one second—in the next it was gone—as if the very books had swallowed it up.

"Mr. Pons, I am not an imaginative woman, and I am not given to hallucinations. I saw what I had seen; there was no question of that. I went around at once to make certain that the windows and doors were locked; all were; nothing had been tampered with. I had seen something, and everything about it suggested a supernatural apparition. I applied to Mr. Harwell. He told me that Mr. Brensham had never made any reference to anything out of the ordinary about the house. He had personally known Mr. Brensham's old uncle, Captain Jason Brensham, from whom he had inherited the house, and the Captain had never once complained of the house. He admitted that it did not seem to be a matter for the regular police, and mentioned Mr. Carnacki as well as yourself. I'm sure you know Mr. Carnacki, whose forte is psychic investigation. He came—and as nearly as I can describe it, he *felt* the library and assured me that there were no supernatural forces at work here. So I applied to you, Mr. Pons, and I do hope you will lay the ghost for me."

Pons smiled almost benignly, which lent his handsome feral face a briefly gargoylesque expression. "My modest powers, I fear, do not permit me to feel the presence of the supernatural, but I must admit to some interest in your little problem," he said thoughtfully. "Let me ask you, on the occasion on which you saw the apparition— last Thursday—were you aware of anyone's breathing?"

"No, Mr. Pons. I don't believe ghosts are held to breathe."

"Ah, Mrs. Ashcroft, in such matters I must defer to your judgment—you appear to have seen a ghost; I have not seen one." His eyes danced. "Let us concentrate for a moment on its disappearance. Was it accompanied by any sound?"

Our client sat for a long moment in deep thought. "I

believe it was, Mr. Pons," she said at last. "Now that I think of it."

"Can you describe it?"

"As best I can recall, it was something like the sound a book dropped on the carpet might make."

"But there was no book on the floor when you turned the light on?"

"I do not remember that there was."

"Will you show me approximately where the specter stood when you saw it?"

She got up with alacrity, crossed to her right, and stood next to the shelving there. She was in a position almost directly across from the entrance to the library from the adjacent room; a light flashed on from the threshold would almost certainly strike the shelving there.

"You see, Mr. Pons—there isn't even a window in this wall through which someone could have escaped if it were unlocked."

"Yes, yes," said Pons with an absent air. "Some ghosts vanish without sound, we are told, and some in a thunderclap. And this one with the sound of a book dropped upon the carpet!" He sat for a few moments, eyes closed, his long tapering fingers tented before him, touching his chin occasionally. He opened his eyes again and asked, "Has anything in the house—other than your books—been disturbed, Mrs. Ashcroft?"

"If you mean my jewelry or the silver—no, Mr. Pons."

"A ghost with a taste for literature! There are indeed all things under the sun. The library has, of course, been cleaned since the visitation?"

"Every Saturday, Mr. Pons."

"Today is Thursday—a week since your experience. Has anything taken place since then, Mrs. Ashcroft?"

"Nothing, Mr. Pons."

"If you will excuse me," he said, coming to his feet, "I would like to examine the room."

Thereupon he began that process of intensive examination which never ceased to amaze and amuse me. He took the position that our client had just left to return to her chair, and stood, I guessed, fixing directions. He gazed at the high windows along the south wall; I concluded that he was estimating the angle of a shaft of moonlight and deducing that the ghost, as seen by Mrs. Jenkins, had been standing at or near the same place when it was observed. Having satisfied himself, he gave his attention to the floor, first squatting there, then coming to his knees and crawling about. Now and then he picked something off the carpet and put it into one of the tiny envelopes he habitually carried. He crept all along the east wall, went around the north, and circled the room in this fashion, while our client watched him with singular interest, saying nothing and making no attempt to conceal her astonishment. He finished at last, and got to his feet once more, rubbing his hands together.

"Pray tell me, Mrs. Ashcroft, can you supply a length of thread of a kind that is not too tensile, that will break readily?"

"What color, Mr. Pons?"

"Trust a lady to think of that!" he said, smiling. "Color is of no object, but if you offer a choice, I prefer black."

"I believe so. Wait here."

Our client rose and left the library.

"Are you expecting to catch a ghost with thread, Pons?" I asked.

"Say rather I expect to test a phenomenon."

"That is one of the simplest devices I have ever known you to use."

"Is it not?" he agreed, nodding. "I submit, however, that the simple is always preferable to the complex."

Mrs. Ashcroft returned, holding out a spool of black thread. "Will this do, Mr. Pons?"

Pons took it, unwound a little of thread, and pulled it apart readily. "Capital!" he answered. "This is adequately soft."

He walked swiftly over to the north wall, took a book off the third shelf, which was at slightly over two feet from the floor, and tied the thread around it. Then he restored the book to its place, setting it down carefully.

After he restored the book to its place, he walked away, unwinding the spool, until he reached the south wall, where he tautened the thread and tied the end around a book there. He now had an almost invisible thread that reached from north to south across the library at a distance of about six feet from the east wall, and within the line of the windows.

He returned the spool of thread to our client. "Now, then, can we be assured that no one will enter the library for a day or two? Perhaps the Saturday cleaning can be dispensed with?"

"Of course it can, Mr. Pons," said Mrs. Ashcroft, clearly mystified.

"Very well, Mrs. Ashcroft. I trust you will notify me at once if the thread is broken—or if any other untoward event occurs. In the meantime, there are a few little inquiries I want to make."

Our client bade us farewell with considerably more perplexity than she had displayed in her recital of the curious events which had befallen her.

Once outside, Pons looked at his watch. "I fancy we may just have time to catch Mr. Harwell at his office, which is just down Sydenham Hill and so within walking distance." He gazed at me, his eyes twinkling. "Coming, Parker?"

I fell into step at his side and for a few moments we walked in silence, Pons striding along with his long arms swinging loosely at his sides, his keen eye darting here and there, as if in perpetual and merciless search of facts with which to substantiate his deductions.

I broke the silence between us. "Pons, you surely don't believe in Mrs. Ashcroft's ghost?"

"What is a ghost?" he replied. "Something seen. Not necessarily supernatural. Agreed?"

"Agreed," I said. "It may be hallucination, illusion, some natural phenomenon misinterpreted."

"So the question is not about the reality of ghosts, but did our client see a ghost or did she not? She believes she did. We are willing to believe that she saw something. Now, it was either a ghost or it was not a ghost."

"Pure logic."

"Let us fall back upon it. Ghost or no ghost, what is its motivation?"

"I thought that plain as a pikestaff," I said dryly. "The purpose is to frighten Mrs. Ashcroft away from the house."

"I submit few such matters are plain as a pikestaff. Why?"

"Someone wishes to gain possession of Mrs. Ashcroft's house."

"Anyone wishing to do so could surely have bought it from the agents before Mrs. Ashcroft did. But let us for the moment assume that you are correct. How, then, did he get in?"

"That remains to be determined."

"Quite right. And we shall determine it. But one other little matter perplexes me in relation to your theory. That is this—if someone were bent upon frightening Mrs. Ashcroft from the house, does it not seem to you singular that we have no evidence that he initiated any of those little scenes where he was observed?"

"I should say it was deuced clever of him."

"It does not seem strange to you that if someone intended to frighten our client from the house, he should permit himself to be seen only by accident? And that after but the briefest of appearances, he should vanish before the full effectiveness of the apparition could be felt?"

"When you put it that way, of course, it is a little farfetched."

"I fear we must abandon your theory, Parker, sound as it is in every other respect."

He stopped suddenly. "I believe this is the address we want. Ah, yes—here we are. Harwell and Chamberlain, 221B."

We mounted the stairs of the ancient but durable building and found ourselves presently in mid-nineteenth-century quarters. A clerk came forward at our entrance.

"Good day, gentlemen. Can we be of service?"

"I am interested in seeing Mr. Roderic Harwell," said Pons.

"I'm sorry, sir, but Mr. Harwell has just left the office

for the rest of the day. Would you care to make an appointment?"

"No, thank you. My business is of some considerable urgency and I shall have to follow him home."

The clerk hesitated momentarily, then said, "I should not think that necessary, sir. You could find him around the corner at the Green Horse. He likes to spend an hour or so at the pub with an old friend or two before going home. Look for a short ruddy gentleman with bushy white sideburns."

Pons thanked him again, and we made our way back down the stairs and out to the street. In only a few minutes we were entering the Green Horse. Despite the crowd in the pub, Pons's quick eyes immediately found the object of our search, sitting at a round table near one wall, in desultory conversation with another gentleman of similar age, close to sixty, wearing, unless I were sadly mistaken, the air of one practicing my own profession.

We made our way to the table.

"Mr. Roderic Harwell?" asked Pons.

"That infernal clerk has given me away again!" cried Harwell, but with such a jovial smile that it was clear he did not mind. "What can I do for you?"

"Sir, you were kind enough to recommend me to Mrs. Margaret Ashcroft."

"Ah, it's Solar Pons, is it? I thought you looked familiar. Sit down, sit down."

His companion hastily rose and excused himself.

"Pray do not leave, Sir," said Pons. "This matter is not of such a nature that you need to disturb your meeting."

Harwell introduced us all around. His companion was Dr. Horace Weston, an old friend he was in the habit of meeting at the Green Horse at the end of the day. We sat between them.

"Now, then," said Harwell when we had made ourselves comfortable. "What'll you have to drink? Some ale? Bitters?"

"Nothing at all, if you please," said Pons.

"As you like. You've been to see Mrs. Ashcroft and heard her story?"

"We have just come from there."

"Well, Mr. Pons, I never knew of anything wrong with the house," said Harwell. "We sold some land in the country for Captain Brensham when he began selling off his property so that he could live as he was accustomed to live. He was a bibliophile of a sort—books about the sea were his speciality—and he lived well. But a recluse in his last years. He timed his life right—died just about the time his funds ran out."

"And Howard Brensham?" asked Pons.

"Different sort of fellow altogether. Quiet too, but you'd find him in the pubs and at the cinema sometimes, watching a stage show. He gambled a little, but carefully. I gather he surprised his uncle by turning out well. He had done a turn in Borstal as a boy. And I suppose he was just as surprised when his uncle asked him to live with him his last years and left everything to him, including the generous insurance he carried."

"I wasn't sure, from what Mrs. Ashcroft said, when Howard Brensham died."

Harwell flashed a glance at his companion. "About seven weeks ago or so, eh?" To Pons, he added, "Dr. Weston was called."

"He had a cerebral thrombosis on the street, Mr. Pons," explained Dr. Weston. "Died in three hours. Very fast. Only forty-seven and no previous history. But then, Captain Brensham died of a heart attack."

"Ah, you attended the Captain, too?"

"Well, not exactly. I had attended him for some bronchial ailments. He took good care of his voice. He liked to sing. But when he had his heart attack and died, I was in France on holiday. I had a young *locum* in and he was called."

"Mrs. Ashcroft's ghost sang," said Harwell thoughtfully. "Something about a 'dead man.'"

"I would not be surprised if it were an old sea chantey," said Pons.

"You don't mean you think it may actually be the Captain's ghost, Mr. Pons?"

"Say, rather, we may be meant to think it is," answered Pons. "How old was he when he died?"

"Sixty-eight or sixty-seven—something like that," said Dr. Weston.

"How long ago?"

"Oh, only two years."

"His nephew hadn't lived with him very long, then, before the old man died?"

"No. Only a year or so," said Harwell. His sudden grin gave him a Dickensian look. "But it was long enough to give him at least one of his uncle's enthusiasms—the sea. He's kept up all the Captain's newspapers and magazines and was still buying books about the sea when he died. Like his uncle, he read very little else. I suppose a turn he had done as a seaman bent him that way. But they were a seafaring family. The Captain's father had been a seaman, too, and Richard—the brother in Rhodesia who inherited the property and sold it through us to Mrs. Ashcroft—had served six years in the India trade."

Pons sat for a few minutes in thoughtful silence. Then he said, "The property has little value."

Harwell looked suddenly unhappy. "Mr. Pons, we tried to dissuade Mrs. Ashcroft. But these Colonials have sentimental impulses no one can curb. Home to Mrs. Ashcroft meant not London, not England, but Sydenham. What could we do? The house was the best we could obtain for her in Sydenham. But it's in a declining neighborhood, and no matter how she refurbishes it, its value is bound to go down."

Pons came abruptly to his feet. "Thank you, Mr. Harwell. And you, Dr. Weston."

We bade them goodbye and went out to find a cab.

Back in our quarters Pons ignored the supper Mrs. Johnson had laid for us and went directly to the corner where he kept his chemical apparatus. There he emptied his pockets of the envelopes he had filled in Mrs. Ashcroft's library, tossed his deerstalker to the top of the bookcase nearby, and began to subject his findings to chemical analysis. I ate supper by myself, knowing that it would be fruitless to urge Pons to join me. After supper I had a patient to look in on. I doubt that Pons heard me leave the room.

On my return in midevening Pons was just finishing.

"Ah, Parker," he greeted me, "I see by the sour expression you're wearing you've been out calling on your crotchety Mr. Barnes."

"While you, I suppose, have been tracking down the identity of Mrs. Ashcroft's ghost?"

"I have turned up indisputable evidence that her visitant is from the nethermost regions," he said triumphantly, and laid before me a tiny fragment of cinder. "Do you suppose we dare conclude that coal is burned in Hell?"

I gazed at him in openmouthed astonishment. His eyes were dancing merrily. He was expecting an outburst of protest from me. I choked it back deliberately; I was becoming familiar indeed with all the little games he played. I said, "Have you determined his identity and his motive?"

"Oh, there's not much mystery in that," he said almost contemptuously. "It's the background in which I am interested."

"Not much mystery in it!" I cried.

"No, no," he answered testily. "The trappings may be a trifle bizarre, but don't let them blind you to the facts, all the essentials of which have been laid before us."

I sat down, determined to expose his trickery. "Pons, it is either a ghost or it is not a ghost."

"I can see no way of disputing that position."

"Then it is not a ghost."

"On what grounds do you say so?"

"Because there is no such thing as a ghost."

"Proof?"

"Proof to the contrary?"

"The premise is yours, not mine. But let us accept it for the nonce. Pray go on."

"Therefore it is a sentient being."

"Ah, that is certainly being cagy," he said, smiling provocatively. "Have you decided what his motive might be?"

"To frighten Mrs. Ashcroft from the house."

"Why? We've been told it's not worth much and will decline in value with every year to come."

"Very well, then. To get his hands on something valuable concealed in the house. Mrs. Ashcroft took it furnished—as it was, you'll remember."

"I remember it very well. I am also aware that the house stood empty for some weeks and anyone who wanted to lay hands on something in it would have had far more opportunity to do so then than he would after tenancy was resumed."

I threw up my hands. "I give up."

"Come, come, Parker. You are looking too deep. Think on it soberly for a while and the facts will rearrange themselves so as to make for but one, and only one, correct solution."

So saying, he turned to the telephone and rang up Inspector Jamison at his home to request him to make a discreet application for exhumation of the remains of Captain Jason Brensham and the examination of those remains by Bernard Spilsbury.

"Would you mind telling me what all that has to do with our client?" I asked when he had finished.

"I submit it is too fine a coincidence to dismiss that a heavily insured old man should conveniently die after he has made a will leaving everything to the nephew he has asked to come live with him," said Pons. "There we have a concrete motive, with nothing ephemeral about it."

"But what's to be gained by an exhumation now? If what you suspect is true, the murderer is already dead, beyond punishment."

Pons smiled enigmatically. "Ah, Parker, I am not so much a seeker after punishment as a seeker after truth. I want the facts. I mean to have them. I shall be spending considerable time tomorrow at the British Museum in search of them."

"Well, you'll find ghosts of another kind there," I said dryly.

"Old maps and newspapers abound with them," he answered agreeably, but said no word in that annoyingly typical fashion of his about what he sought.

I would not ask, only to be told again, "Facts!"

When I walked into our quarters early in the evening of the following Monday, I found Pons standing at the windows, his face aglow with eager anticipation.

"I was afraid you might not get here in time to help lay Mrs. Ashcroft's ghost," he said, without turning.

"But you weren't watching for me," I said, "or you wouldn't still be standing there."

"Ah, I am delighted to note such growth in your deductive faculty," he replied. "I'm waiting for Jamison and Constable Mecker. We may need their help tonight if we are to trap this elusive apparition. Mrs. Ashcroft has sent word that the string across the library was broken last night. —Ah, here they come now."

He turned. "You've had supper, Parker?"

"I dined at the Diogenes Club."

"Come then. The game's afoot."

He led the way down the stairs and out into Praed Street, where a police car had just drawn up to the curb. The door of the car sprang open at our approach and Constable Mecker got out. He was a freshfaced young man whose work Pons had come to regard as very promising, and he greeted us with anticipatory pleasure, stepping aside so that we could enter the car. Inspector Seymour Jamison, a bluff squarefaced man wearing a clipped moustache, occupied the far corner of the seat.

Inspector Jamison spared no words in formal greeting. "How in the devil did you get on to Captain Brensham's poisoning?" he asked gruffly.

"Spilsbury found poison, then?"

"Arsenic. A massive dose. Brensham couldn't have lived much over twelve hours after taking it. How did you know?"

"I had only a very strong assumption," said Pons.

The car was rolling forward now through streets hazed with a light mist and beginning to glow with the yellow lights of the shops, blunting the harsh realities of daylight and lending to London a kind of enchantment I loved. Mecker was at the wheel, which he handled with great skill in the often crowded streets.

Inspector Jamison was persistent. "I hope you haven't got us out on a wild goose chase," he went on. "I have some doubts about following your lead in such matters, Pons."

"When I've misled you, they'll be justified. Not until then. Now, another matter—if related. You'll recall a disappearance in Dulwich two years ago? Elderly man named Ian Narth?"

Jamison sat for a few moments in silence. Then he said, "Man of seventy. Retired seaman. Indigent. No family. Last seen on a tube train near the Crystal Palace. Vanished without trace. Presumed drowned in the Thames and carried out to sea."

"I believe I can find him for you, Jamison."

Jamison snorted. "Now, then, Pons—give it to me short. What's all this about?"

Pons summed up the story of our client's haunted library, while Jamison sat in thoughtful silence.

"Laying ghosts is hardly in my line," he said when Pons had finished.

"Can you find your way to the Sydenham entrance of the abandoned old Nunhead-Crystal Palace High Level Railway Line?" asked Pons.

"Of course."

"If not, I have a map with me. Two, in fact. If you and Mecker will conceal yourself near that entrance, ready to arrest anyone coming out of it, we'll meet you there in from two to three hours' time."

"I hope you know what you're doing, Pons," growled Jamison.

"I share that hope, Jamison." He turned to Mecker and gave him Mrs. Ashcroft's address. "Parker and I will leave you there, Jamison. You'll have plenty of time to reach the tunnel entrance before we begin our exploration at the other end."

"It's murder, then, Pons?"

"I should hardly think that anyone would willingly take so much arsenic unless he meant to commit suicide. No such intention was manifest in Captain Brensham's life—indeed, quite the contrary. He loved the life he led and would not willingly have given it up."

"You're postulating that Ian Narth knew Captain Brensham and his nephew?"

"I am convinced inquiry will prove that to be the case."

Mecker let us out of the police car before Mrs. Ashcroft's house, which loomed with an almost forbiddingly sinister air in the gathering darkness. Light shone wanly from but one window; curtains were drawn over the rest of them at the front of the house, and the entire dwelling seemed to be waiting upon its foredoomed decay.

Mrs. Ashcroft herself answered our ring.

"Oh, Mr. Pons!" she cried at sight of us. "You *did* get my message."

"Indeed, I did, Mrs. Ashcroft. Dr. Parker and I have now come to make an attempt to lay your ghost."

Mrs. Ashcroft paled a little and stepped back to permit us entrance.

"You'll want to see the broken thread, Mr. Pons," she said after she had closed the door.

"If you please."

She swept past us and led us to the library, where she turned up all the lights. The black thread could be seen lying on the carpet, broken through about midway, and away from the east wall.

"Nothing has been disturbed, Mrs. Ashcroft?"

"Nothing. No one has come into this room but me—at my strict order. Except, of course, whoever broke the thread." She shuddered. "It appears to have been broken by something coming out of the wall!"

"Does it not?" agreed Pons.

"No ghost could break that thread," I said.

"There are such phenomena as *poltergeists* which are said to make all kinds of mischief, including the breaking of dishes," said Pons dryly. "If we had that to deal with, the mere breaking of a thread would offer it no problem. You heard nothing, Mrs. Ashcroft?"

"Nothing."

"No rattling of chains, no hollow groans?"

"Nothing, Mr. Pons."

"And not even the sound of a book falling?"

"Such a sound an old house might make at any time, I suppose, Mr. Pons."

He cocked his head suddenly; a glint came into his eyes. "And not, I suppose, a sound like that? Do you hear it?"

"Oh, Mr. Pons," cried Mrs. Ashcroft in a low voice. "That is the sound Mrs. Jenkins heard."

It was the sound of someone singing—singing boisterously. It seemed to come as from a great distance, out of the very books on the walls.

"Fifteen men on a dead man's chest," murmured Pons. "I can barely make out the words. Captain Brensham's collection of sea lore is shelved along this wall, too! A coincidence."

"Mr. Pons! What is it?" asked our client.

"Pray do not disturb yourself, Mrs. Ashcroft. That is hardly a voice from the other side. It has too much body. But we are delaying unnecessarily. Allow me."

So saying, he crossed to the bookshelves at the approximate place where she had reported seeing the apparition that haunted the library. He lifted a dozen books off a shelf and put them to one side. Then he knocked upon the wall behind. It gave back a muffled hollow sound. He nodded in satisfaction and then gave the entire section of shelving the closest scrutiny.

Presently he found what he sought—after having removed half the books from the shelving there—a small lever concealed behind a row of books. He depressed it. Instantly there was a soft thud—like the sound a book might make when it struck the carpet—and the section sagged forward, opening into the room like a door ajar. Mrs. Ashcroft gasped sharply.

"What on earth is that, Mr. Pons?"

"Unless I am very much mistaken, it is a passage to the abandoned right-of-way of the Nunhead-Crystal Palace Line—and the temporary refuge of your library ghost."

He pulled the shelving further into the room, exposing a gaping aperture which led into the high bank behind that wall of the house and down into the earth beneath. Out of the aperture came a voice which was certainly that of an inebriated man, raucously singing. The voice echoed and reverberated as in a cavern below.

"Pray excuse us, Mrs. Ashcroft," said Pons. "Come, Parker."

Pons took a flashlight from his pocket and, crouching, crept into the tunnel. I followed him. The earth was shored up for a little way beyond the opening, then the walls were bare, and here and there I found them narrow for me, though Pons, being slender, managed to slip through with less difficulty. The aperture was not high enough for some distance to enable one to do more than crawl, and it was a descending passage almost from the opening in Mrs. Ashcroft's library.

Ahead of us the singing had stopped suddenly.

"Hist!" warned Pons abruptly.

There was a sound of hurried movement up ahead.

"I fear he has heard us," Pons whispered.

He moved forward again and abruptly stood up. I crowded out to join him. We stood on the right-of-way of the abandoned Nunhead-Crystal Palace Line. The rails were still in place and the railbed was clearly the source of the cinder Pons had produced for my edification. Far ahead of us on the line someone was running.

"No matter," said Pons. "There is only one way for him to go. He could hardly risk going out to where the main line passes. He must go out by way of the Sydenham entrance."

We pressed forward, and soon the light revealed a niche hollowed out of the wall. It contained bedding, a half-eaten loaf of bread, candles, a lantern, books. Outside the opening were dozens of empty wine and brandy bottles.

Pons examined the bedding.

"Just as I thought," he said, straightening up. "This has not been here very long—certainly not longer than two months."

"The time since the younger Brensham's death," I cried.

"You advance, Parker, indeed!"

"Then he and Narth were in it together!"

"Of necessity," said Pons. "Come."

He ran rapidly down the line, I after him.

Up ahead there was a sudden burst of shouting. "Aha!" cried Pons. "They have him!"

After minutes of hard running we burst out of the tunnel at the entrance where Inspector Jamison and Constable Mecker waited—the constable manacled to a wild-looking old man, whose fierce glare was indeed alarming. Graying hair stood out from his head, and his unkempt beard completed a frame of hair around a grimy face out of which blazed two eyes fiery with rage.

"He gave us quite a struggle, Pons," said Jamison, still breathing heavily.

"Capital! Capital!" cried Pons, rubbing his hands together delightedly. "Gentlemen, let me introduce you to as wily an old scoundrel as we've had the pleasure of meeting in a long time. Captain Jason Brensham, swindler of insurance companies and, I regret to say, murderer."

"Narth!" exclaimed Jamison.

"Ah, Jamison, you had your hands on him. But I fear you lost him when you gave him to Spilsbury."

"The problem was elementary enough," said Pons, as he filled his pipe with the abominable shag he habitually smoked and leaned up against the mantel in our quarters later that night. "Mrs. Ashcroft told us everything essential to its solution, and Harwell only confirmed it. The unsolved question was the identity of the victim, and the files of the metropolitan papers gave me a presumptive answer to that in the disappearance of Ian Narth, a man of similar build and age to Captain Brensham.

"Of course, it was manifest at the outset that this motiveless specter was chancing discovery for survival. It was not Jenkins but the Captain who was raiding the food and liquor stocks at his house. The cave, of course, was never intended as a permanent hiding place, but only as a refuge to seek when strangers came to the house or whenever his nephew had some of his friends in. He lived in the house; he had always been reclusive and he changed his way of life but little. His nephew, you will recall Harwell's telling us, continued to subscribe to his magazines and buy the books he wanted, apparently for himself, but obviously for his uncle. The bedding and supplies were obviously moved into the tunnel after the younger Brensham's death.

"The manner and place of the ghost's appearance suggested the opening in the wall. The cinder in the carpet cried aloud of the abandoned Nunhead-Crystal Palace Line, which the maps I studied in the British Museum confirmed ran almost under the house. The Captain actually had more freedom than most dead men, for he could wander out along the line by night if he wished.

"Harwell clearly set forth the motive. The Captain had sold off everything he had to enable him to continue his way of living. He needed money. His insurance policies promised to supply it. He and his nephew together hatched up the plot. Narth was picked as victim, probably out of a circle of acquaintances because, as newspaper descriptions made clear, he had a certain resemblance to the Captain and was, like him, a retired seaman with somewhat parallel tastes.

"They waited until the auspicious occasion when Dr. Weston, who knew the Captain too well to be taken in, was off on a prolonged holiday, lured Narth to the house, killed him with a lethal dose of arsenic, after which they cleaned up the place to eliminate all external trace of poison and its effects, and called in Dr. Weston's *locum* to witness the dying man's last minutes. The Captain was by this time in his cave, and the young doctor took Howard Brensham's word for the symptoms and signed the death certificate, after which the Brenshams had ample funds on which to live as the Captain liked."

"And how close they came to getting away with it!" I cried.

"Indeed! Howard Brensham's unforeseen death—ironically, of a genuine heart attack—was the little detail they had never dreamed of. On similar turns of fate empires have fallen!"

AN ESTIMATE OF RITA
Ed Lacy

The first time I ever saw Rita I didn't much like her. But you know how first impressions are.

Rita walked into our store with her husband and father-in-law—a tall solid-built woman, and pretty. Even togged out in brown twill breeches, a man's shirt and sweater under a heavy hunting jacket, Rita looked feminine and pretty, meaning she had to be right beautiful. When an ankle is trim and slender in a hunting boot—a woman has to be really stacked. Of course, I merely gave her a curious glance, but my six-foot kid brother, Al, why, he actually could not take his eyes off Rita. She seemed about twenty-eight, perhaps a year or so older than her husband, and certainly bigger. At first glance Rita looked like a rangy man in those hunting clothes. But on second glance you saw the strong curves of her figure, the demand of her heavy lips, the bold cool eyes, a sensuous warmth to the clean strong features. In short, on second glance you realized Rita was a lot of powerful gal. I don't know what Al thought on his third—and hundredth look.

We'd seen the men before: they'd stopped at our store last fall. Guess I'd best explain about the store. We're up near the Canadian border; only a spread of thick woods and badlands separates us from Canada. No rivers, guards, or even customs stations. No need for them. This stretch of timber is about the roughest hunk of land and rock you'll ever want to see. Pop used to tell us how during Prohibition some goons figured this would be the ideal spot to send in booze from Canada by backpack. Three of 'em made a try at it—convinced the one guy who finally staggered out alive how wrong the whole idea was. In winter these woods are absolutely impassable. The rest of the year they're filled with queer rock and mud formations, tangled undergrowth, thick trees, and timber rattlers wide as your arm, bears, and mountain cats. There's hardly any trails. Once you get lost, man, you've had it. Couple of ancient Indian trappers are said to live someplace in the woods, but we never see 'em as they sell their skins on the Canadian side.

Ever since I was a kid the woods were nothing. I mean, they were merely a place a person with any sense stayed out of. I know the woods as well as any man. My family have been farming and running this general store for well over a hundred years back. We had a few other farmers for customers, and about got by.

I certainly never figured the 'badlands' would ever do any good. But right after the war some rich fellow comes by and says he's going hunting in the woods. We tried to talk him out of it, but he said he'd done big game hunting in Africa and other places. It ended with me selling him our rifles and rush-ordering boots and ammo. Naturally, this was all very expensive. Well, sir, this man went into the woods and returned a week later with a bearskin, quite happy about the "joy of hunting in virgin woods." He was a talkative type and must have kept talking wherever he went—started a kind of fad. Not that there was ever a great rush of hunters, because to reach us and buy an outfit you have to drop plenty of dollars. But in the fall and spring parties would come up to try for a wolf or a cat. Some of them even flew in, landing their private planes deep in the woods on hidden lakes, where the fish are frantic and plump.

All this proved a big deal for us. We began stocking high-powered rifles, ammo, fancy hunting clothes. We'd put people up for the night before they started out, and when they returned, take care of their station wagons. Like I told you, you had to be loaded with bucks to hunt this way, and we made more money from the hunting parties than we did the rest of the year.

Jim Harris, Rita's father-in-law, was a short and stocky man in his hind-fifties, and he must have married late because his only boy, Jim Junior, looked about twenty-two, but I understood he was a few years older. They were up for the first time last fall, him and his son. Now they were back, and Jim Junior had a wife—Rita. They had one of Ma's big suppers and retired early. The next morning, Monday, they took our jeep and drove off. You see, there's the start of a path and you can drive the jeep about sixteen rugged miles into the woods; then you have to walk. Al once wanted us to build a road, but Al's simple. I explained to him that if there was a road and other improvements, these rich folk wouldn't come up any more; it was the rough-and-tough side which sold them.

The Harris party was due to be gone a week. We didn't think nothing about them, except Al dreaming about Rita, I suppose, until Wednesday afternoon, when the jeep came roaring back. Rita Harris was driving and her husband was stretched across the back seat. She looked wild, her long dark hair undone and hanging to her shoulders. Her face was pale and scratched, her clothes torn, and blood all over her shirt. Jim Junior was in a coma. His head and face was busted, so was his shoulder, right arm, and ribs. He looked death-white, in real bad shape. This Rita got out of the jeep and actually picked Jim Junior up, as if he was a child, carried him to bed while we phoned for a doc.

Up here it takes a doctor about a half a day to drive up—if you're lucky to get Doc Ash from Preston. If he's out or busy, you try Doc Davis over in Little Buff, and he won't come unless it's a hell of an emergency because it means seven hundred and eighty miles of driving and old Doc Davis has no confidence in planes.

Although Rita Harris was on the verge of passing out herself, she sat beside her husband's bed as we waited for Doc Ash. Rita even ate her meals at his bedside, never left him for a second, although me and Al and Ma were around all the time. If big Al wasn't doing nothing else, he'd sit and stare at Rita—like the kid he was.

When she was able to get herself together and talk, Rita told us they'd made their second camp in a rocky gully we call Shale Gut. During the night old man Harris had got up to investigate some animal sounds he heard outside the camp. Rita was sitting by the fire, waiting for the old man to return. He tripped and his rifle went off, shot himself in the belly. Now, a person has to be out of their mind to shoot off a gun with all that loose rock above them, but then, Mr. Harris tripped and shot the gun by accident.

Jim Junior was in his sleeping bag at the time and the vibrations from the shot started a small landslide, crushing him. Now Shale Gut is a good twenty miles from the end of the "road" and that was where the jeep was. Rita with two badly wounded men on her hands, had to make a big decision, because she could only help *one* of the men. So she put Jim Junior on her back and carried him the twenty miles—walking, climbing, crawling, all that night and the next morning, until she reached the jeep. She was lucky she didn't get lost.

Of course, it was a real tough decision to make, knowing whomever she left would certainly die—from animals if not from his wounds. But Jim Senior wouldn't have made it with a belly wound and Jim Junior was her husband. It was a rugged ordeal for her to walk those woods at night, carrying a dying man. I mean, you got to be a hell of a woman (or man) to do that.

Al, and Jake Faro—an Indian farmer who knows the woods best—immediately went out to Shale Gut. (Jake Faro will probably be Al's father-in-law soon, or as soon as Jake's daughter Alice reaches sixteen. It happens Alice Faro is a sweet kid, but even if she wasn't, she'd still be the *only* young gal around.) Me and Ma helped Rita as much as possible, tried to make her take some rest. I kept thinking how wrong I'd been about her. I mean, my first impression of Rita as a kind of hard-looking babe. It took a real woman to carry her man out of those woods.

Even when Doc Ash drove up around suppertime, Rita

refused to leave Jim Junior's bedside. She sat there in a daze, exhausted, haggard-looking from lack of sleep, but never taking her eyes off her husband. He came to once, told Rita how much he loved her, before Doc put him to sleep again with a shot. The Doc begged Rita to take a pill, get some rest. She refused any drugs, but when we brought a cot into the room, she stretched out and had a few hours' sleep, still in her torn bloody clothes. Even Doc Ash, who's pretty cynical, was moved. And it was the first time I ever saw Ma weep. (Ma is my wife, not my mother.) Ma opened the Bible and read, offered a prayer for Rita and Jim Junior.

Doc did what he could, but it seemed Jim Junior was booked to go. We phoned Preston for an ambulance, although Doc doubted if Jim would survive the trip. When Rita heard that—we thought she was sleeping—she went to pieces, hysterically bawling and begging Doc to save her husband. Doc is a fine doctor, but Jim Junior was badly hurt. He'd lost too much blood and the next day he died. Rita didn't cry much then. Instead she seemed in a kind of shock—still sat beside her husband's bed, barely able to answer Doc's questions for the death certificate.

Along about noon Al and Jake Faro returned. They'd found the spot where Jim Senior had shot himself—there was blood about to prove it, his coat, and some other camping stuff—but they couldn't find the body. Now you don't find any better woodsmen than Al and Jake, and they searched the gully from end to end, figuring a bear had taken him away. But they didn't find anything. Of course, a pack of wolves might not leave much to see. When Rita heard about Jim Senior, she really went to pieces—for having left the old guy out there, feeling guilty, I suppose. This time Doc gave her a needle and Ma put her to bed. Rita slept around the clock. There wasn't any reason for her to feel like that; she couldn't have carried both men.

Well, sir, when Rita finally was up and around, wore a dress, with her face rested, she was something. Man, in a dress Rita was all flashy curves. Ma went for Rita's chic clothes, while poor Al stared at her like a lost soul. He was set to ask her to marry him—like that—until Ma talked some horse sense into his empty head, telling him it was not only silly, but hardly the proper time. Meantime, back on the meathouse slab, there was the problem of what to do with Jim Junior. Doc Ash suggested he be buried at once in the little old cemetery at the bend of the main road. We'd called off the ambulance and it would be a long trip by truck to the railroad at Preston. Rita thought it was a good idea, too, for Jim would want to be near the remains of Jim Senior. Jake Faro is a kind of preacher, and Al rushed to make a plain box; so we buried Jim Harris, Junior, in a simple ceremony.

Doc was anxious to return to Preston that night, and Rita suddenly decided to drive back with him—send for Jim Senior's car later. But first she insisted upon ordering a double stone for the grave, stating Jim Junior had died on the nineteenth day of the month and Jim Senior on the sixteenth day. I was on the phone for almost an hour giving exact instructions and making a deal with the stonecutter in Little Buff. Before she left, Rita gave Al her city address and set up a standing reward of five hundred dollars for anybody bringing in the remains of Jim Senior, to be buried beside his son.

Although I well knew Rita was sick of our place, at her leaving my eyes watered, Ma openly bawled, while big Al was shook up and downright ill. Ma kissed Rita and was given one of Rita's ritzy dresses. Al said he'd drive the car to Rita's home for nothing, any time she sent him the word. I just squeezed her hand. And I wondered what this tragedy would do to our business. Well, sir, Doc had about got his car turned around and headed for Preston, when a State Police car came racing up and two fancy-pants troopers jumped out. Darn if they don't arrest brave Rita Harris for murder!

Doc and I couldn't believe it. I mean, after all Rita had been through, this seemed just a little too much. As for Al, well, me and Ma had to tackle Al, keep the idiot from throwing a gun on the troopers. But it all came out like the troopers said, later at the trial.

Seems Jim Senior wasn't one to part with his money easily, despite having plenty of the green stuff. Junior didn't have a dime of his own. Rita—who it turned out had been around before she made this quickie marriage to young Jim—figured the sooner old Mr. Harris died, the quicker her Jim would inherit, and she had Jim Junior jumping through hoops. The hunting trip gave her the idea. So while they were camping in the gully, and when Jim Senior came over to their sleeping bags to say he was going out to see what was prowling around, Jim Junior was already sound asleep. Rita followed the old guy, plugged him in the stomach and was all set to claim it was an accident. But being new to the woods, she didn't realize what the shot would do. When she rushed back to yell accident at Jim Junior, she found him under this small landslide.

Rita did some pretty fast thinking. Under the state law (and she'd looked into that months ago) if her husband died *before* his daddy, then Rita, as Junior's wife, wouldn't get a cent of the father's estate. But if she could keep Jim Junior breathing until Jim Senior died, *and prove it,* then Junior would inherit everything and—as his wife—Rita would get it sooner or later. So Rita made this really superhuman effort to carry Junior out of the woods—and to get him out, if possible, before he died—in order to have witnesses as to the time of his death. She figured the old man would die in a few hours.

Jim Senior wouldn't have lasted that long, except one of the Indian trappers happened to be a mile away, came running when he heard the shot in Shale Gut. He found the wounded man and carried him over the ridge to where he'd seen a guy in a seaplane fishing the lake. They flew the old man to a Canadian hospital. Jim Senior was not only able to tell the police what had happened, but he was up in time to testify against Rita at her trial, two weeks later.

So there it is.

Al still claims it was wrong to send a woman as pretty

as Rita to the electric chair. Even Ma, with her strong streak of righteousness, claimed Rita had to be a darn good woman to carry her husband out of the woods, try to keep him alive, no matter what her motive might be.

Me—I don't know. While I secretly admired her quick thinking and courage, I guess I didn't really like her from the start.

THE FULL TREATMENT
Rog Phillips

The phosphorescent red letters glowing in the darkness said: *"REAL SOUTHERN FRIED CHICKEN* at JIMMY JOE'S in BETHEL 2 MILES."

Hunger added a fraction of an ounce to the pressure of Paul Hamling's foot on the gas. The speedometer needle crept from sixty-five to sixty-eight. The 1950 Mercury motor under the hood of the 1947 Ford purred. The exhaust noise from the slightly defective muffler gave the speeding car an added sound of power.

The next sign leaped out of the darkness a minute later. "BETHEL Pop. 168 CITY LIMITS." Under it on the same square white pole was a bigger sign with a foot high 25 and under it "SPEED LAWS STRICTLY ENFORCED."

Paul took his foot off the gas. The lights of the town weren't visible yet. He could let his speed drift down to twenty-five without using his brakes.

Then he saw the station wagon parked on the shoulder, the soulless intelligence of a rectangular radar eye watching him from its interior. The hair on the nape of his neck rose. He was even with the station wagon before the paralysis of surprise eased off enough for him to put his foot on the brake.

A flashlight's beam suddenly appeared, making rapid motions. Paul was frantically braking as he shot past that. A siren exploded into predatory life. Paul caught a glimpse of the red and white lights of a motorcycle in the rear-view mirror as he finally braked to a stop.

The motorcycle, siren screaming, pulled in front of

him. Its rider was resplendent in the very smartest of motorcycle cop uniforms, complete with white crash helmet with a blue cross in a red circle.

It was a ludicrous uniform for a man so short and so slight of build. He could not have been more than five feet two, nor weighed more than one-twenty. But there was nothing ludicrous about his prominent cleft chin, his small thin-lipped mouth, his narrow-set eyes, or the small cannon that dangled from his right hip.

He came toward the car, flashing his light briefly into the car, directly into Paul's face, then lowering it slightly. "Let's have your driver's license," he said.

"Yes, sir," Paul said. He took out his billfold and extracted the license from its plastic window and held it out.

"Paul Hamling, huh?" The cop turned the flashlight full into Paul's eyes again for a second. "Age twenty-six. You live in Chicago?"

"Yes, sir," Paul said.

"You leave there this morning?"

"No, of course not," Paul said. "It's about twelve hundred miles—"

"At the rate you were traveling you could have," the cop said. "The radar clocked you at a hundred and twelve."

"That's impossible!" Paul said.

"Are you calling me a liar?"

"My speedometer said sixty-eight," Paul said carefully.

"Faulty speedometer," the cop said. "And one headlight out."

"I didn't know a headlight was out," Paul said.

"I'll take your word for that," the cop said in a kindlier tone. He took a ticket book from his breast pocket. "I'll have to give you a ticket for speeding. Twenty-five from a hundred and twelve is eighty-seven dollars. You have a choice of paying it now or staying overnight in jail until court opens in the morning. Court costs are twelve dollars. You can save that by paying now, too."

"What if I don't have that much money?" Paul said bitterly.

"Brother, you'd better have," the cop said. "If you don't, you'll have to work it out on the road gang at three dollars a day, and a buck of that'll go on storage for your car."

"Eighty-seven?" Paul said.

"That's right."

Paul counted out four twenties, a five, and two ones, and held them out, his hand shaking with anger. "I want a receipt," he said.

The cop took the money and stuffed it in his pants pocket. "No receipt," he said. "Now drive along slow into town and pull into the service station."

"What for?" Paul demanded.

"To get a new headlight and your speedometer fixed. You aren't going anyplace until you get that done."

There was a family resemblance to the cop in the service station attendant's face. "The headlamp will be four bucks and fixing the speedometer will be fifteen," he said. "You might as well go down the street to Jimmy-Joe's for a bite to eat. It'll take an hour, anyway."

"I'd just as soon stay and watch you take out the speedometer," Paul said.

"Suit yourself." The man slid into the front seat, twisted around until he was draped under the dashboard with his feet over the back seat. Five minutes later he had the speedometer free. "I've had a lot of practice," he said with modest pride, displaying the unit.

"I'll bet you have at that!" Paul said. He followed the attendant over to a bench and watched until the speedometer was partly disassembled. "I think I will get something to eat," he said.

Jimmy-Joe's was crowded. All the teen-agers in Bethel seemed to be there, occupying the booths. Paul sat down at the deserted counter.

Jimmy-Joe occupied a throne behind the cash register. A faded and dispirited woman of fifty waited on Paul.

"The Southern fried chicken," Paul said, noting the

family resemblance of Jimmy-Joe to the cop and to the service station man.

"Sorry. We're all out of it," the waitress said. She opened a menu and put it on the counter.

It was a printed fountain menu with a mimeographed insert, soiled by much handling and yellowed along the borders by age.

"I'll have the roast beef," Paul said. "And coffee."

The waitress brought the coffee. The jukebox erupted to ear-shattering life with an adenoidal male singer whining his accompaniment to a git-tar. Paul sipped the coffee cautiously. It was hot and good. He took a bold swallow.

The waitress brought his roast beef dinner. It was thin slices of roast beef and chunks of white potatoes, generously covered with a brown gravy that glistened coldly in the reflected rays of the overhead lights.

Paul tasted the food cautiously. The gravy and potatoes were room temperature, the roast beef slightly colder. He glanced in the direction of the cash register. Jimmy-Joe was watching him. Paul grinned at the man, pushed the plate away, and lit a cigarette.

He finished his coffee leisurely. As he strolled toward the cash register, he glanced at his check. It listed roast beef, a dollar eighty, and coffee, ten cents.

Paul laid the check carefully on the counter and took a dime out of his pocket. "The coffee was very good," he said quietly, "but the roast beef was ice-cold and so were the potatoes and gravy. I couldn't eat them." He placed the dime on the counter. "I'm just paying for the coffee."

"Well now, we'll just see about that," Jimmy-Joe said, getting off his high stool. "Wait right here." He went down the length of the counter to the kitchen, was gone for about five seconds, then came back. "My wife is the cook, mister," he said. "She says your food was hot."

"I say it was cold," Paul said.

"Are you calling my wife a liar?" Jimmy-Joe said.

"If she said my food was hot, yes," Paul said.

"What seems to be the trouble?" a familiar voice said behind Paul.

Paul turned. The motorcycle cop stood there.

"You got here pretty fast," Paul said.

"This stranger refuses to pay his bill, Donny-George," Jimmy-Joe said. "And he just called my wife a liar."

"You're just alookin' for trouble, aren't you, Mr. Hamling?" the bantam cop said, resting his hand on the butt of the small cannon. "Now I'd suggest you pay your bill and apologize for calling Aunt Martha a liar."

Paul hesitated, then took out his billfold and extracted two one-dollar bills. Jimmy-Joe took them and slid Paul's dime toward him.

"Here's your change, Mister," he said.

"Give it to the waitress for a tip," Paul said. He took out another dollar bill and laid it on the counter. "Give this to your wife—with my apologies," he said.

"Well now, that's mighty nice of you, mister," Jimmy-Joe said.

"I'm glad you think so," Paul said.

Donny-George opened the door and said, "I'll just walk back to the service station with you—sort of keep you out of trouble." He smiled. "It would be a shame if you wound up on the road gang now. A traffic violation isn't so bad. You can work it out. But assault and battery carries six months to a year. If Jimmy-Joe had come out from behind the counter and poked you for calling his wife a liar, and you'd poked him back—" Donny-George shook his helmeted head sadly.

They reached the service station. Paul glanced in his car. The speedometer window was empty.

The service station man was sitting inside the station reading a battered hunting magazine.

"Isn't my speedometer fixed yet?" Paul said.

"Nope," the man said. "Have to send to Springfield tomorrow for some parts. Can't fix it till they get here."

"Well, couldn't I—?" Paul saw the expression on Donny-George's face. "No, I suppose you won't let me."

"That's right," Donny-George said. "Now, you have to have someplace to stay for the night, and we don't have a hotel."

"So?" Paul said.

"There's a house down the street about three blocks," Donny-George said, "where you can rent a room for the night, reasonably."

"A relative of yours?" Paul said.

"In a way," Donny-George said. "Nora's the widow of my uncle Georgey-Frank. She has to take in roomers for a living. And Nellie—that's her daughter—is my cousin."

"That should be recommendation enough," Paul said. "Does she serve meals too, or do I have to eat at Jimmy-Joe's?"

"She might fix you something," Donny-George said.

The house was a two-story frame dwelling set back from the street behind a row of locust trees; on one of the trees was a sign: ROOMS FOR RENT BY DAY OR WEEK.

Paul Hamling, suitcase in hand, went up the walk to the porch and knocked. The door was opened by a girl. Her prominent chin, close set brown eyes, and small thin-lipped mouth were somewhat softened by a cute nose. She wore a ponytail, instead of a white enamel crash helmet, and a gingham dress. She was clearly a more recent stamping from the same mold that had formed Donny-George. Fifteen or possibly sixteen years old.

She looked Paul up and down with an open frankness more commonly found in certain types of men looking girls up and down. Paul said, "You must be Nellie. Your cousin Donny-George said I could get a room here for the night. I'm Paul Hamling."

"Tell the gentleman to come in, child!" a woman said, appearing from the kitchen and wiping her hands on her apron.

"And you must be Donny-George's aunt," Paul said with hearty enthusiasm. "Donny-George said you might fix me something to eat. They ran out of hot food at Jimmy-Joe's before I got there."

"I might," the woman said. She was slightly taller than her daughter—perhaps five feet three—on the plump side, with the type of figure where bosom and stomach merge to form an imposing front. Her hair was black and done up in a bun on top of her head. Her face lacked the Donny-George stamp, but it bore a striking family resemblance to the waitress in Jimmy-Joe's. She went to a large oak commode and opened a well-worn ledger book. "First you'll have to register," she said. "It'll be three dollars for the room and a dollar for your supper."

"That's very reasonable," Paul murmured, writing his name and address on the first vacant line.

"From Chicago, huh?" the woman said. "Your car outside?"

"Uh, no," Paul said. "I have to wait until tomorrow for some parts to fix the speedometer."

The girl, Nellie, burst into high-pitched laughter.

"That'll be enough of that, Nellie," her mother said. "Show Mr. Hamling to his room."

"Okay," Nellie said. "Come on, Mr. Hamling."

"Your supper'll be ready soon as you wash up," Aunt Nora said. "And I'll take the money now."

"Oh. Of course," Paul said. He counted out four dollars. "Is that correct?"

"Unless you want to take advantage of our weekly rate."

Paul picked up his suitcase and climbed the stairs toward Nellie who was waiting on the upper landing.

"Twenty-five dollars a week, room and board," Aunt Nora called after him.

"No, thanks," Paul said, looking down at her, "I won't be here that long."

Nellie opened a door. "This is your room," she said. "The bathroom's that door down the hall." She pointed and then started away.

"Just a minute, Nellie," Paul said.

The girl turned. He was holding a dollar bill out toward her.

"What's that for?" she said suspiciously, backing away.

"A tip," Paul said.

"What on earth for?" Nellie said, laughing nervously. "I didn't do nothin' but show you your room."

"You did far more than that," Paul said. "You're the only one I've met in Bethel that didn't cost me money. Now is that right? You should have your slice of my bankroll, too!"

"If you say so," Nellie said, taking the bill cautiously. She looked at it, her small thin-lipped mouth curved downward unhappily. Then, impulsively, she whispered, "You should get out of town! Don't waste a minute. Just git!" Then she turned and scurried down the stairs.

Paul watched her until she was out of sight. And when he went into his room, he was frowning. Had she meant he should abandon his car and take to the road as a hitch-hiker? He almost felt like it, but that was absurd. He shrugged off her warning. She was, after all, just a kid.

He thought about it while he went down the hall to the bathroom and took a shower and shaved. Everything that could happen to him in this speed-trap town of Bethel had already happened, he decided.

"What else can happen?" he asked his reflection in the bathroom mirror with lifted eyebrows, and answered himself, "Nothing!" Tomorrow morning he would go to the service station and get his car, and drive at a speed of twenty miles an hour until he reached the city limits; then he could forget Bethel. And good riddance!

Thus reassured, he went down to eat his belated dinner.

A stranger sat at the dining-room table. Not quite a stranger, because of his prominent chin, small thin-lipped mouth, and narrow-set eyes. But it was as though some cosmic caricaturist, having faithfully reproduced the familiar face, then went overboard. Bushy black eyebrows and a thick mane were tacked on above. Below on the neck was a wing collar and shoestring tie, below that was a white shirt front and a single-button coat that was a dusty shade of black and had black velvet lapels. A gray glove was on the left hand, its mate lay on the table. Matching gray spats adorned the ankles below the black trousers that had black satin stripes down the sides. To complete the picture of sartorial elegance was a black cane shaped like a dwarf pool cue, with an ornate gold head, and which was leaning against the edge of the table.

It was not so much the clothing as the exaggerated dignity of the man which struck Paul as indescribably ludicrous. He burst out laughing.

"What's so funny?" the man growled in an orator's voice.

"Sorry," Paul gasped. "You. I can't help it."

Paul ducked the wild swing of the cane and was suddenly sobered by the intense rage in the man's narrow-set eyes.

"Now wait a minute!" Paul said, getting hold of the head of the cane. "I didn't mean anything personal."

The man kicked Paul's shin with the point of his patent leather shoe. This was extremely painful, so Paul jerked the cane out of the man's hand and shoved him away.

The man fell backwards with a violence that later on seemed to Paul to be far out of proportion to the force of the shove. He knocked over two chairs and brought up against the wall with a thump that shook the house. While Paul stared, the man quietly closed his eyes and fell limply to one side.

At that moment Aunt Nora came into the dining room from the kitchen. Paul had taken an unconscious step toward the stranger, still holding the cane. Aunt Nora screamed and dropped the cup and saucer she was carrying.

It was a nerve-shattering scream, and, in the midst of it, the front door slammed open. Donny-George, looking like a pint-size stormtrooper, advanced into the room with drawn cannon.

"He's killed *Theodore!*" Aunt Nora shouted. "With Theodore's own walkin' stick, too! I seen him do it!"

A significant groan came from the lips of Theodore.

"He's still alive, Aunt Nora," Donny-George said. "Call Doc and Big Leroy." He looked at Paul. "So," he said softly, "attempted murder. And you had to pick as your victim, the *Mayor of Bethel himself!*"

They came. The doctor first, with his black bag. He

glanced with brief curiosity at Paul, before going over to the motionless figure of Bethel's Mayor. Then Big Leroy, the Police Chief, arrived.

One glance at Big Leroy and Paul Hamling lost whatever hope he might have had. It was not so much Big Leroy's size as it was his face and eyes. If Donny-George and Jimmy-Joe and Nellie and Mayor Theodore were stampings from the same mold, Big Leroy's features were the mold itself, leathered and much used, and his narrow-set eyes were those of a man who could kill or horsewhip with perfect calm.

The doctor looked up at Big Leroy and said, "The Mayor'll live, but it may be close."

Donny-George spoke his piece. "This is quite a boy we've caught us, Uncle Leroy. He comes barreling into town at a hundred and twelve; he tries to get out of paying for his supper at Jimmy-Joe's; then he tries to kill the Mayor with the Mayor's own walkin' stick."

"Take him to the jailhouse, Nephew," Big Leroy said. "If he tries to escape, shoot his legs out from under him. We want this boy alive. You hear?"

Paul made a try. "I don't suppose it would do any good to tell you I wasn't going a hundred and twelve, that the food at Jimmy-Joe's wasn't fit to eat, and that all I did was protect myself when the Mayor tried to hit me with his cane because I couldn't help laughing at his getup."

"Are you calling Donny-George a liar?" Big Leroy said softly.

Donny-George said, "He called Aunt Martha a liar, too."

"You can have your say in court tomorrow, boy—through your lawyer," Big Leroy said. "See that he gets a lawyer, Donny-George."

The jailhouse was a beautiful brick building on a sidestreet, fronted by a well-kept lawn. Over the entrance was a sign that said BETHEL CITY HALL.

The jail part was in the basement. The jailer resembled

Donny-George except that he was taller and thinner and in his forties. He emptied Paul's pockets, carefully listing everything and dropping the different items in an envelope. "Three hundred and forty dollars," he said after counting the currency in Paul's billfold.

"Then he can pay for the best lawyer in town," Donny-George said.

The jail cell had a wet concrete floor. Paul was pushed into the cell, his wrists finally freed of handcuffs. The overhead light outside the bars went out a few minutes later, leaving him in almost total darkness.

Wearily he lay down on the cot welded to the wall.

Soon after he awoke in the morning, the jailer appeared and slid a rectangular tray under the door. Hunger forced Paul to gulp down the eggs and fried potatoes and to ignore their rancid taste.

The jailer returned for the tray, and handed Paul a pencil and slip of paper. "Sign this," he said.

Paul read what had been scrawled on the paper. It was an authorization for the jailer to pay the sum of two hundred and fifty dollars to one Johny-Jake Bemis for services rendered.

"Johny-Jake will be your lawyer," the jailer said. And then added in a confidential tone, "If anyone can get you out of here, he can."

Paul signed.

Johny-Jake looked very much like Donny-George except that he was about three inches taller, wore a business suit, and had an eager personality.

"All I'm going to try to do today is get you out of here," he said. "Attempting to kill Mayor Theodore is quite a serious offense—not that there aren't others who wouldn't like to try it. Bail's apt to be quite high. How much can you lay your hands on?"

"How high do you think the bail will be?" Paul asked.

"I don't rightly know," Johny-Jake said. "Uncle—that is, Judge Ostrand might make it anything from five hundred to fifteen thousand dollars. Once he sets bail he won't change his mind, so I'd better have some idea of the most you can lay your hands on."

"Five hundred or fifteen thousand," Paul said. "I can't get it."

"Too bad," Johny-Jake said. He stepped back from the bars. "Well, I'll try to earn my fee anyway."

"Doesn't it matter that I'm innocent?"

"They have you dead to rights." Johny-Jake shook his head sadly. "You'd better get some money somewhere or you'll never get out. See you in court." He turned and left.

Paul sat on the bunk and stared at the wet floor. Hours later the jailer and Donny-George appeared. The diminutive cop kept his cannon pointed at Paul's stomach while the jailer put on the handcuffs.

Paul was led upstairs and into a courtroom. There were new faces with close-set eyes, small thin-lipped mouths, and prominent chins. One of them was in the judge's chair.

Big Leroy, the doctor, and Donny-George quickly outlined their evidence. Johny-Jake, Paul's lawyer, whispered to Paul, "This is only the preliminary hearing. Unc— the Judge will set a date for the trial, probably this fall. *Then* I step in to demand your release on bail."

"The prisoner will stand trail in this court starting the first Monday of October," the judge said.

"But, your Honor!" Johny-Jake said, springing to his feet. "That's three months away! Three months of confinement in a jail cell! I demand bail be set so my client can be released until the date of the trial!"

"Very well," the judge said. "Bail is set at six thousand four hundred and twenty-two dollars. Failure to appear at the date of the trial will mean confiscation of the bail and an arrest warrant." He rapped his gavel, stood up, and went through the doorway at his back.

"I was sure I could get you out on bail!" Johny-Jake said, beaming with professional pride. "In fact, I was so sure that I took the liberty of asking Uncle Davey-Jack to be in court."

"That's right," a stranger—with narrow-set eyes, a small thin-lipped mouth, and prominent chin—said, coming over and seizing Paul's hand and pumping it several times. "I'm president of our local bank. We don't want you to stay in that jail cell downstairs another night. It's a disgrace to the community and we civic-minded citizens have been trying to get it improved for years, but traffic fines and bail forfeitures are just about the only new money, worth speaking of, coming into the city treasury."

"I see," Paul said.

"I happen to have with me," the banker said, withdrawing some papers from the breast pocket of his coat, "the necessary papers to get you out on bail before the day is out. All it requires is for you to open an account in our bank, write a check on that account for the correct amount of the bail, and send a telegram to your bank in Chicago instructing them to transfer the money from your account there by return wire. All perfectly legal and binding." He laid the papers out before Paul as he talked.

"I don't like it!" Donny-George shouted, slamming his gleaming crash helmet against the table. "He almost killed Mayor Theodore. And if he gets out on bail, he won't come back for trial!"

"Of course he'll come back," Johny-Jake, Paul's lawyer, said. "If he doesn't, he'll forfeit his bail."

"He'll forfeit his bail all right," Donny-George said, scowling. "He won't stand trial and go to jail for ten years."

"Ten years!" Johny-Jake said. "I'll bet you a hundred dollars I can get him off with no more than four!"

"I'll just take you up on that bet, Cousin," Donny-George said. "His car's ready to roll right on out of town as soon as he pays the nineteen bucks he owes Jerry-Phil for fixing it. And that's just what he'll do."

"What if he don't, Cousin?" Johny-Jake said. "What if he just sticks around until the trial?"

"Then he'd better just watch his step because I'm going to be following him every minute. But I'm betting he'll skip."

"Well," Johny-Jake taunted, "you can't stop him if he does."

"I know that," Donny-George said. "That's what's eatin' me."

Paul took the pen the banker was holding out. He filled in the application for a checking account. He hesitated over the check, then signed it.

"What do I write on this?" Paul said, pointing to the telegraph blank.

"A telegram to your bank requesting that they transfer six thousand four hundred and twenty-two dollars to your account in my bank," Davey-Jack said. "Then as soon as the money comes your check is good. I transfer the money to the City of Bethel, and you're free to go."

"There's only one thing that puzzles me," Paul said slowly.

"What's that?" Davey-Jack said.

"Who pays the cost of this telegraph transfer? It must amount to twenty or thirty dollars."

"A very good question," the banker said, frowning. "The bank can't pay it very well."

"He has ninety bucks in cash," Donny-George said. "Nineteen of that goes to Jerry-Phil. That leaves seventy-one."

"Fine! Fine!" the banker said, beaming. "I'll let you know the telegraph charges and you can take care of them from that balance of yours."

Paul slammed down the pen and gripped the edge of the table, his lips pressed tightly together.

"Of course," the banker said, "if you want to save the telegraph charges you can write a check on your Chicago bank, and we'll all wait until it clears. About five days, I would say...."

Bitterly, Paul picked up the pen and began to write.

"First National Bank of Chicago," he wrote. "Please close out my account and send the entire six thousand four hundred and twenty-two dollars by collect telegraph money order for deposit to my account in the Bethel State Bank."

The phosphorescent red letters glowing in the darkness

said: *"REAL SOUTHERN FRIED CHICKEN* at JIMMY JOE'S in BETHEL 2 MILES."

Hunger added a fraction of an ounce to the pressure of David Miller's foot on the gas. The speedometer needle crept from fifty-eight to sixty-one. The rebuilt motor under the hood of the fifty-four Chevy purred contentedly.

The next sign leaped out of the darkness a minute later. "BETHEL Pop. 168 CITY LIMITS."

Seconds later, the jaws of the town of Bethel would close upon this fresh morsel of tourist flesh, while far to the northwest, with the distance growing greater every minute, the picked bones of what was left (financially speaking) of Paul Hamling hunched over the wheel of his '47 Ford, headed back to Chicago, interested only in getting there before the few dollars he had left to his name vanished completely.

Suddenly a sign materialized beside the road. CITY LIMITS. Tires screamed as Paul's foot came down hard on the brake pedal and the speedometer needle dropped from sixty-five to slightly over twenty.

Beads of perspiration glistened on Paul Hamling's forehead. How many such signs were there between him and Chicago? Hundreds. Thousands!

His sweaty hands gripped the wheel. A field of corn moved slowly by as he crept toward the distant lights of an approaching town. . . .

ANOTHER DAY, ANOTHER MURDER
Lawrence Treat

Neither of the two cops could have told how this habit of theirs started, or why.

What they did was watch wreckers pull down the row of tenements where the housing development was going to be built. Whenever they had a chance, they drove over there and parked. Sometimes they got out of the car and sometimes they didn't. They bet nickels on when a wall would come down or which worker would step out next for a smoke or how long between wheelbarrow loads. They got to know some of the wrecking crew by sight and spoke to them casually, *Hello* and *How's it going* and stuff like that.

Bass was a big, plump, broad-shouldered guy; his eyes were very light blue. Salmon was tall and rangy. He had buck teeth; so his mouth was never quite closed. He sniffed a lot and had a dry nasal voice.

Bass and Salmon, detectives. The rest of the boys called them the fish patrol and kidded the pants off them. The result was that Bass and Salmon stayed away from the precinct house as much as they could. They were stuck with each other, but they got along nicely and made a good team.

On that particular day, they were busy all morning and didn't get over to the construction site until around two o'clock. They parked across the street from number 748, where the main work was going on. They watched a load of plaster, brick, and broken cement come roaring down a chute and into a truck.

Salmon cut the motor. Bass coughed and said, "That junk. It gets into your lungs, doesn't it?"

Salmon agreed. Then they both stepped out of the car and started to cross the street.

The truck driver yelled at them. "Hey," he said. "You come for the excitement?"

"What excitement?" Salmon asked.

"Guy found some jewels and ran off with them."

"You kidding?" Bass said.

"Ask anybody," the truck driver said. "They'll tell you."

Salmon glanced at his partner. "I'll check in," he said. He walked over to the car, picked up the two-way radio phone, and told the precinct dispatcher that he and Bass were leaving the car for a few minutes on an investigation.

Bass waited, staring at the boarding with which the ancient buildings were fenced in, the warped lumber and old doors and disintegrating plywood. When Salmon returned, the two of them headed for the shack from which the foreman, Bill Donlan, superintended the wrecking operation. He saw them coming and stood, a big bloated man, filling the doorway.

"Hi," he said, in a rough bass. "Anything I can do for you?"

"We're after the treasure," Bass said, grinning. "Who found it?"

"Oh, that," Donlan said. "Tony Amalfi. Maybe you can get it straight; I can't. Come on."

He picked up a baseball bat before he crossed the broken sidewalk and stepped into what had once been a store. The smell of damp decay was strong.

"Watch your step," Donlan said. He slapped the bat against a plank to test its solidity. "You never know when this stuff is rotted out."

He led the way up a couple of narrow flights of stairs that no longer had banisters. The third floor was roofless, and he picked his way over the rubbish-strewn floor and headed for a gap in the wall. He crossed a couple of buildings in various stages of ruin and reached one on which a gang was working.

He called out in his deep rasping voice, "Hey, you guys. These officers want to talk to you."

Salmon glanced at the workmen, then at the walls of a room that had once been blue. Big chunks of plaster had been ripped off and the wooden lathing was exposed. A partly dismantled fireplace was open to the sky.

Bass did most of the questioning. Tony Amalfi had been taking down the chimney when he'd suddenly yelled out. The other workers thought he was hurt, but he'd merely reached into a hole in the chimney and removed a small black box. He'd stood there, examining the contents. Jewel box, they thought, but they weren't sure. He'd snapped it shut before any of them could see inside it.

They all had theories—the box contained jewelry or money or old documents, something like that. But the only certainties were that Tony had found something, had been excited, had put the stuff in his lunchbox and walked off the job.

Salmon and Bass examined the chimney hiding place. It measured a couple of brick-lengths each way.

"Tony's a crazy guy," Donlan said. "Wait till he comes back, I'll get it out of him."

"Where does he live?" Salmon asked.

"Come on back to the office and I'll look it up."

That was all there was to it. Salmon and Bass got the address and returned to the car. They were busy the rest of the afternoon and had no time to follow up on Tony Amalfi. Nor did it seem important. He didn't have the connections for disposing of expensive jewelry. If he tried to get away with something valuable, he'd be caught. And if the thing wasn't worth much, who cared? Besides, Donlan had said he'd handle it. So some time tomorrow, they'd stop by and ask him about it.

The next morning they had a robbery to investigate, nothing out of the ordinary, but it would take them an hour or so. They were on the way there when the dispatcher called them. Salmon was driving, so Bass took the call. The dispatcher ordered them up to an alley off Merrill Street, where a body had been found.

The alley was a deadend between two buildings, one of which contained a pizza restaurant. The cop on the beat was holding off a small crowd that kept shoving forward in order to get a look. Salmon and Bass cleared the alley and walked back. Some garbage pails partly hid the body of a muscular little guy in a brown suit. He was lying on his stomach, and his head was bashed in.

The uniformed cop explained, "The restaurant people put their garbage out in the evening and leave it in the alley overnight. In the morning the porter lugs it out to the sidewalk, where it gets picked up around ten o'clock. When he came out this morning, he saw this. Says he didn't touch anything."

Bass bent down and felt the wrist of the corpse. He stood up quickly. "Feels cold," he said. "Killed some time during the night."

"Killed over there," Salmon said. He pointed to some stains near the mouth of the alley. "Dragged back and dumped where nobody'd notice him for awhile."

Bass grimaced, drew back, and stared at the body. The face was partly hidden by the outstretched arm. "I've seen that guy somewhere," he said.

"You and your memory," Salmon said, squinting. His lips balled out more than usual as he forced himself to bend down and examine what he could see of the face. He stood up with relief. "Yeah," he said. "Seems like I've seen him, too."

Bass swung around and walked rapidly to the rear of the alley. Salmon rocked on his heels and let his eyes drag themselves along the surface of the pavement and come to rest on the body. The garbage pail must have been knocked over the night before, because cheese paste from the pizzas was smeared on the ground and spattered against the brick wall. With his fingernail, Salmon dislodged a small blob. It had dried out and hardened like cement, but it was also powdery and flaked off into nothing.

The crowd kept watching him expectantly. He heard somebody say, "What is it? What's he got?"

"Cheese," somebody answered.

Then another voice exploded in a guffaw. "Cheese it," it said, "the cops!"

The crowd laughed, but with a jeering note that made Salmon uncomfortable. He supposed they wanted him to do something dramatic—or at least interesting—and were tired of waiting. But he never could figure out civilians. Either they were scared of you or else they hated you for no reason.

With a gesture of disdain, Salmon opened his jacket, took a deep breath and let his holstered gun show. This display of power gave him a certain satisfaction. Stony-faced, he pulled the jacket lapels together again, smoothed down his coat, and buttoned it.

When Bass came back from the other end of the alley, Salmon said in a low voice, "I'm sure it's him. You know who I mean?"

Bass gave a decisive nod. "Right," he said.

Neither of them mentioned Tony Amalfi's name, but they both felt that Tony must have found a genuine treasure and been killed on account of it.

"He always showed up first with a wheelbarrow," Bass said. "Won me quite a few nickels."

Salmon grunted, moved to the wall opposite the restaurant, and leaned against the brick. There was nothing more to do until the lieutenant and the headquarters brass showed up and took charge. But Bass pranced around energetically, while his eyes made quick, darting glances at everything. Suddenly Salmon called to him.

"Look," Salmon said, pointing. "Guy stepped in some garbage and left us a nice footprint. That heel—perfect, huh?"

Bass jerked to attention, started to march forward and stopped himself. He lifted his foot awkwardly and studied the bottom of his shoe.

"Mine," he said tersely. "Just stepped in the stuff."

He rubbed his shoe methodically to scrape off the goo. A couple of minutes later, the first siren sounded.

The lieutenant listened to what Salmon and Bass had to say and then brought them over to the commissioner.

"These boys of mine are right on the ball," the lieutenant said. "They know who the decedent was and why he was killed. Now, if we can just learn what Amalfi found, we're on our way. Otherwise, this case can mean trouble."

"Thorough conscientious police work will do the trick," the commissioner said pompously. He gave Salmon and Bass the privilege of his personal attention. "Men," he said in a stentorian tone, "I know you'll do honor to the department. What are your names?"

Bass stuttered out his answer and the commissioner repeated the names in surprise.

"Well, they're easy enough to remember," he boomed out, and laughed. "But don't go after any red herrings, you hear, because I'll be keeping an eye on you."

Salmon nodded, turned, and started elbowing his way through the crowd. He felt a tug at his sleeve and he looked down at a small boy.

"Mister," the boy said, "I found this. It was behind one of those cartons." He pointed to some rubbish at the entrance to the alley, and he handed Salmon a green lunchbox.

Salmon examined the box. It had a mottled surface, the kind that won't take fingerprints, and there was a smear of cheese near one corner. There was nothing inside.

"Thanks, sonny," Salmon said and kept on going. He put the lunchbox in the trunk of the car and got in behind the wheel. He figured he'd look like a jackass if he went back and admitted that a kid had spotted something which he and Bass had missed—and, it was likely, the kid had found it before they arrived on the scene. Besides, he couldn't take any more of the commissioner's hot air.

After a couple of minutes, Bass climbed into the front seat of the car. "Glad to be clear of that guy," he said. "Him and his sense of humor." Bass snorted with contempt. "You know what he said after you left? He wanted us to report to him direct, so he'd be sure we didn't pull any boners."

"No kidding?" Salmon said. He started the car and raced the motor. "Can't he read the manual? Don't he know we're working out of the precinct?"

"That's what the lieutenant told him; so His Nibs said okay, just so we made an arrest before morning. Said that ought to be easy, with the start we got."

"Didn't tell us who to arrest, did he?" Salmon asked drily.

"Sure he did. He said get the killer, or else." Bass tapped his partner's arm. "Or else means back in uniform."

"He can't do that," Salmon said angrily, "except for cause. That's what the manual says. We could go to court on that."

"And get our pictures in the paper? Salmon and Bass. We couldn't show our faces after the ribbing we'd take."

"Yeah," Salmon said with distaste. "So what do we do now?"

"Go to Amalfi's. Lieutenant's going to check on who lived in that apartment where the stuff was found. He'll let us know, as soon as he can run it down."

"Right," Salmon said.

He shot the car forward and headed for the boulevard. Neither he nor Bass mentioned the commissioner again, but they were both sullen, edgy, and anticipated trouble.

Tony Amalfi's house was in a development at the other end of town. His wife opened the door. She had a pretty enough face, and later on—when they were talking about her—Bass figured her waist at fifty inches, while Salmon held out for forty-five. They never did find out.

"You come about Tony?" she asked, as soon as they'd identified themselves.

"What about Tony?" Bass asked.

"Did something happen to him?" she asked anxiously. "He wasn't home all night. I've been worried."

"Where'd he go?"

"He didn't say. Officer, did something happen? *Tell me.*"

Bass looked at Salmon and Salmon looked at Bass.

"He found something on the job," Bass said. "What was it?"

"I don't know. He came back early, around five, and I cleaned his lunchbox. He stayed near the phone and he got two calls." She let out her breath in a sigh. "Nobody calls Tony that early, he's never home before six."

"Who called him?"

"I don't know. I was in the kitchen."

"When did he go out again?"

"Right after dinner. He took his lunchbox and said he might get home late, but Tony doesn't stay out all night. Not him. Tell me—what happened?"

"He got killed," Salmon said quietly. And turning to Bass, said, "Better ask one of the neighbors to come over."

On the way back to the car, Salmon remembered the lunchbox. "I got it in the trunk," he said. "I'll get it, so you can see it."

Bass glanced at the lunchbox without interest. "Anything inside it?"

"No."

"Better let Mrs. Amalfi take a look at it. Find out if it's Tony's."

Salmon nodded, picked up the lunchbox, and went back to the house. When he returned he said, "It's his all right." He made out an identification tag and tied it onto the handle. Bass watched, then climbed into the car and picked up the phone to report.

The dispatcher had a message. "The apartment Amalfi found the stuff in," the dispatcher said, "belonged to a man named Richard Lopez. Landlord says Lopez moved out a year ago, owing rent. Employed by the telephone company. Lieutenant says to find out what you can from the company."

"Right," Bass said.

Salmon started to turn the ignition key, but Bass stopped him. "Wait a minute," Bass said, frowning. "This guy Lopez, Richard Lopez. We had a bulletin on him. Let me think."

"You can think while I'm driving, can't you?"

"I'll place the guy after a while," Bass said. "While you were inside, this woman next door—she told me there was a car parked across the road last night. Lights were off, but somebody was sitting in it, smoking. Over there, by those trees."

"What kind of car?"

Bass shrugged. "Two-tone with a white trunk. And big fins."

Salmon punched the door open. "Let's have a look," he said.

They marched over to the clump of trees and examined the surface of the adjacent road. There was a small patch of oil slick on the macadam, and the shoulder showed tire marks. The two detectives studied the soil carefully.

"Can't identify tires from that," Salmon said. "No detail. What time did the car leave?"

"She thought around eleven. I don't see any cigarette butts, either."

"Ashtray," Salmon said laconically, and headed back to the car.

He drove jerkily and faster than usual. Bass stared through the windshield and was busy with his own thoughts. He said suddenly, "Richard Lopez. I got it now. A Missing Persons bulletin. No follow-up that I can remember."

"Then there was none," Salmon said. "Better tell the lieutenant."

Bass leaned forward to call the precinct.

The guy they saw at the phone company was a district manager or an exchange superintendent or a personnel supervisor, they didn't get his title straight, or care. He was polite enough and he dug up Lopez's record.

"He hasn't been with us for more than a year," the phone guy said.

"Why not?" Salmon asked.

"It doesn't say."

"What does it say?"

"Nothing."

"Can I have a look at that?" Salmon asked.

"It's confidential."

Salmon stood up irritably. His worry, his anger at the commissioner, all his pent-up feelings came to a head. "Let's have that paper," he said. "Confidential stuff—I don't buy that line."

"Officer," the phone guy said. "You have no right—"

Salmon grabbed the sheet out of the man's hand. It

read, "Discharged for cause." He slapped the sheet of paper down on the desk and said, "What was the cause?"

"I don't know."

"Listen, buster—you want trouble, you'll get it."

Bass slid between the two men. "Skip it," he said. "Let the lieutenant handle him."

Salmon swung around. "Sure," he said. "I got maybe an idea, anyhow."

Salmon didn't mention what it was, but he would have given heavy odds that Bass had the same idea. Wiretap.

The rest of the day they tried to forget the commissioner, and they worked the way cops work. They made no smart deductions and concocted no theories. They knew if they waited long enough, witnesses would turn up, police files would be consulted, important information would drop in their laps. Other men were busy with other leads, and the lieutenant would tie everything together. Patience and a minimum of imagination—that was their dish. The lieutenant would go to bat for them. He was paid to worry; they weren't. Still—

Salmon ticketed the lunchbox and turned it in for the lab boys to examine. He signed for it, and he and Bass drove off. They proceeded quietly on their rounds.

The next item that dropped in their laps came from the dispatcher. "Proceed to the Quick-Service Television Shop, 1817 North, and question Peter Milano. Amalfi tried to contact him yesterday."

After Bass had repeated the address, the dispatcher's voice dropped to a casual tone. "Hey," he said, "what's with you and the commissioner? He called a little while ago and said he wanted the pair of you in his office first thing in the morning. Said he liked fish for breakfast. You been making jokes with him?"

"Just mind your own business," Salmon said.

The dispatcher laughed. "My, my!" he said, "aren't we touchy!"

Salmon slammed down the phone.

On the way to the Quick-Service Television Shop he and Bass simmered down.

Pete Milano, young, black-eyed, was waiting for them.

He said he was Tony Amalfi's nephew and that Tony had dropped in on him yesterday afternoon around two-thirty.

"I wasn't here," Milano said. "He left word he'd be down at the corner place for a while—my uncle liked his beer—and that he had to see me."

"About what?" Bass asked.

"He didn't say. I got back a little after five and I called him. He asked if he could come up and use my tape recorder, but I had a service call to make, and then a date with my girl for that night. I tried to stall him off, but he said it was important and that he'd be up right after dinner. Well, he never got here."

"How long did you wait?" Bass asked.

"Till around eight-thirty. My girl—"

"So maybe he did get here, after you left."

"If he did," Milano said, "he'd have gone down to the corner for a beer. And I'd have seen him, because that's where I was."

"Did he say what he wanted to hear on your machine? Did he say anything about the tape?"

"Nothing. Officer, he was such an innocent little guy, he couldn't be involved in anything crooked."

"What makes you think there was something crooked?" Salmon asked.

"Well. . . ." Milano blinked uncomfortably, as if he was sorry he'd made the remark. "He was killed, wasn't he?"

Bass, fussing around the far corner of the shop, said suddenly, "You do all kinds of repair work, don't you?"

"Anything with wires, I can fix it."

"You and Lopez?" Bass said casually.

Milano looked startled. "Who's Lopez?" he asked.

Bass didn't answer. He glanced at Salmon and started out. Salmon followed him to the car and said, "He didn't bite on that one, but who knows? So how about a beer?"

"The beer'll keep," Bass said. "We got a session with the lieutenant ahead of us and he can smell a beer breath a mile off."

"Yeah," said Salmon.

At the precinct the lieutenant was waiting for them in

his office, and they went right in. He was strictly business.

"I got the medical and the lab reports here," he said, "and there's one little item you better think about, because the commissioner's likely to mention it." He glared coldly. "They found a fingerprint on that lunchbox, and you know whose it is? One of my own detectives!"

"They're cockeyed," Salmon said angrily. "That surface won't take prints. Impossible."

"Some cheese got rubbed on it, and that's what took the print."

"Oh," Salmon said. "Look, Lieutenant—those things happen—"

"They shouldn't," the lieutenant said crisply. "Particularly when the commissioner is on your neck."

"The lab boys could have skipped it," Bass said.

The lieutenant cleared his throat. "Well, let's get down to business. They found wood splinters in Amalfi's skull, so we know he was hit with some kind of a club. Lab says it was hardwood stained brown. He got killed around eleven or twelve, maybe a little earlier but not after midnight. Now—what did you boys come up with?"

He listened attentively while they spoke. He kept thumping his feet against the desk, which annoyed Salmon. Bass, however, seemed to enjoy the sound.

"Any leads on Lopez?" Bass asked.

The lieutenant shook his head. "He just dropped out of sight. No trace of him."

"Could have left town," Salmon remarked.

"And the state and the country," the lieutenant added. "And this physical world, too."

The detectives tried to look sorrowful, without success. The lieutenant stopped thumping.

"It's beginning to shape up," he said. "There was this wiretapping business a year ago."

He didn't have to tell them about that. The lieutenant had been the guy who broke the case and he'd exposed a few cops who had been in on the racket. A departmental shakeup had followed, and the lieutenant had gotten his big promotion from the ranks.

"I don't remember coming across Lopez's name," he said thoughtfully, "but he could have been one of the mechanics that hooked up wires. The phone company did some investigating of their own and fired quite a few people. I guess Lopez was one of them."

"We figured it that way," Salmon said.

"Let's say Lopez got hold of one of the tapes that was a recording of a phone conversation," the lieutenant said. "It incriminated somebody. When Lopez got fired, he needed money and decided to shake this somebody down. But instead of collecting, he got knocked off."

"And left the tape, or a copy of it, in his apartment," Bass said. "Hidden in the chimney, until Tony found it."

"And Tony got in touch with this same somebody who'd knocked off Lopez," the lieutenant said, "and tried to put the bite on him. That tells us the motive for killing Tony. And I'd say the killer got the tape and destroyed it. That's where we stand, right now."

"How," said Salmon, "did Tony know who this guy was? Tony hadn't heard the tape played because he never got together with his nephew."

"That's what the nephew says," Bass said mildly.

"Let's cut the guesswork," the lieutenant said. "We know Tony got two calls yesterday and one of them was from his nephew. The second was from somebody who knew Tony had gone home early and maybe knew Tony had found that tape. Well, who qualifies?"

"There was the gang working on the job with him," Salmon said, "but I can't see how they'd tie in. Just a bunch of bricklayers."

The lieutenant leaned back. "I think we're getting somewhere," he said. "Donlan. Bring him in."

Salmon stood up dutifully.

Bass said. "About that lab report—could it tell if those splinters came from a baseball bat?"

"Maybe," the lieutenant said. "Why?"

"Donlan had one at his shack. He used it to test the planking. Want us to get hold of it?"

"I'll send someone else for it," the lieutenant said. "And

you'd better have dinner first. Anyway, I want to get a line on Donlan before you bring him in."

He picked up the phone and was working as Salmon and Bass left the room.

Donlan's house was a lot fancier than anything you'd expect a construction foreman to have. Donlan opened the door himself and said in his rasping voice, "My family's away, down in Florida, so I'm all alone. Glad to see you, boys. What's on your mind?"

"Lieutenant wants to talk to you," Bass said.

"What about?"

"He'll tell you," Salmon said. "Come on."

"Now look, boys, don't be in such a hurry. Let's sit down and have a drink, and we can talk things over."

"No soap," Bass said.

Donlan stiffened. "I got a right to know," he said hoarsely.

Neither of the cops answered, but they moved in on him from both sides, ready for trouble, each of them knowing exactly what the other one would do.

Bass held back a couple of feet and slid his hand underneath his jacket and rested his fingers on his gun.

Salmon stepped forward, grabbed Donlan by the arm and spun him around. "Come on," he said, "and stop arguing."

Before they took Donlan in Bass opened the garage doors of Donlan's house. He saw a two-tone car with a white trunk and big fins. He closed the doors. When he marched over to Salmon, he gave a half-wink.

Back at the precinct, it was routine. The questioning, the relay of cops, the gradual breaking down. At eight o'clock, Donlan was saying he'd been home alone the night before looking at TV, that he'd never phoned Tony or thought of Tony or even guessed that Tony had found a tape. As for the baseball bat that had been in his shack, Donlan couldn't explain its disappearance. Somebody must have taken it, he said. Maybe to frame him.

By nine the lieutenant had Donlan involved in last year's wiretapping and Donlan was making vague admissions about paying somebody off for keeping quiet about padded payroll and labor kickbacks.

And by ten the lieutenant had Donlan reeling and Donlan began making more admissions. Yes, he'd spoken to Tony when Tony had walked off yesterday. Yes, he knew what Tony had found; he'd figured Tony might be onto a good thing and he'd wanted a piece of it, so he'd phoned Tony later in the afternoon and Tony had promised to bring the tape, but Tony hadn't kept his promise. Yes, the car across the road had been Donlan's. He'd gone to find Tony, but he insisted that he'd missed Tony and had never seen him or spoken to him since the phonecall. Donlan claimed he'd waited from eight until after eleven, when he finally gave up and went home. And that was the story he stuck to for the next hour.

With no confession in sight for a while, the lieutenant took Bass and Salmon into his office for a coffee break. They were tired, brain-weary, and not too hopeful.

"We got him on the ropes, but not knocked out," the lieutenant said. He pushed the pile of reports out of his way, so that he'd have elbow room to stir his coffee. "Even if the lab proves Tony was killed with a baseball bat, how do we prove the bat was Donlan's and that Donlan swung it? What we need right now is a bright idea."

Salmon fingered the reports. He was an unhappy guy, being on the spot with the commissioner. It was just his luck to get his fingerprint on the one spot on the lunch box that would take a print. And now he had an idea all right, but he wasn't sure that he had the nerve to come out with it. Guessing was no good, unless you could back up your guess with proof.

"The funny thing is," he said, slowly, carefully, "I believe that last story of Donlan's."

"Huh?" Bass said, surprised. "Why?"

"Because," Salmon answered, still slowly, as if he were groping for something, "Donlan admits he left Tony's house around eleven and came home. That leaves him wide open. If he's guilty, why didn't he claim he stayed there until one or two in the morning? That would make sense."

The lieutenant sipped his coffee. "What are you driving at?" he asked. "The nephew?"

Salmon lowered his eyes and fidgeted with the reports. The one on top was about the fingerprint on pizza cheese. He read the brief sentences and his heart suddenly lurched. He knew, knew definitely, his hunch was right.

"No," Salmon said. "I mean us. Bass and me—we also knew all about Tony's finding that tape."

"Go ahead," the lieutenant said.

"You hooked a lot of cops in the wiretap," Salmon said, "but it looks like you missed out on at least one. The one who got Lopez—and Tony Amalfi."

"Go on," the lieutenant said.

"Donlan was framed all right—by somebody who knew he had a baseball bat and who used it. As for me, last night I went to a birthday party where a dozen people saw me all evening. What about you, Bass? Where were you?"

"You're off your rocker," Bass said. "What about evidence?"

"Your footprint was there in the alley. That's evidence."

"I explained that."

"But it got me thinking. And now here's this fingerprint. I thought it was mine, but it says here in the report that the print's yours. And from that time the kid gave me the lunchbox you never even touched it. Besides, when I got the box, that cheese was too hard to take a print; the cheese crumbled when you touched it. But when the garbage pail was knocked over around midnight, the cheese was undoubtedly soft, and that's when you took the incriminating tape out of the lunchbox, after you killed Tony...."

Bass gaped and started stammering a denial.

Salmon, watching happily, wondered who his next partner would be. Someone, he hoped, with a nice ordinary name—like Rumplemeyer, say—so the boys couldn't make jokes.

THE LIVING DOLL
Richard O. Lewis

The reason I was having a relaxing beer in Patti's Place that evening was because it had been a long, hard day at Tafney's; long, because of the extra four hours I had had to put in that day; and hard, because of one Mr. Teems, general manager, who had been hopping around my stockroom all day like a one-locust plague, giving orders where none were needed and failing to give any where they might have been of some value.

Mr. Teems, like many egotists with small accomplishments, took his job with a deadly earnestness that brooked no humor. Immaculately clad, even to cutaway coat, he strode from floor to floor and from department to department, a frozen smile on his face for the customers and an ill-concealed frown for any clerk who seemed not to be displaying sufficient "customer-sales consciousness," a term he had dreamed up all by himself in one of his odd moments.

For the greater part of the year Mr. Teems didn't get too much in the way of anyone or obstruct to any great extent the normal flow of business, but when December began to roll around, he fell into a state of rapid metamorphosis. His mincing step became quicker and jerkier. He rubbed the back of an index finger more often across the hair-thin line of mustache that graced his upper lip and placed that index finger more and more frequently to the side of his temple, an outward manifestation of the creative thought processes which were supposed to be occurring within the confines of his narrow skull.

Everyone in the store, of course, knew precisely what

was happening: Mr. Teems was mentally designing the annual million-dollar Christmas display of jewelry and gemstones, a pretentious display for which the Tafney Company had long been noted.

After Mr. Teems's first week of mental travail there always followed another week of frenzied group planning. Designs of the intended display were hastily drawn and just as hastily discarded. More designs came and went or came and were changed beyond recognition until, finally, Mr. Teems himself gave birth to a brainchild that was of sufficient merit to be acceptable to his vanity. Strangely enough, the final plan always turned out to be precisely like the one that had been used during the preceding years, except for certain innovations such as a new paint job for the props and new outfits for some of the dwarfs.

I don't know if the display was worth the million dollars accredited to it, but I do know that the star which always graced the top of the Christmas tree in the center of the display window was undoubtedly worth several hundred grand, a tidy little fortune for anyone who might be lucky enough to have it in his possession.

I am not a thief by nature, but every man has his price, and a few thousand dollars would come in mighty handy. Many times during the five years I had been in charge of the stockroom of Tafney's—and, therefore, had been Mr. Teems's right-hand boy in the final assembling of the display, the task that was now absorbing long hours—my thoughts had wandered toward that tantalizing bauble of encrusted gems. Now, as I sat in Patti's Place, nursing my second bottle of relaxation, the same thoughts kept tapping away at my brain with the persistence of Poe's morbid raven.

Anyway, the whole setup offered an intriguing challenge. Protecting the street side of the display window was an ornamental steel grill, which, in turn, was connected to an alarm that was triggered to sound off at the slightest provocation. Besides that, police cars patrolled the street at irregular intervals, and spectators paused to gaze through the window during nearly all the hours of day and night. From the inside of the store the window could be entered only through a pair of double doors of steel, doors which could be firmly barred and time-locked against any intrusion.

Though the display window seemed impregnable, the Tafney Company protected themselves still further by insuring the gems for their full value; and each year the insurance company, for its own protection, placed an armed guard in the store during the night hours when the establishment was closed to the public.

Yes, it was an interesting challenge, and I could not help but wonder what would happen to the pompous, egotistical Mr. Teems if, after all the precautions against every conceivable eventuality, that star should vanish into thin air some night from the top of the tree. Yet, the possibility of that event ever occurring was so remote. . . .

My musing was suddenly penetrated by the tinny clatter of a piano, and as I looked in that direction a small girl came dancing out on the little stage. She wore a pinafore over a short dress that reached only to the knees of her ruffled pantalets. A floppy hat shaded one eye, and a long boa of white feathers was draped over her shoulders and dropped to her toes.

After once across the stage and back, she stopped, struck a pose, and began singing in a contralto voice that was amazingly low and husky.

"I don't want to grow up to be a lay-dee. . . ."

She didn't look to be more than five years old.

"Lay-dees have to wear such cum-ber-some things. . . ."

She took off the hat and flung it aside, exposing a tight coiffure of golden curls.

"They are tight and hot and so unhealth-ee. . . ." Her pinafore went skittering away toward the discarded hat.

"Just give me the lighter things—like di-a-mond rings. . . ." She held up a left hand that glittered and sparkled beneath the lights.

By the time she had divested most of her raiment except the feathered boa, which she handled with great dexterity, I realized this was no five-year-old I was watching. Finishing her song, and now clad in but the scantiest of attire, she went into an acrobatic dance.

It was when she was doing a series of contortions that the idea struck me. It hit me so suddenly that I sprang half out of my chair, upsetting my beer across the table. This was it!

A waiter came rushing up. "Anything wrong, Mac?"

"N-no," I said. "I—I just had a brilliant idea."

"Well, try not to have any more of 'em," he mumbled, wiping up the spillage. "One an evening is enough."

I flipped the pencil and order pad from his shirt pocket, found a dry spot on the table, and scribbled a note. "What's her name?" I asked, gesturing toward the stage.

He shrugged. "She's billed as Minneta, The Living Doll."

"Give her this," I said, handing him the pad, along with a folded bill, "and tell her where to find me."

A few minutes later The Living Doll appeared at my table. Her face was elfin as she peered questioningly up at me, and she was clad in a silken wraparound garment that did little to hide what she had so recently displayed. She seemed no taller than one of Tafney's Christmas dwarfs.

"Are you the one who speaks of big money?" she asked.

"Big-big money!" I said.

In one graceful move she left the floor and sat on the table directly in front of me. Her eyes were now almost on a level with mine, and I could see they were greenish with little flecks of brown. Devilishly impish!

"How old are you?" I asked, more from curiosity than anything else.

"Old enough to have a thirst," she said, signaling the waiter.

I ordered another beer, and she got a gin something-or-other and took a long appreciative swallow.

"How big is big-big money?" she asked, eyeing me over the rim of her glass.

"Big-big-big money!" I assured her.

"Legit?" She took another long drink.

"A one-night performance," I told her. "The greatest performance of your career."

"Keep talking."

Suddenly I realized I didn't actually have a plan. All I had was a nebulous idea that might be whipped into shape—or might not pan out at all. It would require some thinking, and I needed her help in the thinking.

Two couples had seated themselves at the table next to ours. "I don't have all the angles figured yet," I said. "Let's get out of here. Go somewhere—"

"Look, buddy," she said, drawing back, "I've heard a lot better lines than that. Now, if you've got something on the ball, let's have it. If not, call me up sometime when you do." She finished her drink and set the glass on the table.

I grabbed her wrist, and found it surprisingly sturdy for its size. "No!" I pleaded. "Don't go! Listen! This deal can't wait! It's got to start moving by tomorrow morning and we've got to plan it together. Tonight!"

I felt her relax a bit, and I remembered one of the lines of her song. "... *give me the lighter things—like di-a-mond rings....*"

I raised her hand. "Look," I said, "how would you like to have all the cut diamonds you could hold in this hot little fist of yours—and more?"

That did it. She looked at her hand and then at me, and I could see that the song had meant something to her beyond mere words.

"You on the level?" she asked, finally.

I nodded. "Scout's honor! We'll go to my apartment—"

"Just a minute." She drew her wrist from my grasp. "There's something you should know, just in case you turn out to be a phony. I have a brother and he is not exactly what you might call a midget!"

"We'll talk," I assured her. "You can leave at any time."

I got to my feet and lifted her down from the table. "Better get your gear," I suggested. "If things work out, you may not want to come back."

An hour—and a half bottle of gin—later, we had most of the details worked out. Surprisingly, the plan had taken form almost on its own accord. She was now holding out for a fifty-fifty split, claiming she would be running all the risk.

I gave her another glass of gin and explained to her that my risk was fully as great as her own and, too, that the idea had been mine. "A sixty-five-thirty-five deal should be fair enough," I said, "considering all the circumstances."

She leaned back, resting her head against my shoulder, and grinned up at me pixielike. "All right," she agreed.

The next morning I took her into the stockroom with me where Mr. Teems was already prancing about, giving unnecessary orders, and introduced her to him. "Mr. Teems," I said, "this is Alice, my little niece."

She made an awkward curtsy that brought the hem of her dress nearly to the floor.

Mr. Teems looked down his thin nose at her in a manner that clearly indicated he was far too busy to be bothered by infants.

"I'll just have her for a few days," I explained, "while my sister is away."

Childlike, little "Alice" was immediately attracted to the seven dwarfs that were standing in line waiting to be transported to the display window. She fingered the material of their costumes, noted their tiny hats, and paid particular attention to their painted faces. Then she went over and sat down beside an empty gift-wrapped box that was also destined to become a part of the display.

During lunch hour I hurried her off to a store a few blocks away and bought her the materials she pointed out, along with shears, needles, thread, and a few other necessities. Then I taxied her back to my apartment and left her there to her own devices.

She went with me again the next afternoon, a stuffed handbag suspended over one shoulder by a strap. The dwarfs and most of the other props had already reached their appointed places in the display window where Mr.

Teems was now officiously holding forth.

I carried in the rest of the display—toys, dolls, empty gift-wrapped boxes of various sizes, rubber balls gaudily painted—and placed them under the tree in the manner indicated by Mr. Teems' chart. When all was finally in order, Mr. Teems alone remained in the citadel to give the scene its final touch, the million-dollar display of jewelry, after which the steel doors would be barred and locked and the key handed over to an official of the insurance company.

With the help of Robbie, my young assistant, I cleaned the stockroom of the rubble that had accumulated during the last few hectic days, tossed the debris into the incinerator that graced the rear wall, ignited it, opened the draft, and clanged shut the iron door. Then I washed up and went across the street to the cafeteria for a cup of coffee.

At precisely eight P.M. Mr. Teems and I, along with a half dozen more of the store's personnel, were gathered on the street outside the curtained display window. A wintry wind had sprung up and little puffs of snow were skittering about the sidewalk.

Mr. Teems gave a signal to someone at the door who gave a signal to someone in the store who, in turn, gave a signal to someone else who pressed a button to set the heavy curtain into motion, and the rest of us gave out with a suitable number of "ohs" and "ahs" to gratify the ego of Mr. Teems as the display was slowly unveiled to all who cared to behold.

In the center of the dimly lighted scene was the Christmas tree with toys and boxes arranged at its base. At the far right-hand side was a doorway over which was painted WORKSHOP, and from the doorway a dwarf was advancing in jerky motion along a hidden track. In his extended hands he held a plush box containing a solitaire and a diamond-encrusted wedding band, tilted at the proper angle so the spectators in the street could get an unobstructed view. After traversing the entire length of the window, the dwarf paused before an oversized Santa

Claus who gave three mechanical nods of approval. Then, turning about and following another hidden track, the elf-like figure disappeared behind the Christmas tree, obviously to send the gift upon its way.

Another dwarf and another followed at irregular intervals, each bearing a glittering gift for Santa's gearshift approval, until seven in all had made the journey. Then the cycle was repeated.

Mechanical dolls sat here and there, but did little more than move their heads from side to side and give an occasional wink of a glassy eye.

Dominating all was the star atop the tree. In the center of its velvet face was a blood-red ruby. Surrounding the ruby was a circle of sapphires, and extending outward from the circle into each of the five points of the star were three converging rows of graduated diamonds. The other side of the flat star was nearly identical. Concealed red and blue lights were focused upon the star in such a manner that while it turned slowly about on its spindle, bringing first one side and then the other into view, the thousands of facets of the clustered gems filled the entire scene with a scintillating snowstorm of refracted lights that showered down over the gems in the tree and in the hands of the jerky dwarfs.

Yes, it was a glittering, beautiful—and expensive—display, and we all took turns shaking the hand of Mr. Teems, genius, and gushing out our congratulations.

Once clear of the crowd that was rapidly gathering, I raised the collar of my coat, snapped the brim of my hat down, faced into the wind, and entered the first movie theater that presented itself.

Some three hours later I was seated near the broad windows of a cafeteria, a cup of coffee and a folded newspaper on the table before me, and a clear view of the Tafney display directly across the street.

It was now near midnight, the storm had increased a bit, and there were but a few late stragglers upon the street. Only occasionally did anyone pause to give the Tafney display the attention it so richly deserved.

I lit a cigarette, sipped my coffee, unfolded my newspaper, and waited, as jittery as the backer of a Broadway production on opening night.

Suddenly, and without preliminaries, the lid of a large gift box snapped back and an elfin figure popped up. The figure wore the same kind of attire as the mechanical dwarfs and had the same painted face and the same pointed nose. It remained frozen and immobile as someone paused to gaze into the window.

I glanced quickly about me. There was only one other customer seated near the windows, a book propped up on the table before him. It was extremely doubtful he was even aware of the Tafney exhibit.

My gaze swept back to the scene again. The onlooker had gone, and the elf was now out of the box and walking jerkily mechanically along the hidden track toward Santa, for all the world like one of the dwarfs. It didn't pause to receive Santa's nods of approval, but turned sharply about and disappeared behind the Christmas tree.

I wanted to laugh but checked myself. I knew what would happen to the jewels of each dwarf as it passed from sight behind that tree, so I was not surprised when, as the cycle began to repeat itself, the gift box in the hands of each dwarf that came from the workshop door was now tightly closed—and empty.

But I *was* surprised when one of the dwarfs swerved haltingly from the beaten trail, took up a position under the tree, and wheeled around to face the window. For the moment I had failed to distinguish the real from the unreal.

Three women, muffled in furs, had paused to gaze at the display. A patrol car rolled slowly by without pausing or changing course. No one paid particular heed to the elfin figure that had now become a part of the background, its head moving jerkily from side to side, an eye closing and opening occasionally in a mechanical wink.

Yes, Minneta, The Living Doll, was indeed giving the finest performance of her career!

When the women left, Minneta went into action again,

moving about as if directed by an inner system of gears. Within minutes, the baubles from the lower branches of the tree—necklaces, brooches, rings, diamond-studded watches—had disappeared into the hidden pockets of her tiny costume.

Then, slowly and haltingly, freezing into place when anyone passed by or paused at the window, she began ascending, step by step, the pyramid of gift-wrapped boxes near the tree. As she neared the top, I forgot to breathe. This was the final scene of the drama, the climax of the production. Here, before the very eyes of all, the boldest jewel theft of all time was in progress, a theft that would go down through the pages of history as a classic, a brilliant masterpiece of mystery.

A doll-like hand reached up toward the star and paused. The elfin face was turned directly toward me, and I am certain I saw an eye close in an impish wink. Then the hand plucked the prize from its spindle, and the swirling snow storm of variegated lights came to an abrupt end.

I glanced quickly about me again, and my heart suddenly stopped beating. The man with the book had chosen this particular moment to look up from his reading. I couldn't see his face, but from the tilt of his head it seemed impossible that he should not be aware of the change in the scene across the street.

I waited. Then my pent-up breath flowed out again in a long quivering sigh as he methodically turned a page and lowered his head slowly toward it.

Two minutes later the elf was back in its box, and the lid had flipped shut.

I got stiffly up from the table, my legs nearly paralyzed from the tension I had been under. There was now nothing more to do until I reported for work in the morning at the usual time. By then the theft would be known, there would be an investigation, a certain amount of confusion. I had but to mingle with the hubbub and, at a propitious moment, have my "niece" appear unobtrusively at my side, her filled handbag slung from its shoulder strap. I would then take her lovingly by her little hand and lead her gently away—and that would be that.

But it didn't turn out quite that way. When I passed the display window the next morning, I saw that the curtains had been drawn shut which meant, of course, that the theft had been discovered. But when I entered the store, there was no hubbub in progress, no confusion. The steel doors of the window stood partly open, and a uniformed policeman was standing quietly beside them. There were a few clerks here and there, their faces pale and drawn, their heads held at half mast. It was as if a funeral were in progress.

Miss Prentis, from Hosiery, spotted me and came scurrying up, wringing her hands. "Oh, Mr. Jones!" she sobbed. "Something terrible has happened! The window! The jewels! Gone! Vanished into thin air!"

I let my face show what I hoped was the proper amount of amazement and concern.

"The police patrol saw that something was wrong with the window early this morning—and they called Mr. Teems—and he called some of us—and the people from the insurance company came—and there was a thorough police investigation and...."

"The thief!" I said, cutting in on her babbling. "Did—did they catch the thief?"

"Thief! Why, Mr. Jones, you know that no one could get in or out of that window! The jewels just vanished! Just like—like magic!"

Well, so far so good. At least Minneta hadn't been discovered as yet. Now all I had to do was get rid of Miss Prentis and wait for the right moment.

I started for the steel doors, Miss Prentis trailing me. The policeman stepped aside, and one glance through the doors showed quite plainly why he hadn't bothered to stop me. What had once been a scene of beauty was now a shambles. The tree was on its side, two dwarfs lay at grotesque angles, the false front of the "workshop" had been torn completely away, Santa had vanished, and nearly all the gifts from under the tree—including a certain large gift box—were gone. It was as if a tornado had struck the place. I felt a chill of fear course through me.

"Mr. Teems! Poor man!" It was Miss Prentis again. She had thrust her head in through the door. "He went into a regular tantrum! He pulled his hair! He screamed! He tore things out! Carried them away—"

I turned quickly, nearly knocking her down. "Where did he take them? Where did he carry them to?"

"The stockroom," she said, struggling to regain her balance. "He carried everything there and—"

I started toward the stockroom. Maybe things would work out all right after all.

"—and threw them into the incinerator!"

I stopped and wheeled about. "He did *what?*" I shouted.

"Poor man!" Miss Prentis raised both hands to the sides of her head, "He was completely bereft of his senses, a regular madman! Throwing everything into the incinerator! They took him away in an ambulance just a few minutes ago—in a complete state of shock. . . ."

I didn't listen any more. I raced to the back of the store, pushed open the door to the stockroom and rushed in. The floor was littered with pine needles, tinsel, a few scraps of paper and ribbon. Nothing more.

I leaped to the door of the incinerator and flung it open. A gust of living flame lashed out across my face, and I clanged the door shut again.

Suddenly the room spun in one direction, my stomach in another, and I staggered to a wall and held myself up.

I was only dimly conscious of finally groping my way through the store and into the street.

"Poor man!" someone was saying as I left. It was probably Miss Prentis. "I don't know what is going to become of us all!"

In my apartment I opened a fresh bottle of gin, sat down on the divan, and stared into space. Finally, I found myself looking at the silken garment lying on the divan beside me. I picked it up, found the little suitcase, and tossed the garment into it, along with a few other odds and ends and a few scraps of material she had left lying about. I tucked the suitcase under the divan and out of sight. Sooner or later, I would have to get rid of it. I wondered how long it would be before someone missed her and set into motion a search. She had said something about having a brother.

I didn't leave the apartment for two days, except just long enough to get a newspaper and a fresh supply of gin.

The newspaper had played it big, given it nearly half of the front page. A fortune in jewels disappearing while spectators watched and patrol cars patroled! The perfect crime! And Mr. Teems, under sedation at City Hospital, a possible nervous collapse. . . .

I tossed the paper aside. Mr. Teems be damned! A typical egocentric: shatter the ego and there is nothing left! Nothing at all.

It was nearly two weeks before I could drag myself back to work in the stockroom, and even then I could not force myself to glance in the direction of the incinerator.

Fortunately, there was much work to be done. Robbie had fallen far behind during my absence, and the bulletin board was cluttered with requests from the various departments. I glanced at one of them, then selected a box and set to work.

"Too bad about Mr. Teems," said Robbie, hammering away at a crate behind me.

I didn't answer. I didn't care what happened to Mr. Teems, just so long as it was all bad.

"Nervous breakdown. Doctors ordered him to take a complete rest, away from everything, somewhere in the sunshine."

I couldn't care less.

"Some of us went down to the airport last week to see him off to Mexico," Robbie continued. "Him and his little nephew."

My hammer paused in midair.

"Cute little tyke, that nephew. Purty as a living doll. . . ."

I had quit listening. My brain had suddenly become a madhouse filled with tumbling questions.

What would an egocentric do on the opening night of his masterpiece? Would he go quietly home and crawl into bed? Or would he stand across the street and watch the awed reactions of the passersby? And would the unfolding of a certain drama suddenly fill his egotistical being with greed and avarice?

Had Mr. Teems thrown a *real* fit next morning in the store? Had he tossed *everything* into the incinerator?

Or had Mr. Teems purposefully created a lot of confusion during which he had carefully emptied out the contents of one large gift box, threatened the contents with exposure, made a quick deal, and let the contents slip quietly away out the back door of the stockroom?

I sat down weakly on the edge of a packing case and let the hammer slide from my fingers. I shook my head, sighed, and looked at the closed door of the incinerator. It was quite possible that I would never *really* know. . . .

THE FLAT MALE
Frank Sisk

Reaching deftly behind the jug of formaldehyde, Thaddeus Conway brought forth from the closet shelf a bottle of his own brand of embalming fluid. It was a fifth of Pennsylvania rye now reduced to about half of its original contents. Uncorking, Thaddeus set a mustached lip to the task of further diminishment. The apple in his scrawny throat bobbed twice. He caught his breath with a shudder and then sighed, "Aaah, better, better...."

At that a four-noted chime rang discreetly in the distance, *"How dry I am."* Or so it seemed to say to Thaddeus.

"Want me to get it, Thad?" asked a man's voice from behind the half-open door to the preparation room.

"No, John. I'm on the way." He replaced the bottle of rye on the shelf. At a nearby sink he drew a glass of water and swallowed an ounce distastefully. He then looked at himself in the mirror above the sink. His sharp nose was nearly as red as the carnation in his left lapel.

There had been a real nip in the air at the cemetery that morning, he reminded himself. Bad burial weather, if there was any such thing as good.

Again the distant chimes caroled *"How dry I am"* and Thaddeus, sober-faced as befit his profession, moved on quiet shoes of black patent leather to answer.

At the big door of darkened oak stood a small woman in her late middle years. Many who approached the mortuary establishment of F. X. Conway & Son wore an expression of stunned grief or unquenchable sorrow, but this woman looked essentially brisk, even businesslike. She also looked like a lady of some refinement. Thaddeus based this last assessment on a practiced glance at her apparel and accessories. Not too expensive, but in good taste and of good quality.

"I am Thaddeus Conway, madam," he announced most mellifluously. "Will you step inside?"

"Thank you," the woman said. "My name is Cora Peddington and I do need your assistance."

"Whatever the circumstances, madam, it will be my pleasure to assist. This way if you will."

The pert little lady accompanied him to the Statistic Room, so named by his recently departed father, and he seated her in a deep leather chair which nearly engulfed her to the midriff. Such a chair, in Dad's opinion, trapped a person into telling the truth.

"May I offer you coffee as we converse? Or tea?" The inflection in his voice recalled Dad's on similar occasions, and Thaddeus resented it in spite of himself.

"Tea will be fine," the woman said.

"With or without, Mrs. Peddington? It is *Mrs.* Peddington?"

"Yes it is. With lemon and without cream."

Thaddeus pressed a white button on the wall which actuated a buzzer in the preparation room, thereby informing John to set aside the embalming apparatus and put on the water to boil.

"I'd like to smoke if I may," Mrs. Peddington said.

"You most certainly may," Thaddeus responded.

"But not in this chair," she said. "If you will help extricate me, I'll take the wooden chair by the window."

Proffering a hand, Thaddeus classified this little lady as one who might have outwitted his father. He supplied her with a light for the cigarette and an ashtray. Then, settling himself in the swivel chair, which stood in front of a rolltop desk, he turned and bent a sympathetic gaze upon her.

"I suppose I may as well get to the point," said Mrs. Peddington.

"My time is at your disposal." Thaddeus swiveled the

chair a couple of inches and reached for a pad of yellow paper.

"I am looking for a good economical undertaker," Mrs. Peddington continued.

Thaddeus extracted a ballpoint pen from the inner pocket of his coat. "Undertaker" was a term he abhorred, and when modified by "economical," it was a treacherous phrase. He smiled blandly. "We are extremely flexible here, madam. Let me assure you of that at the outset."

"Good," said Mrs. Peddington. "That's more than one can say for some of your competitors. If that's the word."

Thaddeus began to feel the need for a drink. "You've dealt, then, with other morticians in the past?"

"I've been dealing with them this morning," said Mrs. Peddington.

"Please forgive me, madam, but I don't seem to follow you."

"It's simple enough, Mr. Conway. I've got to cut costs to the bone. As a result, I must shop around."

"Shop around?" Something new had been added to the professional lexicon, and Thaddeus knew it would have shocked dear old Dad out of countenance. "Shop around? Well, yes, of course. Naturally."

"I'm glad you understand," said Mrs. Peddington. "None of the others did, really."

"Well, that's understandable, too," said Thaddeus. "Some of us are more progressive than others. But before we proceed with the financial aspects of the matter, I should like to get a few of the pertinent data together, biographical and the like. For the obituary, you know, and certain statistical records."

"Of course."

"First, may I assume that we're talking about—ah— Mr. Peddington, who is your husband?"

"Oh, definitely." Mrs. Peddington's small smile was rueful. "I forgot to mention him, didn't I?"

"I'm afraid so." Thaddeus began to jot on the pad. "He has left us?"

Mrs. Peddington cocked her head birdlike. "Left us?"

"In a manner of speaking."

"Oh, I see what you mean. Yes. You may say he has left us."

Thaddeus set down his pen and said, quite formally, "Permit me to convey my sincere condolences, madam. It is a moment like this that. . . ." He let the sentence melt to a mumble under the rather flabbergasted look in Mrs. Peddington's eyes. Unlike his late parent, Thaddeus was often beset by doubts as to the importance of what he was doing. Sometimes he felt he would have been happier as a floorwalker or a bartender, and this was one of those times. "Well, now," he said, retrieving his pen, "we may as well begin with your husband's full name."

"Adam L. Peddington."

"Age?"

"Fifty-one."

"Address?"

"Eleven Briarwood Gardens."

Thaddeus was acquainted with this luxury-apartment complex. Residence there hardly indicated the need for cut-rate funeral service unless the Peddingtons were a butler-housekeeper team.

"Occupation?" he asked.

"Adam is comptroller—*was* comptroller, I should say, of Videlectronics Corporation."

This made the reason for economy more elusive than ever, for Videlectronics was large and still growing. Its comptroller would be a man of ample means. But rather than probe that area at the moment, Thaddeus shifted to another level of questioning. "Did he leave suddenly, Mrs. Peddington, or was he taken by a lingering illness?"

"No, it was quite sudden, quite sudden." An odd light, almost of amusement, shone briefly in her eyes. "One could call it precipitate."

"It can be a blessing that way," said Thaddeus, reverential. "A blessing on both sides. And just how did he go?"

Mrs. Peddington stamped her cigarette into its ash. "Out the window," she said.

"Here today and gone tomorrow," said Thaddeus, and then appeared to hear himself and Mrs. Peddington in counterpoint. "Did you say Mr. Peddington went *out the window?*"

"The window in our living room, yes."

"Oh, my," said Thaddeus.

"It opens out onto a tiny balcony as a rule," said Mrs. Peddington. "But the balcony was removed a few days ago when it was discovered that several of the supporting lag bolts—I believe that's what they're called—had rusted away at the mortise."

"Oh, my," repeated Thaddeus.

"It presented a hazard as it was," said Mrs. Peddington. "And so it was removed until a new balcony could be installed. Unfortunately, I forgot to tell this to Adam. He's so seldom at home these days. But this morning he wanted a breath of crisp air, as he called it—"

"It was nippy earlier," said Thaddeus, transfixed.

"—and before I realized what he was doing, he pushed open the window and stepped out."

"And this—this caused his death?"

"Instantly. Our apartment is on the top floor, the tenth."

"Oh, my," said Thaddeus, shivering.

At this moment John entered the Statistic Room, bearing a silver tray. Wordlessly he set it on a table convenient to Thaddeus, then retired. Thaddeus needed the respite. He poured tea for his guest and coffee for himself. Holding the cup a few inches from his mustache, he sniffed appreciatively: the sweet smell of rye mingled complementarily with the steamy aroma of coffee. John was on the ball.

As they sipped Thaddeus directed the conversation away from the immediate question and learned that the Peddingtons had been married twenty years and had no children. Besides his wife, Mr. Peddington was survived only by a sister in Canada and a few nephews whom he had never seen.

"Well, you had twenty years together," said Thaddeus with his father's pseudophilosophic intonation. "That's more than many of us have. Twenty years make many memories." He placed his cup on the saucer, wondering if the rye was making him talk like this.

"Adam is all—*was* all business," said Mrs. Peddington. "I won't be a hypocrite about it. Twenty years of living with a business machine, that's what it amounts to."

"Takes all kinds," said Thaddeus, quaffing deep of the cup.

"When we were first married, we had to save every penny for his night-school course. After he became an accountant we saved for a house, which we finally bought, only to sell almost immediately at a profit. The profits went into other real estate, then into stock-option plans. We never had a honeymoon."

"Nor I," said Thaddeus who had not yet even been married.

"I won't mourn him," said Mrs. Peddington. "That would be hypocritical. Frankly, Mr. Conway, we have been far from close together during these last years. Each time his company promoted him, the gulf between us grew wider. He preferred younger women as he got older."

"A common failing, I fear," said Thaddeus. "Worldly success does not guarantee happiness. This, by the way, leads me to wonder about the contradictions in your situation, madam."

"What contradictions are those?"

"Well, obviously Mr. Peddington was on the way up, so to speak, before he went out and down. This would seem to mean money, if I may say so."

"It does mean money. I don't know how much. Adam excluded me from his financial secrets. But I should guess he is rich or very close to it."

"I am at a loss then to understand why you, as his widow, are so concerned with cutting the cost of his funeral to the bone, as you put it. Not that I believe in extravagance at such times, but—"

"I have no choice," said Mrs. Peddington. "I *must* cut the cost to the bone."

"But you inherit, don't you?"

"Not immediately. My husband always professed a strong antipathy for rich widows. He felt that, between the time of their husbands' deaths and the time they gained control of the legacies, a purgative period should ensue. This would give the widows a more balanced view of the past and the future. Or so he often said. In my case his will stipulates that I inherit nothing except the money from his life insurance for a period of two years after his death."

"Life insurance, ah," said Thaddeus. This was something more up his professional alley. "Well, there we have it."

"Perhaps not," said Mrs. Peddington.

"Life insurance, certainly, is immediately collectable."

"Yes, true," said Mrs. Peddington. "But my husband's will further stipulates that I must live exclusively on this life-insurance money for two years after his death. I must not work to supplement this money. I must not borrow. I may beg if I wish, or use any monies I may possess at the time of his death. But I must not pawn any personal items, such as jewelry. Not that I have much jewelry."

"An unusual document," commented Thaddeus. "What are the consequences of just ignoring it?"

"Clear. I inherit, in that case, only a tenth of the estate, the remainder going to his sister and her sons."

"How much insurance did he leave?"

"Two thousand dollars is the face value."

"You mean you are expected to live on two thousand dollars for two years?" Thaddeus made a mental calculation. "Why my dear lady, that is only about twenty dollars a week."

"I know. Adam was quite businesslike about it when he pointed this out to me. When we were first married, he was earning two thousand a year. We lived on it and saved money besides."

"But the cost of living was much lower in those days."

"Also the cost of dying."

"But two thousand dollars, madam, is ridiculous. You can't possibly survive, except by charity."

"I do have nearly five hundred in a secret savings account. That's one thing he doesn't—didn't know about."

"Every little bit helps."

"Oh, and the insurance policy does carry a double-indemnity clause. So that makes it four thousand in case of accidental death, doesn't it?"

"Yes," said Thaddeus, reaching again for the coffee, lukewarm though it was.

"And falling from a tenth-story window upon a balcony which isn't there—that's usually construed as an accidental death, I believe."

"I believe so," said Thaddeus.

Mrs. Peddington opened her handbag and produced a small spiral-bound notebook and a silver pencil. "Shall we discuss basic costs now, Mr. Conway?"

Thaddeus heaved a sigh and nodded. "To begin with, Mrs. Peddington, in most instances of violent death, such as a fatal fall, certain cosmetic services are required to restore the features of the deceased to a semblance of—"

"We can dispense with that," said Mrs. Peddington briskly, making a note in her book.

"I see. A closed-casket ceremony."

"I don't plan on a casket at all."

"If not a casket, then what, madam?"

"A basket should do, I think. Do they come with lids?"

Thaddeus sighed sadly. "Yes, they do come with lids."

"Fine."

"Now, as to his burial attire, do you wish to supply it, or would you prefer to leave it to our discretion?"

"Why not let him go as he is?"

"Well, it's never done, I can assure you of that. Whatever the poor man was wearing when he fell is probably all—ah—rumpled or worse."

"Probably a bloody mess," said Mrs. Peddington. "No earthly good to anyone else. So we'll let him take it with him. Adam would really like the economics of it. He hated waste."

"Oh, my! Well, next we must decide on the place of interment. Unless you already subscribe to a memorial association."

"We'll cremate him," said Mrs. Peddington. "Adam respected the value of real estate."

An hour later, as he reached behind the jug of formaldehyde, Thaddeus said to John, "This afternoon we may have to go out and pick up a flat male."

John answered from the preparation room. "In the city?"

"Yes, but I'm not sure where yet."

"High diver?"

"I hate to say this, John, but I have a funny feeling that his wife pushed him."

"That little dame up front with you?"

"No other." Thaddeus sluiced his throat with rye and nearly decided this time he was in the wrong business. "Little but wiry. Mind like a steel trap, John. Lived for twenty years with this glorified bookkeeper. Miser type, rest his soul. Taught her how to pinch pennies."

"Can't we pick him up now, Thad? I'm finished with this one, just about."

"Not till we hear from the little lady, John."

"I don't get it, Thad."

"If we're low bidder—" Thaddeus shook his head slowly and gravely as if commiserating with a fast-fading image of himself as the dutiful son of F. X. Conway. "If we're low bidder, John, we'll get the body. The little lady is home now comparing the cost figures from four funeral directors. Her husband should be proud of her."

"F. X. must be turning over in his grave right about this time."

"Amen," said Thaddeus, setting the bottle of rye reluctantly back on the shelf.

The afternoon went pleasantly. Thaddeus drank beer and watched television. John ran the vacuum cleaner haphazardly from room to room. It was nearly six o'clock before they realized it, and then it was the sound of a siren that alerted them to the time.

Thaddeus looked at his wristwatch as the shrill sound grew closer, closer. John looked out the front window.

"Fire engine?" asked Thaddeus.

"Ambulance," said John. "Police ambulance, and coming right up our driveway, Thad."

"Well, since we don't operate a hospital," said Thaddeus, "I guess Mrs. Peddington is awarding the body to us."

"First time I ever heard of the cops running taxi service like this," said John, going to the door.

"That's true," said Thaddeus, puzzled. "Unusual."

After the remains of Adam L. Peddington, contained in a long burlap sack, were deposited in the preparation room, Thaddeus invited the ambulance driver and his assistant to join him in a drink. They accepted. He broached a fresh bottle of rye and even brought out glasses and ice.

When the glasses were aloft, Thaddeus said, "I'm much obliged to you boys for transporting the corpse from the morgue or wherever it was."

"Morgue!" exclaimed the driver. "We picked it off the street."

"As soon as the coroner gave his okay," said the assistant.

"You mean to say the city let a body lay around the street all day?" asked Thaddeus incredulously.

"All day, hell!" said the driver. "The guy fell out a window a little more than an hour ago." He looked at his watch. "The cops got there before he stopped bouncing and we got there almost as soon. Then the coroner came with the medical examiner, like they'd both been standing around the corner. Right, Moe?"

"Right," said Moe. "Good booze you got here."

The driver continued, "The whole investigation was finished in fifty, fifty-five minutes. Moe and me had the bundle ready to drive to the morgue when the wife comes up with the coroner, and they tell us to take it here and get a receipt."

"A receipt," murmured Thaddeus, sitting down at the table in front of his empty glass. As he wrote he tried to whistle *"How dry I am"* but his lips were too dry.

CHAVISKI'S CHRISTMAS
Edwin P. Hicks

Joe Chaviski, retired chief of detectives, sniffed the smoke and disinfectant that permeated the grim gray atmosphere of the Fort Sanders police station and city jail. It was so sweet to him that he filled his mighty lungs a second time. This was his youth again—this was living as he had known it for thirty years as a member of the force.

Detective Chief Marty Sauer, who was once one of his "boys," came into the station smoking a big black cigar. "Joe, what are you doing down here on Christmas Eve? Last place I'd be tonight if I could get away."

"You can," Joe said. "That's the reason I came down—so one or more of you boys could take off and be with your wife and kids."

Sauer stuck out his hand. "Wish I could take you up on that, Joe."

"Go on home, Marty. I'll take over," Chaviski offered.

Sauer didn't go. Instead, he went over to a bench and picked up the afternoon paper.

Detective Johnnie Hopp came in. "Well I'll be—Joe Chaviski! Merry Christmas, Joe. I thought you'd be home popping corn or maybe out of town visiting relatives."

"Have a cigar, Johnnie," Joe said, pulling a long black one from his pocket.

"Is this a Fidel special?" Hopp asked. "Won't explode on me, now, Joe?"

"What do you rummies think I am? This ain't April Fool. You think I'd give you an exploding cigar at Christmas?"

"Well, no—not at Christmas." Hopp lighted up. He

took a couple of puffs and then held the cigar at arm's length. It didn't explode. "Gee, thanks, Joe," he said.

"Of all the uncouth, ungrateful ignoramuses," Joe stormed, glaring with his old fervor, "you're the worst! Don't you respect a friend's gift?"

"Sorry, Joe. I really am. This is a darn good cigar."

"I came down here thinking I could take over somebody's run for an hour or so, let the boys take turns going home to be with their kids on Christmas Eve. All I get is insults."

"Chief's got a schedule worked out," Hopp said. "I get off at eight-thirty and go home for an hour. All the boys get off sometime tonight. Day shift's coming back to help out."

"Okay, okay," Joe said. "Don't mention it. I come down here to be good to some guy. Might as well go on back home and listen to the Christmas carols. That's all there is on television. I'll be glad when Christmas is over."

Joe didn't go home. It was the last place he wanted to be tonight. It was so barren and empty—his wife, Lucy, had been dead seven years now. Christmas had meant so much to Lucy. They had never had children, so she'd take a dozen or more youngsters from the orphanage into their home for a real Christmas. Joe had always groaned when the bills came in, but the happiness that Lucy had given the children was worth it. Of course it was always his lot to work on Christmas Eve, but like all the boys he had got off duty for an hour, and Lucy had him play Santa Claus and distribute the gifts. He'd change into a Santa Claus suit in the garage—and with his two hundred and fifty pounds it needed no padding.

Now Joe's home rang with emptiness instead of the happy laughter of little children. He hadn't put up any Christmas decorations, and the packages he had received earlier in the week from Charlie Taylor, his nephew in St. Louis, and from Emma Howard, his niece in Memphis, still lay unopened on the living-room table. Joe had mailed out his presents ten days ago and had posted his Christmas cards the week before. He had also mailed a sizable contribution for presents at the orphans' home. Now, on Christmas Eve, he had wandered down to the police station to grouch and cuss and joke with the boys —to be with other humans on the most terrible night of the year for a retired and lonely man.

Desk Sergeant Jack Haley had a fruitcake wrapped in foil on his desk, beside a big electric percolator. "Help yourself, Joe," he said. Joe cut a piece of cake and filled a paper cup with hot black coffee. "Cream and sugar over there," Haley said.

"No, thanks, I like it black."

Motor Patrolmen Pete Rauser and Charlie Henryetta came in with a drunk. They booked him, searched him, turned his billfold, watch, and pocketknife over to Haley, who also served as night jailer, and then put him in the runaround. "Go to sleep," said Rauser, "and sober up."

Henryetta cracked a pecan and began eating it. Rauser went to the telephone and dialed his wife. "How are the kids? Tell them I'll be home in a little while—oh, about half an hour. Fix me some eggnog."

Night Chief Merle Henson came in. "Hello, Joe. Glad to see you."

"I came down thinking I might take over for someone, let one of the boys go home to his family."

Henson nodded. "Thanks, Joe. Appreciate it. But we got a schedule all worked out."

"Hell of a thing about that three-year-old being kidnapped over at Tulsa last night," said Marty Sauer, putting down the paper. "We watched the bridge all last night. Stopped every car coming from Oklahoma. He either had already got through or headed somewhere else out of Sallisaw."

"Anything new on it?" Joe asked.

"No, nothing," Chief Henson said, "except we got a picture of the kid, special delivery, about thirty minutes ago from the Tulsa police department. Posted on the bulletin board."

Joe swore. Kidnapping—at Christmas! He waddled over to the bulletin board and looked at the poster hurriedly prepared by the Tulsa police. A dark-haired tot, wearing a cowboy suit and a brace of toy six-shooters almost as big as he was, looked back at Joe from the poster. The child's name was Jimmy Wells.

His father, the bulletin stated, was a Tulsa oilman. The parents were separated. It had been a spectacular kidnapping. The father had sent his chauffeur for the boy around ten A.M. the day before, and he was to spend the rest of the day and night with the father, and be returned to his mother the next day—Christmas Eve.

Two hours later the body of Wells' chauffeur had been found in a Tulsa city park.

Three hours after that Sequoyah County officers had come upon the abandoned Wells car on U.S. 64, just west of Sallisaw, Oklahoma. A crudely scrawled note demanding a hundred-thousand-dollars' ransom had been pinned to the front seat of the car. The note threatened death to the child if the police were informed—silly, because it was almost certain that officers would either find the car or be notified the moment someone else found it. Sallisaw was about twenty miles west of Fort Sanders on the Arkansas-Oklahoma state line, but the kidnappers could have gone in any direction from there.

Joe scrutinized the bulletins and posters on other criminals—killers, safecrackers, forgers, extortionists, and escaped convicts wanted by the FBI and police departments throughout the Southwest—but always his eyes came back to the three-year-old boy who was in the hands of a killer-kidnapper.

A couple more drunks were brought in; one was wild, cursing and screaming. There was an accident far out on the old Greenwood Road. Far out! Joe was living out there twenty years ago. Old Greenwood Road was now paved and in a heavily populated part of the city. The city limits had pushed much farther south.

Joe found the station filling with trim young men in snappy police uniforms, shining boots and shoes, gleaming helmets, badges, belt buckles, and efficient-looking guns. It was eight-thirty. Some of the boys were leaving for their homes. The others had come in to relieve them.

Marty Sauer winked. "Come on, Joe, let's go out and cruise around and maybe get a cup of coffee. Johnnie Hopp's mother and sister got in tonight and they're leaving again tomorrow. He won't have much time to see them so I sent him home whether Chief likes it or not. I knew you'd be glad to ride with me."

"That's what I came for," Joe said.

"Got your gun?"

"Sure. I always carry my gun."

This was more like it! This was living again for Joe. They cruised Main Street. Shopping was almost over. Some of the stores already had closed, but a few were still open and last-minute wild-eyed shoppers were rushing here and there. Salvation Army lads and lassies shivered as they kept the Christmas pots boiling beneath their tripods, hoping to pick up a few belated coins to help pay for tomorrow's Christmas dinners for the poor and homeless. Icy winds whipped around streetcorners and set the strings of decorative lights to dancing. Night fog swept in from the river accompanied by gusts of sleet. Weary salesclerks looked at the clocks on the walls of their stores, wanting to get home to be with their own families —and the spirit of Christmas took over the Holy Night.

They cruised the length of the avenue, turned back, and went up a sidestreet. Everything seemed in order. One or two drunks were weaving along the sidewalks in the west part of town, but Sauer paid no attention to them. Ordinarily, Joe knew, Sauer very likely would have stopped and picked them up. A swaying drunk crossing a street at night was a traffic menace. He might be killed or hurt or cause someone else to be hurt trying to avoid hitting him. But tonight, Christmas Eve, Sauer wasn't seeing them. Traffic was thinning down. Maybe they would stay on the sidewalk and safely get to wherever they were going.

They drove across the river bridge into Oklahoma, turned around under the overpass, and came back over the bridge. The Christmas decorations over the avenue were beautiful. How many, many Christmas Eves had he spent just like this when he was on the force—cruising the streets of the city, looking for prowlers—and before that, in his rookie days as a patrolman, walking his beat, trying the back doors of business houses for break-ins, checking the restaurants, the honkytonks, the railroad and bus stations.

Now Marty and Joe cruised the alleys behind the big wholesale buildings in the west end of town, their eyes and flashlights covering every window, every back door. Joe's big paw settled on Marty's wrist. "Over there. The steps at the end of the warehouse loading dock. I saw something move."

Sauer shot the car toward the dock, turning the headlights on upper beam. A dark shadow parted from the side of the steps and scurried into the darkness beneath the dock. Joe leaped out of the cruiser on one side and Sauer on the other, their handguns drawn.

"Don't shoot! Don't shoot!" The crackling voice of an old man came to them from beneath the dock.

"Come out from under there with your hands up!" Sauer commanded.

"Okay, don't shoot," the old man whined. A thin, grizzled, and dirty man of about seventy crawled out of the shadows.

"Well, hello there!" Sauer said. "It's Fisherman Frankie. Frankie, what the devil are you up to?"

"Ain't up to nothin'," said the old man. "On my way to my houseboat to play Santa for my grandson."

"Yeah? Why did you duck under that dock?"

"Well, sir, Mr. Sauer, I guess it was jest habit. A feller up the street give me a couple of swigs of good whiskey, it bein' Christmas—and me, when I been drinkin' and I see a cop comin', I jest natchelly run and hide, and that's the truth."

Sauer's flashlight was merciless, revealing a seamed and wrinkled old face, red from the biting wind—but the old eyes squinting out from beneath straggly white hair and a craggy thrust of forehead were keen as a knife blade—and calculating.

"I'll hold him," Joe said. "You better take a look behind those steps."

"Why, Mr. Joe Chaviski," Frankie said. "I ain't seen you in a coon's age. Got me a sack of stuff the Salvation Army give me under there, that's all."

"Uh-huh," said Joe. "We'll see." Old Frankie was a petty thief, a river rat. He made the legitimate part of his living as a professional fisherman on the river—if you forgot the fact that he never bought a professional license, or any fishing license at all, in his whole life. The rest of the time he lived either by what he could "pick up" or off the city while sitting out jail sentences. It had been like this when Joe Chaviski was on his first beat on the force—and it would be like that until Frankie was too old to get about.

Marty Sauer came out from under the dock with a towsack loaded with packages. "Salvation Army is getting highfalutin' these days to giftwrap all its stuff for charity," he said. "Don't you think so, Joe?"

"Not all of it come from the Salvation Army," Frankie said. "I got a lot of friends give me things at Christmas."

Sauer motioned to the car. "Okay, get in the back seat, Frankie. We're going riding."

The old fellow got in the car protesting. "I got a grandson visitin'. He's just a little mite of a feller. I tole him Santa would bring him some things tonight. Now what is he goin' to think?"

"He's not alone down there, is he?"

"Nope. The ole woman's with him. But he's going to be mighty disappointed. He'll think his grandpappy plumb lied to him. He won't never trust no Santa no more."

At the station they unloaded Frankie's sack upon the top of Haley's desk. There was a silk dress from one of the leading department stores, a toy bulldozer, a box of chocolates and a box of hard candy, a football, a can of mixed nuts, a water pistol, a popgun, a near child-size doll, and a toy airplane. There was a necklace of imitation pearls and a matching set of earrings, a set of doll dishes, an electric alarm clock, a Boy Scout knife, and two boxes of 12-gauge shotgun shells. Most of the items were gift-wrapped and they came from different stores.

"Frankie, Frankie," Joe said, "you and I have got along all these years. Why did you have to go and make us put you in jail on Christmas Eve?"

"You think I stole those things?"

"We know darn well you did," Joe said. "Now what is that *other* little boy going to do, who was expecting that football you got here, and that popgun, and that toy bulldozer? What's the lady going to do when she finds that dress missing—or that little girl when she doesn't get her baby doll in the morning? Frankie, I'm ashamed of you."

"I don't know what you're talking about, Mr. Joe. That dress was give to me fer my wife. I got some friends in this here town, I have. And them toys was for my little grandson. My boy Jed brought him along from Californie. Jed don't get home very often."

Sauer handed Joe a paper which Haley had just given him. The list contained a number of items reported stolen from parked cars. "They've been phoned in during the last thirty minutes. Late shoppers. They left their cars unlocked as per usual."

Practically everything reported stolen from the cars now lay on the sergeant's desk.

"Lock him up," Sauer said. "Charge grand larceny."

"Mr. Sauer," old Frankie whined, "have a heart. First time I ever seen my grandson. What'll he think of me? All I got is two dollars. Won't some of you go buy him a leetle present of some kind? I hate to let that li'l feller down. Me an' the ole woman don't want nothin' fer Christmas. I didn't pick up that stuff fer us. I just grabbed what I could, hopin' to get something for the boy."

"Where is the boy?" Joe inquired.

"Down in my houseboat. You know the place where the old wharf used to be years ago, jest above the ole railroad bridge."

Joe nodded. "Marty and I'll try to pick up some toys

somewhere for him. Don't know where—everything's closed by now. But we'll find him some toys somewhere."

Old Frankie held out his hand—a gnarled old hand as hard as a stick of oak. "Thank you, Joe. I don't give a damn what happens to me, just so that leetle boy gets somethin' fer Christmas. His daddy had to leave just as soon as he dropped him off last night. He'll be back tomorrow, or the day after, but I don't know whether he'll bring the kid anything or not."

Joe and Sauer consulted with Night Chief Henson, and then passed the word over the police radio that a little boy wasn't going to have much of a Christmas because his grandfather was locked up in jail—where he was liable to be for some time. The police were asked to "kick in" with a small and suitable gift from the toys they had bought for their own children.

The appeal couldn't have done better if it had been person-to-person to Santa Claus himself. One by one the boys began appearing at the station with a toy—a teddy bear, a box of blocks, a little mechanical duck, a tiny train, a popgun, and on and on. For good measure, the police wives donated candy, fruit, cookies, and articles of clothing. Joe grinned with pleasure.

Chief Henson surveyed the pile of gifts on Marty Sauer's desk. "Okay," he said, "who's going to play Santa Claus? You ought to do it, Marty—you and Joe. I know Joe will go along."

"Wait a minute," Joe said, "look at the time. It's ten-thirty. That little boy has been asleep for hours. We can't go down there and wake him up this time of night."

"That's right, Joe," the chief said. "But somebody ought to go down there and tell Frankie's old lady where he is. She might be missing him—it being Christmas and him not getting back with anything."

Some of the boys chuckled. "I'll go tell her," Sauer said. "You want to come along, Joe?"

They drove down to the end of the pavement on Parker Avenue and got out of the car. Old Frankie's houseboat was anchored down at the foot of the natural wharf, a hundred feet or so above the old Missouri Pacific bridge. The dirt road that led down to the wharf was muddy from recent rains, and a car was liable to bog down. Joe and Sauer made their way slowly down to the boat, walking carefully over the sleet-covered slate walk which was part of the old wharf. Frankie's boat was tied up to iron rings hammered into crevices of the rock. There was no light on in the boat, and a single twelve-inch plank led from the slate rock to the boat—a crude and slippery gangplank.

"Hello there in the boat, Mrs. Frankie," Sauer shouted. After the third call, there was a spurt of yellow light inside, and a moment later a gaunt gray-haired old woman appeared in the door. She was wearing a long flannel nightgown and was holding a lighted lantern.

"Who is it?"

"Detective Sauer of the police department—and Joe Chaviski," Sauer said. "Frankie ran into a little trouble. We've got him up there in jail."

"What fer?"

"Going through cars."

The old woman remained silent.

"We thought you might be uneasy when he didn't get back tonight."

"I shore thank ye for letting me know."

"You've got your little grandson on the boat, haven't you?" Joe said.

"I shore have. Cutest little feller you ever seen. He's sound asleep."

"The police department heard about it, and we want to bring down some presents for him in the morning."

"That shore would be nice."

"What time do you think the boy will be awake?"

" 'Bout eight o'clock, I reckon."

"Good," said Joe. "We'll be back in the morning."

"Okay," said the old woman. "I'll have some fresh coffee bilin'."

"Fresh coffee, Joe," Sauer said, when they had climbed back up the muddy road to their car. "Where you reckon they get the water? From the river?"

"Well, it will be 'biled,' " Joe said. "I hope you fellows won't forget to get those things down to her in the morning like we promised."

"Where do you get that 'you fellows' stuff? That's your job. The whole idea was yours."

"The heck with you. This is the police department's party. I'm not having anything to do with it."

"Oh no? You be down here at eight o'clock in the morning to go with me," Sauer said. "And that's an order."

At the station Joe started for his car to go home.

"And say," Sauer said, "you still got that Santa Claus suit? Why don't you do it up right and wear it in the morning. Don't want to let that kid down just because his granddad got caught and had to go to jail."

Joe got in his car and gunned it out of the parking area. When he got home, he opened the packages his folks had sent him. The package from his nephew contained a pair of gloves too small for his hands. The package from his niece contained a bright red tie. Joe never wore a red tie in his life. He carefully did the packages up again. He'd take them down to old Frankie's place in the morning and leave them there for the old scoundrel whenever he got out of jail. Maybe they'd reduce the charges to petty larceny.

Then, on an inspiration, Joe went to the clothes closet —it had been Lucy's closet—and fished one of Lucy's good dresses out of a moth-proof bag. The dress had been hanging there since the summer before Lucy went away. He folded the dress and gift-wrapped it, using some of the paper that had been left over from the presents he had sent the families of his niece and nephew. Lucy's dress was of good quality. Maybe it wasn't in the latest style, but poor old Mrs. Frankie wouldn't know the difference.

Joe turned in, but he couldn't quickly get to sleep. There was something troubling him and he wasn't quite sure what it was.

He was up at six in the morning and cooked a Christmas breakfast of ham and eggs, toast, hot coffee, and a side dish of instant oatmeal. Then Joe rummaged at the bottom of an old trunk in his bedroom and drew out the Santa Claus suit—the suit he had used when Lucy entertained the orphans years ago. Any grandson of Fisherman Frankie—and son of Jed Frankie—was bound to be underprivileged. Maybe Lucy was watching Joe approvingly now.

He pulled on the suit, and it was a tight fit. He pulled on the black boots, and even dug out the white whiskers, but he placed the whiskers in the front seat of his car. No need of putting them on until the last minute—the darn things had always tickled. It was a quarter of eight when he strode into the police station.

He was greeted by a chorus of "Ho, ho, ho's!" delivered in unison by the boys who were there.

"Where the devil is Sauer?" he asked Pete Scoville, day desk sergeant.

"Why, Joe, he works at night. He might be down later, though."

"You wait until I get my hands on him!" Joe roared. "Well, some of you fellows got to go with me to old Frankie's place. I'm not taking this thing on all by myself."

The report of a safecracking at a supermarket came in, quickly followed by automobile accidents in widely separated parts of town. The station was cleared of policemen in a jiffy.

Sergeant Scoville looked at Joe and shrugged. "Looks like you're a solitary Santa Claus," he said.

"All right. Where's that darn towsack Frankie had his stuff in last night?"

The sergeant found it and helped him load everything into it that the boys had donated for the Frankie kid's Christmas. Joe was shouldering the pack when Scoville handed him a cigar wrapped in a Christmas card. There was a note in the card: "Merry Christmas, Santa Joe. See you later. I'm sleeping. P.S. Have this cigar on me. Marty."

Swearing to himself, Joe lugged the sack out to the car. It was like old times. He lit Marty's cigar. It exploded! Joe shook his fist at Scoville, who was watching from the door of the police station.

He drove to the end of the pavement above the old wharf and parked the car. He put on the ticklish Santa Claus whiskers, hefted the sack of presents to his back, carried the package containing Lucy's dress under his arm, and started the descent to the houseboat. Last night's freeze had put a crust on the surface of the muddy wharf road, but the last fifty feet over the slate rock was slippery with ice.

Joe reached the plank that led from the rocks to the boat and halloed until Mrs. Frankie opened the door. She was wearing a faded Mother Hubbard this morning, and she had combed her hair and done it up in a bun. "Morning, Mr. Chaviski," she said. "Coffee's ready. Watch yore step on that plank. It's plumb icy."

Joe minced across the plank like a great cat trying to avoid getting its feet wet. A small child was seated at a table inside the houseboat, but until Joe's eyes adjusted all he could make out was the outline of the tot's head. "I want my mommy," said a little voice.

Joe "Ho-ho-ho'd" in his best Santa Claus voice and began putting the toys on the table before the boy, drawing the presents out of the sack one by one. He handed the package containing Lucy's dress to Mrs. Frankie. "A present from my wife," he said.

"Thankee," said the old lady. "That was real thoughty of her."

"I want my mommy," wailed the little fellow. He had been spooning something that looked like oatmeal and milk out of a bowl. Great tears ran down the child's face.

"My boy Jed brung little Junior here so his wife couldn't get her hands on him," Mrs. Frankie said. "They've split up, and he had to hide the boy away from her lawyers. Jed'll be here any time now. He said he'd be back early Christmas morning and maybe take the boy away ag'in."

Joe selected a cuddly teddy bear from the pile of gifts and pushed it toward the youngster. The child stopped crying and grabbed the toy with a gurgle of delight.

"Lor'-a-mercy!" said the old woman. "I wish my poor man was here. I never seed so many purties in my life. None of my kids ever had more than one toy, and I brung up eight of them. Quite a job, too, when we was livin' on the river all the time."

Joe looked at the youngster, now over his timidity and diving into the other toys on the table. Eight little ones brought up in a one-room box on the water like this! There were two cots, a bare table, and two chairs, one with the back broken off. Heat was furnished by a woodburning range at the far end of the cabin. Wall decorations consisted of smelly fishnets and coils of trotline cord. Stored beneath the table was a sack of welfare commodities and a Christmas box of groceries from the Salvation Army.

Mrs. Frankie shrieked with delight. She had opened Joe's package, and held the dress at arm's length admiring it, then ran her hand lovingly across the front, patting it fondly. "Tell your old lady—tell Mrs. Chaviski it's the only silk dress I ever had in my life," she said. Joe wished Lucy could have heard her say it in person.

Joe got up to leave, but she insisted he have some coffee. She poured it into a tin cup and he drank it down without a qualm about germs and water pollution. The coffee was so hot and strong he knew no germ could survive.

Joe picked up the child and held him in his arms. "Daddy, Daddy," the tot crooned. "Take me Mommy."

"I'll do that, sonny," he said. "I'll do that very thing. Daddy will come see you right away. You be a good boy till Daddy comes."

"Mr. Chaviski, my mister always said you was a good cop. I wish you'd do what you could to get him out of jail. It's tough on a ole woman like me trying to get along without no man. Them Salvation Army vittles is all the food we'uns have got."

"I'll do what I can," Joe said. "Maybe we can get the charge reduced to petty larceny." He picked up the package containing the red tie and the one with the gloves. "These are gifts for Frankie. I'll take them to him in the jail."

Joe made his way carefully back to the car, drove it about a block and parked behind some shrubbery. He had brought the towsack back to the car with him, and now he took the mats from the floor of his car and stuffed them into the sack. He lowered the windows an inch or two on each side of the car to let the fresh air in and started the heater. It might be a long wait, and it was still plenty cold at a little past nine o'clock.

He had an idea that Jed would be coming, just like his mother had said, and that he would come across the old railroad bridge. That bridge had been built before Jed Frankie's father had been born. Jed and his brothers and sisters had played in the shadow of that bridge all their lives—and the only bath water they had ever known was the muddy Arkansas River water that swirled about its base.

Thirty minutes Joe waited. The Santa Claus suit, tight and uncomfortable as it was, helped keep him warm. He did not remove the whiskers. He even forgot they tickled. Darn it—if he just had some vanilla ice cream—just a pint carton of it. But he dared not drive off to get some. Across the river at the end of the old railroad bridge a car could park in the cottonwood saplings and never be detected from the highway. Jed knew both sides of the river along the Arkansas-Oklahoma border like the back of his hand.

Another thirty minutes passed, and then he saw the dark figure on the bridge halfway across. It was Jed all right. He was tall and lean like his father, except he wasn't bent over like Fisherman Frankie. Jed stopped at the end of the bridge and appeared to melt into one of the big steel end girders. Joe could see his head turning slowly as he peered warily about.

Now he was coming on—and Joe was out of his car, with his bulging sack on his back. They met at the cut, where the dirt road led down to the natural wharf.

"Santa Claus!" Jed said. "What the devil are you doing down here in this part of town. Slumming?"

"Salvation Army," Joe said. "Got some stuff for Mr. and Mrs. Frankie in the houseboat down there. First time I ever called on folks in a houseboat." Joe was carrying the gift packages for old man Frankie in his hands, the gaily wrapped package with the gloves and the one with the red tie.

"Them's my folks," Jed said. "Old Santa Claus wouldn't have a present for a little boy like me? Say a bottle of bonded bourbon?"

"No, I'm afraid not," Joe said, "but here's a pair of gloves and a nice red tie."

Joe shoved the packages toward Jed and suddenly pressed them against his body. The black barrel of a .38 revolver, lashed to the glove package with a pretty red ribbon, jammed into Jed's flesh.

"It's all up, Jed," Joe said. He took two guns off the astonished Frankie.

At the police station a harassed Detective Chief Marty Sauer nearly dropped the telephone when he saw Joe Chaviski, bursting at the seams in a tight-fitting Santa Claus suit, herding a handcuffed Jed Frankie into the jail ahead of him, followed by Fisherman Frankie's wife lugging a black-haired little boy of three in her arms.

"He ain't no son of mine no more," old Mrs. Frankie was saying, emphasizing her declaration with choice oaths.

"What the devil you doing?" Marty Sauer said.

"I wanted you to go along with me, you hook-ruben," said Joe, "but no, you'd rather play with explosive cigars." He nodded to the jailer, then when the barred door opened, pushed Jed Frankie through and slammed the door shut after him. "You're not going anywhere, Frankie, so sit over there. We'll book you and take the cuffs off in a minute or two."

Chaviski sat down in Sauer's chair, reached for the telephone, and placed a collect call to the Tulsa police department.

"Chaviski, Fort Sanders police. Hello, Captain, Merry

Christmas to you. You got a young oilman over there and a young mother you think a three-year-old boy might possibly bring together again? Sure we got him. You didn't pay out the hundred-thousand-dollar ransom, did you? Sure, we got the kidnapper too. What am I doing back on the force? Oh, when they got something tough they can't figure out, they call in the old man. Three hours? You make your boys watch out for slick spots on the highway and bring the mother and father both. I promised the kid they'd be here. Okay, Captain. Need anything else, don't fool with the police department over here—just call Joe Chaviski."

Marty Sauer bent down beside Chaviski, pulled out one of the drawers of the desk. There was a box of cigars, and there was a card on it: "To Joe Chaviski from the boys at the Police Department."

"And not a darn one of them is going to explode," Sauer said.

THE CASE OF THE HELPLESS MAN
Douglas Farr

"Uncle Rudolph," Karen asked, "you can hear me, can't you?"

She was sitting beside him on the big bed, and now she leaned closer suddenly, so that their faces were only inches apart. Karen was pretty, in her dark way, but now her expression was hard, calculating. And she hadn't asked the question solicitously, or out of curiosity either. She had a purpose in her which he didn't yet comprehend, but could only sense somehow was evil.

"Yes, you can hear me," she went on. "I can tell from the expression in your eyes."

He felt helpless, frustrated. He had never liked or trusted Karen. In the old days he would have told her to get off his bed and mind her manners. But since his stroke he couldn't tell anybody what to do.

He could just sit there—as he'd been sitting every day for the past two weeks—propped up by his pillows. It had been George—dear, kind George—who had suggested the pillows, so that the invalid would have something to stare at beside the blank ceiling.

So he could look around him—as far as his eyes could turn, that is, because he was unable to move his head. He could hear too. But that was all. Everything else in him was dead, motionless, paralyzed. His voice was silent. His hands lay on the coverlet like those of a corpse.

"But you can't do anything, can you, Uncle Rudolph?" The malice was obvious in Karen's voice now. There was unconcealed wickedness in her eyes and in the little smile which twitched at the corners of her mouth.

140   THE CASE OF THE HELPLESS MAN

For a moment he was physically afraid, feeling the ignominious helplessness of a prisoner gagged and tied and at the mercy of a torturer. Her long red-tinted fingernails could scratch at his face, pierce his eyes, and shut off one of his last two avenues of communication with the world. But then he sneered at his fears, inwardly, silently. Karen might want some kind of vengeance for some imagined hurt, but she would never dare to take such vengeance. After all, George was in the house.

"None of the doctors think that you'll ever recover, Uncle Rudolph."

Was she really so callous and cruel as to gloat over his situation? Yet she was doing precisely that—gloating. Why did she hate him so much?

Then it was as if he had asked the question aloud. Because the answer started to come. "So I have to take matters into my own hands, Uncle Rudolph. You've shown entirely too much favoritism toward George. Especially in the will. But you'll never be able to change your will now, Uncle. I'll have to correct the errors for you."

Yes, that was it, of course. Karen had always resented George. Even though she had no right to resent him. Being Paul's son, George had always been a gentleman, both naturally and consciously. Bertram's offspring was quite another matter, Karen was too much like her father, cold, selfish. He had endured her out of the same sense of duty that had caused him to endure Bertram.

But what about his will? Staring into Karen's face, he tried to think back. Yes, his will. Childless himself, he had naturally left everything to his brothers' descendants. But not equally. Two thirds would go to George, only one third to Karen. It was certainly fair since it was his own money. If he hadn't felt a sense of duty, he wouldn't have left Bertram's child anything.

"What's the matter, Uncle? You know, it's simply remarkable how much emotion you manage to convey with just your eyes. It's so obvious that you disagree with my point of view. George is your favorite, and you think that rich uncles should be allowed to have favorites. Well, we'll see."

She slipped off the bed and he watched her as she walked toward the door. Her dress, he thought, was unnecessarily tight. She'd never have worn a dress like that in front of him a few weeks ago. Now she was. . . .

But why was he thinking about unimportant things like Karen's dress? There was the will. And Karen was up to something. The feeling of helplessness swept over him in a bitter tide.

She was gone for two or three minutes. When she returned, George came with her. Or rather, she carried him. George was on his feet, but unsteadily, and his left arm was draped around Karen's shoulders, and her right arm encircled his waist. He was not a large man, but he was bigger than his cousin, and all his weight seemed to be on her. She was managing nicely, however, guiding his laggard feet, urging him across the room, then depositing him finally into a sitting position in the armchair that was at one side of the foot of the bed and for the old man's visitors.

Rudolph Iser stared incredulously at his nephew. George's once handsome face was vacant, expressionless, animal-like, entirely without any semblance of intelligence or humanity. His nice brown eyes were open, but they stared blankly at nowhere, and his lower jaw hung slackly, dangling.

"Look, Uncle Rudolph," Karen said, breathing a little hard from her exertions, "good old George is drunk."

Angrily but silently the old man denied her claim. Drunk, no! It was impossible. George didn't drink at all; much less would he drink to excess. If he was drunk now, it was Karen's fault. He didn't know exactly how she had accomplished such a thing. He only knew that she was full of trickery and guile, and that George must somehow have fallen prey to her.

But Karen was already busy elsewhere. She went straight to the tall bureau, and without hesitation opened one of the drawers. He couldn't see which one because the bureau was on the extreme periphery of his field of vision, and he was unable to turn his head to follow her movements. So he also didn't see what she took from the drawer. He didn't see it till she came back and stood beside his bed.

His gun! The small revolver that he'd always kept in the third drawer. He wanted to shout at her that the gun wasn't hers, it was his, and he didn't want her to meddle with it or even to touch it.

But he couldn't shout, of course. He could only watch her, first in anger and finally with a kind of fascination, as she checked to see if the weapon was loaded, and then having handled it, began cleaning and wiping it carefully with a handkerchief.

The thought passed through his mind that she was going to fire the gun and he would be her target. A kind of longing followed the thought, a longing to die. And then shame for his own cowardice overcame the death-desire. He had to thwart Karen's evil purpose, whatever it was.

Now she stood still for a moment, surveying George. Then she sat down beside him on the bed. But differently than before, not facing him, but rather facing the same direction as he, toward George. She moved quickly and efficiently now, and he could scarcely follow or understand her movements.

First she took one of his extra pillows, placed his right arm on it, so that the pillow supported his wrist. She still had the gun, held it carefully in the handkerchief, and she put it into his right hand, the butt against the heel of his thumb, curling his forefinger inside the trigger guard. Then her hand, smaller and so much softer, over his bony old claw. Her forefinger, slim, smooth, over his gnarled forefinger. And finally pointing the gun toward George.

Still foolishly uncomprehending, the old man could feel only a nameless dread. Karen edged closer to him on the bed, till their shoulders touched. Still closer, till her cheek was against his and he could feel her warm breath on his cold skin. In front of his eyes was the gun. He was staring along the barrel, and Karen—he reasoned—was doing the same thing, with the sight seeming to point at George.

Full realization flooded into the old man's brain. He

wanted to shout a warning to his nephew. George, George, she's going to kill you. . . .

But no sound came from his lips. Instead, the silence was shattered by the roar of the gun. Just one shot, but making an enormous noise that boomed and reverberated like a bomb burst.

George had been sitting in the chair limply. His body jerked and straightened under the impact of the bullet. On the front of his shirt, right at his heart, a red stain appeared, small at first, then growing slowly wider and wetter. Then, after a moment of the whole body's twitching, the head fell forward on the chest, seemed to drag the torso behind it. First the head and arms, then the trunk came forward, sagged from the chair and out of sight onto the floor.

Very gently Karen disengaged her hand from the old man's, rose from the bed, and walked the few steps to where her cousin lay. She gazed down at him for a long time. When she turned back toward her uncle, there was a smile of diabolical pleasure on her face.

"Poor dear Uncle," she announced, "I'm afraid you've killed your favorite relative. . . ."

The plainclothes detective was a friendly-looking man of medium height, a little pudgy, with a round plain face, undistinguished, unimpressive. Yet to Rudolph Iser there appeared an encouraging glimmer of intelligence in this newcomer's eyes.

Karen merely stood on the threshold and gestured into the room. The detective paused in the doorway for a moment, surveying the scene. Then he walked swiftly toward the foot of the bed and knelt down, almost out of Rudolph Iser's sight. Examining the body, of course, and then rising and saying, "He's dead all right."

Then he walked around to the right side of the bed and stood staring down at the occupant. His expression revealed that he obviously considered this a strange sight —a motionless, silent old man in the bed, his right arm propped up with a pillow folded under the wrist, a revolver in his right hand, his forefinger still curled around the trigger. Without touching anything, the detective bent down, put his nose close to the muzzle of the gun, and inhaled.

Then he stood up again, scratching his head in frank puzzlement, and spoke to Karen over his shoulder. "You say this man is completely paralyzed, can't move or talk, but can only hear and see?"

"As far as we know," Karen answered. She was putting on a magnificent act. Her face was tearstained and pale, as if she'd witnessed something that was both a shock and a sorrow to her. She lingered in the doorway, pretending to be reluctant to enter the room, to come any closer to this awful scene of death. "I heard the shot and came upstairs and I found this room exactly as it is now."

"Okay, you can go, Miss Iser," the detective said.

But Karen hesitated. Did she seem uneasy about having to leave, not being able to stay here and explain everything to the police? Rudolph saw the uncertainty in her. "If there's anything I can do. . . ." she began.

"Just go downstairs and let my boys in when they come," the detective told her. "The whole homicide crew is on its way. You can go down and wait for them, Miss Iser. And shut the door as you leave, please."

She was being dismissed and she had no alternative but to obey. She stepped back into the hall, shutting the door as instructed, and Rudolph Iser was left alone with the detective.

There was a brief silence between them. By directing his eyes upward and as far as possible to the right, Rudolph could see the man's face. It was a soft face, almost kind. Only the voice had been harsh.

But now the voice softened too. "I'm Lieutenant Dorsic," the detective said. "And I understand your name is Rudolph Iser." It was a pleasant voice, soothing after the terror and the excitement. "You're completely paralyzed, but somehow or other, you're supposed to have shot your nephew George."

The old man listened, hoping that some of his emotion

was communicating in his eyes. Hadn't Karen said that she'd seen emotion in his eyes? He exerted all his frail energy now to tell this policeman that things weren't as they seemed.

And maybe he got through to him. Or maybe Lieutenant Dorsic was just an intelligent man. Anyway he said, "But this whole setup looks fishy to me."

The old man's heart pounded furiously, as furiously as it had when the gun had roared in his ears. Karen had thought she was clever, but here was a policeman who was more clever. He would discover the truth.

"Your niece," Dorsic went on, "has given me a pretty thorough rundown on the situation. You had ruled this house with a hand of iron till your recent stroke. George was your favorite because he obeyed you. And you rewarded George by putting him down in your will for two thirds of your estate. But then after your stroke George began misbehaving. Drinking especially. And you had always detested drinking. Karen suggests that when you saw George drunk you got so angry that you became capable of some physical movement. Enough to shoot George anyway. Granted that for some reason George brought you the gun and then very conveniently made himself a target. Your niece didn't suggest that part of it, but that's the way it would have had to happen. That's why I'm skeptical, old-timer. Of course, I'm going to check with your doctors to see just how paralyzed you are. But even though you might have been able to fire a gun, I doubt that you could have climbed out of that bed and gone after the gun."

This policeman is very intelligent, the old man exulted. He will discover that the evildoer is Karen and then he will see to it that she is punished. And I want her punished. . . .

Dorsic was staring at the gun now with utter concentration. "Mr. Iser," he said, "if ever a murderer were caught red-handed, it's you. But appearances can be deceiving, can't they? So even though the gun is in your hand and the corpse at the foot of your bed, this may not be the whole or true story."

Dorsic's eyes, hard and glittering bright now, shifted to the old man's face. "Mr. Iser," he said, "you know what happened. But you can't tell me, because you can't speak. But I've noticed that you can move your eyes. Up and down, for instance, to say yes. From side to side to say no. How about it? While we're waiting for my crew, shall we play a little guessing game? You just answer yes or no with movements of your eyes, and I'll try to guess the right questions to ask."

Of course, the old man agreed silently. Yet not so silently, because his poor heart was pounding with such violence that surely the sound of its heavy beating must be audible. So simple to answer questions. Why hadn't Karen foreseen that?

"Let's start with the big question," Dorsic began. "Technically your hand fired the gun, let's say. But did you intend it that way? Are you guilty of murder?"

The old man shifted his eyes left and right as far as he could. No, he answered.

"Okay. Somebody else is guilty. How? Did somebody else put the gun in your hand and fire it for you?"

Yes, yes, yes. Again and again, emphatically, yes.

"Let me guess who. Your niece?"

Yes, oh, yes.

"Well, we're off to a good start." Dorsic pondered briefly. "Quite possible. If a paralyzed man is completely helpless, why can't someone stick a gun in his hand and fire it? We could run a paraffin test, and it would show that your hand fired the gun. Next question, old-timer. Did your niece deliberately get your nephew drunk, do you think, in order to provide you with an apparent reason for wanting to kill him, and also to guarantee that he would be a cooperative target?"

Yes, yes. It was so simple, so easy. This detective was inspired. Karen's little plan was completely shattered. If only he could see her face when the detective accused her of murder. She'd have to confess.

But the old man's elation wasn't mirrored in Dorsic's face. The face was thoughtful, almost glum. He spoke slowly, more to himself than to the invalid. "Now we have a nice theory, but we've got to prove it. We have your word against your niece's word. The doctors might help. If they can state that beyond a shadow of a doubt you would have been unable to pull that trigger. But could any doctor make such a definite statement? I'm not so sure. If they would hedge just a little, even hint that your emotional upset over your nephew's drunkenness might have spurred you to great, unusual effort, then the medical testimony wouldn't be worth two cents."

But I can't move, the old man protested. If I could have moved one muscle I would have tried to save George.

Dorsic was silent again. He and the old man, the sick and the well, the chained and the free, stared intently at each other for a long time.

"Mr. Iser," Dorsic said finally, "the things a court would call evidence—fingerprints, paraffin test, the gun actually in your hand—are all against you. Not that we'd dream of yanking you out of that bed and trying you for murder. But we have no evidence against your niece. Beyond your accusation, that is. And I'm afraid that wouldn't be enough."

Happily triumphant only a moment before, Rudolph Iser now experienced a return of his former despair. There had to be a way to prove Karen's guilt. There had to be justice. But if this clever detective couldn't bring it about, who could?

Dorsic was staring at the gun now. "The paraffin test wouldn't be any good on her hand if she held her hand over yours. Flesh doesn't take fingerprints, so her prints wouldn't be on your hand. And unless she was careless—which I doubt—they won't be on the gun itself either. That girl was smarter than I am, old-timer. You and I know she did it. But we can't prove a thing."

Dorsic shook his head, obviously displeased with his own failure. "I could question her, even accuse her, hope she would break down. But a woman who could manufacture this setup can't be expected to break down. Look, old pal, I'll give plenty of thought to this problem, and I promise you I'll do whatever I can. Meanwhile, I'm going to leave everything as is. I want to be especially careful with that gun. I'll let an expert relieve you of it, just in case our girl was careless. You don't mind holding it there a little longer, do you? I'm going to ask a few questions anyway."

But the detective didn't sound or look hopeful as he turned and left the room, closing the door behind him. And he left the old man in a state of panic.

Because Rudolph Iser had just thought of one thing they could do to fight back against Karen. If they couldn't charge her with the guilt of her crime, they could at least rob her of that crime's rewards. Rudolph Iser could change his will.

Bring me Maddox my lawyer, he shouted. But the shout had neither words nor sound. It simply echoed and reechoed, crashed and reverberated, inside the old man's skull.

Please . . . please . . . hear me . . . listen to me . . . my lawyer . . . I might not live very much longer . . . Mr. Dorsic . . . Mr. Dorsic . . . if you can't outsmart Karen, don't waste your time trying . . . think of what's important . . . forget about clues . . . think about the will . . . I'll be satisfied just to change the will.

No sound. Not a whisper. Just the futile beating of his shouts against the wall of bone inside of which he lived. And that beating more and more overwhelmed, drowned out, by the rising roar of his blood rushing to and from his weakened heart.

And then he began to realize the most awful, the most defeating truth of all. He was dying. The strain had been too much. Before Dorsic could return—long, long before Maddox could get here and be made to understand —there would be two corpses in this room. And Karen would win, completely, once and for all.

Then came the pain, the final thrust of exquisite agony, that blotted out consciousness of everything but itself. Merciful pain perhaps, destroying thoughts of George, of Karen, of revenge. Focusing on itself, then consuming itself. A pain that contained its own power of self-destruction. It brought death, and death annihilates everything. . . .

But if there is a soul, and that soul endures after the death of the body, then Rudolph Iser's soul endured. If that soul had striven against his niece Karen during life, then certainly it would have continued striving even after life had ebbed away. Surely a man's paramount interests and desires do not alter completely with his passage into eternity. But if—if—a dead man's wishes cannot determine the course of things in the living world, then at least Rudolph Iser lingered on the scene to observe and hope.

The homicide crew was late in arriving. It was, in fact, detained by another murder, rather gory and complicated, farther uptown. Dorsic's companion, a Sergeant Mowery, had been given the job of trying to contact Rudolph Iser's doctors by telephone. The doctors weren't immediately available, and Sergeant Mowery stayed at the phone, pursuing them with messages.

Dorsic meanwhile interviewed his suspect. Dorsic questioned Karen Iser for a full five minutes, intelligently, skillfully, using all the resources of his long experience at his trade. But the interview accomplished nothing beyond a repetition of the facts Karen had first related. She knew it and Dorsic knew it. And when he went outside to wait for his crew, he went as a defeated man.

Released from the library, which had served as the interrogation room, Karen's vindictive nature took her upstairs to her uncle's bedroom. Not to meddle with the picture of the crime, which was already as perfect as necessary, but merely to look in on the invalid. She entered the bedroom furtively, closed the door behind her, then stood there, looking at a scene which hadn't changed since she'd left it.

"Well, Uncle," she said, "did you and the detective have a nice chat?"

The old man didn't answer. He merely sat there in his

bed, staring stonily back at her. The gun and the pillow and the chair and the corpse at the foot of the bed were all in their proper places, bold, bald, unquestionable evidence of a murder.

"It must have been an interesting chat," Karen went on, "and that detective is a smart boy. But then I wasn't counting on a dumb one. I'd fully expected that the police would have certain suspicions. After all, you are paralyzed, Uncle. It's hard for a completely paralyzed man to commit a murder. But what can even a smart detective do against all this evidence here? And there is no other evidence. Absolutely nothing to point to me. Do you know something though, Uncle? That detective may be smart, but he's not very good at hiding his thoughts. It was very obvious that he believes I'm the guilty party. But he can't prove it, and it frustrates him horribly. What do you think of that, Uncle? The detective believes I did it. He knows I did it. But he can't prove what he knows. So I'm going to get away with it, Uncle. Did you hear me, Uncle? I'm going to get away with it."

She walked closer, till she stood just over the corpse of the man she'd murdered, and she shouted the question and the statement of triumph again. She didn't know she was addressing a dead man. "Did you hear me? I'm going to get away with it!"

One of two things happened then. Or perhaps both actually. One—Rudolph Iser's lurking, brooding revengeful spirit burst through the barriers between its own immaterial world and reentered for one brief second the world of tangible objects, and worked its will upon one of those objects. Two—*rigor mortis,* operating swiftly in the dry, almost fleshless corpse of Rudolph Iser, caused the contraction of the muscles in the right hand of that corpse.

The revolver in the hand fired. The little gun had been preaimed, of course, at chair-level, but the unresisted recoil action took care of that. It was a perfect shot. . . .

FAT JOW AND THE SUNG TUSK
Robert Alan Blair

The theft of the Sung Tusk was discovered by Fat Jow, coming early down the steep narrow street through the chill fog of morning. As he turned in at the door of his herb shop, he glanced past toward the art and novelty shop a few doors below and discerned what appeared to be a large black disc attached to its plate-glass window. Chuckling at his overactive imagination, he proceeded to unlock his shop door. Halfway in, he paused and looked again. Then, to quell his sudden curiosity, he shuffled the few extra steps downhill and his amusement departed, for he found a neat round hole cut in the glass. The removed circle, the marks of twin suction-cups still faintly visible, lay on the cloth at the base of the window beside a shattered glass case which had contained the Sung Tusk.

The De Young Museum had appraised the tusk at $50,000, but it was beyond price for its sentimental place in the heart of Chinatown, and was as irreplaceable a fixture as the Buddhist Temple or the steel statue of Dr. Sun Yat-sen. Carved from the tusk of an elephant by an unknown artisan of the Sung dynasty, it depicted in exquisite detail a procession of elephants draped with tasseled brocades, bearing elaborate pagodas in which rode infinitesimal men, themselves decked in the most minutely worked ivory finery.

Fat Jow hurried back to his shop, and to the wall telephone behind his counter. He called not the police, but the importer himself, a late riser whose wife must arouse him. The Oriental mind, prompted by centuries of oppression to suspect authority, looks first within itself, or to others of its kind, for solutions to problems which would cause the Occidental to notify the police. Chinatown merchants, incorrigible gamblers all in a society which presumes to outlaw gambling, consult the police only when they must.

Fat Jow had another reason for calling the importer. In the past he would have ignored him, but no longer could he condemn the importer outright for his continuing sporadic traffic in refugees from Red China, because through the importer had come little Hsiang Yuen to brighten the days of his great-uncle Fat Jow. And the price? Fat Jow had been required to assist the importer in soliciting from apprehensive Chinese-American families sums of ransom for relatives still in China.

The importer came to the phone, and Fat Jow said, "Did you know that the Sung Tusk was taken during the night?"

"Ai!" said the importer. "I shall be there soon."

Within the half-hour he arrived, and Fat Jow joined him before the window. "It can never be replaced," moaned the importer. "How can a money value be placed upon it?"

"Bewailing the loss accomplishes nothing," grunted Fat Jow. "I would study motives."

"Profit," said the importer uncomfortably. "What else?"

Fat Jow studied his lean pinched features. "The method of entry suggests a certain technical skill, while his selection of the tusk implies a deficiency in his knowledge of antiquities. The tusk is so well known that no connoisseur would dare to buy it, at any price."

"What are you saying?" complained the importer. "You speak in riddles."

Fat Jow stroked his wisp of beard. A possibility had not escaped him: that the importer himself, in league with the Red Chinese seeking to reclaim a national treasure, might have engineered the theft. "You of course will offer no objection if I offer my poor assistance to recover the tusk?"

The importer was trapped. He said sourly, "It is more than I deserve."

"Agreed. I recommend a circumspect approach to the authorities."

"I had not thought to trouble the police about a matter which concerns Chinatown alone," muttered the importer. "Perhaps a few discreet inquiries, locally...."

"You must report it, you know. The Sung Tusk is too important to drop from sight without explanation. There may be a way to smoke out the thief. Will you participate in a small subterfuge?"

The importer was less than enthusiastic. "I will do what I can."

"We shall make use of the press," declared Fat Jow.

The story appeared on the front page of the morning paper, more notable for its novelty than its significance, and the final paragraph: "The tusk is said to carry the Sung curse, only recently identified by epidemiologists as a rare Asiatic virus. Dry and dormant, it may survive indefinitely; when brought into contact with warm living tissue, it revives and becomes active in the host organism. Symptoms of its presence are accelerated pulse, dry throat, shallow breathing. The glass case which contained the tusk was protection for the public as well as for the tusk. No cure is known, but the virus may be controlled by a folk-remedy known to Chinese herbalists."

Detective Lieutenant Cogswell, a folded copy of the morning paper tucked under his arm, came to the herb shop during the midmorning. "This little gem yours?" he asked.

Fat Jow inclined his head, eyes partially closed. "You flatter me; I was not aware that my journalistic style was so readily identifiable."

"Very cute. What d'you think you're trying to do?"

"Expand your list of suspects. I have notified all herbalists in the Bay Area to report to the police any calls describing these symptoms. But you need not thank me."

Cogswell grunted. "And there's not a grain of truth in it, is there?"

"No matter. An unenlightened thief, reading the article, may develop the symptoms."

"It's just crazy enough to work. *We're* sure getting nowhere. This case is full of contradictions. The skill is professional; but no professional would leave all those prints on the glass. We're checking them out, but it's little enough to go on. You have any more angles?"

"One which pales all others, Lieutenant. Had you considered a political motive?"

"Political?" Cogswell drew out the word, tasting it.

"A diversionary feint, to draw official attention away from a larger matter."

"Do you know something?" asked Cogswell suspiciously.

"Nothing." Fat Jow would not outline his private conjecture about the importer, without knowing more. "It is but a possibility which you cannot overlook."

Cogswell pursed his lips in thought. "One of the boys did bring up the Red Chinese, but only in terms of the tusk itself. What are you getting at? You're onto something."

"It is merely my imagination, sir. If you will, compare notes with other police departments around the Bay, offer this general theory as a starting point, and let them suggest potential targets for the Reds. The tusk, as a symbol of the Sung dynasty, represents the first great surge of the common people toward participation in government at the local level, and thus might be sought by the Reds for more than its value as art or antiquity. But they would hardly launch a recovery mission with only the tusk as its objective."

"Well!" said Cogswell, newly impressed. "I came in here on a Chinatown robbery. It seems to be getting bigger."

"It well may be," assented Fat Jow.

Cogswell jerked open the door. "I've got some work to do; I'll keep you posted." He hurried out, the pendant bells jangling behind him.

In the evening Fat Jow's grandnephew Hsiang Yuen failed to arrive home on schedule from the Chinese classes which follow the public school day. Although there was no reason to connect it with the Sung Tusk, a certain uneasiness persistently reminded Fat Jow of the cause-and-effect illusion, if only for the simple positioning of the events in time: theft, newspaper article, failure of the child to appear. He did not forget that the Red Chinese, who once had released the child to him, could at any time reclaim him, despite all indications that they had imposed no conditions for his remaining with Fat Jow.

He loved the boy and was hard put to visualize his tranquil and solitary existence as it had been when he was not with him. Hsiang Yuen had responded with vigor to his new life, and already had acquired considerable skill at the baseball, a mysterious activity both strenuous and vocal to which many Occidentals are addicted as avidly as are the Orientals to gambling.

Hsiang Yuen had become an essential part of Fat Jow's life, so simultaneously was he concerned for the boy's lateness and also warmed that there was someone to be concerned for, someone to listen for, someone to miss.

An hour after the boy's customary time for appearance, the telephone rang. A woman's voice, low and well-modulated, asked in Cantonese, "Do you know me?"

"Of course," he whispered, at once fearful that her return to San Francisco somehow threatened Hsiang Yuen. Dunya Skarin had been instrumental in sending him the boy from China, and he was grateful to her, but her return, in the face of federal authorities ready to apprehend her, meant a risk well worth taking. But for what?

"Are you now thoroughly worried about Hsiang Yuen?" she asked. "He is with me. You may come get him."

"He is not harmed?"

Her voice held a mild hint of reproach. "We are old friends, Hsiang Yuen and I. Did I not take him from the refugee camp? Come to the St. Francis yacht basin by the Marina Green, and look along the breakwater for a cabin cruiser named *Celestial III*. Ask no questions, simply come. Hsiang Yuen will be on deck. He is not hungry; we have had supper."

After a hasty and solitary meal, Fat Jow set out walking through the crisp sparkle of early evening, that butterfly-wing-blue time of unreality which attends the setting of the sun in a fog-free sea; down the long slope of Pacific Heights to the northern tip of the peninsula, along the Marina Green in view of the red steel lacework of the Golden Gate Bridge.

The St. Francis yacht harbor is a coronet set upon the brow of the city, its jewels the multiple ranks of moored yachts, both sail and power, gleaming in fresh paint and polished brightwork. The *Celestial III* was an imposing deepwater powercraft, bow-on to the stone breakwater between strips of floating dock. At its wheel abaft the foredeck Hsiang Yuen, in a yachting cap too large for him, had lost himself in an adventure on the high seas. As Fat Jow came down the narrow steps to the dock, the child dropped back into the present and came to the rail to assist him. "Come aboard, Uncle," he said, eyes glowing. "Is it not splendid?"

Fat Jow's intended sternness softened at the infectious excitement in the small voice. "How did you come here?" he asked.

"The importer met me at the school. I came with him, for he is my friend."

True; Fat Jow's initial introduction to the Reds had come through the importer, who later had brought Hsiang Yuen from Vancouver to San Francisco.

Dunya Skarin, a statuesque Eurasian of rare beauty, tall in flowing pajamas of flowered silk, her glossy black hair cascading softly about her shoulders, appeared in the cabin companionway. "My friend," she smiled spontaneously and warmly, extending both hands. "I was not entirely confident that you would not send the police in your stead."

He held her hands, enjoying their smooth cool touch. "Not I. I owe you far too much to betray you. I have not yet had the opportunity of thanking you for your kindness in sending me the boy."

Her smile saddened. "I have not misjudged you, then. Perhaps you will neither thank me nor call me kind when you know why I am here." She beckoned him down the short ladder into a spacious well-appointed cabin, waved him to one of the bunks, stood at the ladder with arms folded. "The importer tells me you have taken an interest in the Sung Tusk."

"What is the nature of *your* interest?" he asked blandly.

She ignored his question. "That nonsense about the virus was a hoax, was it not?"

"Why, have you experienced the symptoms?"

"You have now observed the ease with which Hsiang Yuen was brought here. You will cease further participation in this case, while informing me of the progress of the police in their investigation."

She need not elaborate; Fat Jow recalled well her words: "Children vanish every day from the streets of large cities." As the son of a deceased Red Army hero Hsiang Yuen would be welcomed in China, and in honor of the memory and fond wish of his father would be enrolled in the Red Guard.

Fat Jow said wearily, "I was not so naïve as to believe there would be no further price to pay for the ransom of Hsiang Yuen."

Her manner was kindly, regretful. "It is not I who ask it, you know. My superiors recognize your efficacy in Chinatown and with the local authorities, and orders were issued to insure your neutrality."

"How many sins are committed under the guise of obeying orders!" he said bitterly.

"I am sorry, although you may not believe that."

"I believe it; but it makes silence no easier."

Dunya came to sit upon the bunk beside him. "You understand. If our conversation here were witnessed, I should be reprimanded for my unforgivable lack of firmness with you. But I feel that I know you too well to attempt either cajolery or threats. How much simpler if you were to join with a will! When can I make you see that you are on the wrong side?"

"Please define 'wrong,' " shrugged Fat Jow. "Explain how you are on the 'right' side, when your father brought you here as a child and educated you in American schools."

Her eyes rounded. "You know this?"

"There is a fairly extensive dossier on you. Your White Russian father fled Shanghai with you in 1949, ahead of the advancing Red Army. Your Chinese mother remained behind, eventually to become a Party official. Why your choice?"

She stood, returned slowly to the ladder, turned. "I can tell you, I suppose. As I grew older my mother's letters proved more persuasive than my father's arguments. His thinking was not organized, he had no clear purpose, and he was discouraged by the chill reception he found among the bourgeois citizens of your San Francisco. His flight was an escape, not a quest. When he died, I returned to my mother, and my familiarity with this region became useful to the Party. I have a purpose my father never had, for I am serving. Yours is a mad faltering society, whose peak of achievement is winning the envy of one's fellows: a better house, a bigger car, the whitest wash on the block. Where in this great American dream is service to society?"

"The incentive of service," said Fat Jow, "is diminished by obligation. The American dream offers a choice; it does not command 'do right.' One must be master of his destiny, whether for good or evil, with no paternalism dictating. You, conditioned to obedience, faced with the need for an independent decision, must turn to some authority to make the decision for you."

"People are inadequate to make their own decisions," Dunya said.

"And who is the authority? Some superman? With his personal prejudices and weaknesses, is he qualified to decide for anyone but himself? I am barely capable of managing my own life; how can I trust another organism as harried and secretly insecure as I? Planning is good, within bounds; but if too rigid, it dilutes the spice of uncertainty with bland expediency."

She smiled. "You are a persuasive speaker."

"If one is confirmed in his direction, it is not for me to turn him from it. I insist, however, that the choice be his to make. Surrounding himself with others of a similar mind, he keeps his doubts at a distance."

"But I have no doubts," said Dunya. "It is said that no power on earth can stop an idea whose time has come. Every atom of my person insists that I am part of such an idea."

"Which either may or may not be. Time itself has a way of blunting the edges of ideas or subtly altering their direction. It is presumptuous of one society to oppose, compete with, or seek to overthrow another. Let me allude to the ancient parable of the foolish old man who would remove the mountains. He set his sons to chopping away at the mountains with hoes, and when ridiculed, said that his sons and grandsons, working patiently through the generations, would in time complete the removal. Is he not a better model for these quiet ones who study the paths to unity, than for the fiery zealots who bend their energies wastefully toward competition? More can be accomplished by forces allied than by forces opposed."

Dunya stared. "Have you been reading Chairman Mao?"

"One must understand the toxic substances if he is to concoct an effective antitoxin. Mao has no monopoly of vision."

"I do regret," said Dunya with quiet sincerity, "that you and I are on opposite sides of a political barrier. You are so firm in your convictions . . . can I trust you?"

"You had reason to trust me before and nothing has changed. I am ever in your debt and would not see you come to harm."

"Will you at some moment consider the debt discharged and betray me?"

Fat Jow shook his head slowly. "While Hsiang Yuen is with me, the debt is not discharged. You see, I too have my bargaining points, if I wish to employ them."

"These are not arguments which I can present to my superiors," worried Dunya.

"I am concerned not with them, but with negotiations between you and me as individuals; next, between myself and the authorities. If I mislead them by neglecting to tell them of you, then your mission has a better chance of success and does not affect me directly. But if I mislead you, obstructing your mission, it does affect me, for it threatens the loss of Hsiang Yuen. He is my past, present, and future in a single small package. Can I sacrifice him?"

"Please forgive me for doubting you." She stepped aside from the ladder, gestured up the companionway. "Go now, take the child, and leave town for a few weeks. I shall say that I missed you."

"Thank you," he said, gently smiling, "but no. Unless I bow to the will of your superiors, my life would be unending fear of reprisal. I know that you acted on impulse in sending Hsiang Yuen to me, and your superiors have since reconsidered value-received from me in exchange for the boy. I treasure his company; the joy of keeping him with me is worth much. We may call my previous efforts for the Party but a down payment."

"It is a difficult decision you make."

"And yours, to suggest that I take the boy away, was both difficult and indiscreet. Is it not a punishable offense if you fail to enlist my cooperation?"

She seemed to go slack and her voice softened. "What becomes of me is not one of my arguments."

"To me it is. Although we represent opposing camps, I respect you."

She straightened her shoulders. "How ironic, that you volunteer your cooperation. I cannot report it, for they will not believe. You have seen the police?"

"I have, once only as yet." He related briefly but fully his single exchange with Cogswell, adding an apologetic note: "Had I known you were implicated, I should not have turned him in the direction of a political motive."

"No matter," she said absently, "the damage is done. I shall require no more than another day at the most. Try to learn something more tomorrow morning and let me know no later than midday." She motioned again up the companionway. "Go now, and do not come to the boat again. Call the importer, he will get a message to me." As Fat Jow passed her she grasped his hand. "Good luck."

He patted her arm. "It is more appropriate that I wish

it to you. You are not in an enviable position."

Fat Jow and Hsiang Yuen walked slowly home through the evening. The boy remained silent most of the way, sensing that his great-uncle was troubled. As they turned into the final block to the Baxter mansion, he said, "If they want me to go back to China, it is not really so bad."

Fat Jow looked down at him. "Would you want to go?"

"I want to stay with you, Uncle. But if it makes trouble for you, I can go back."

"You will stay," said Fat Jow grimly. "May I depend upon your saying nothing of our visit?"

"Yes, Uncle, if you wish."

"You must tell no one that Miss Skarin is here. I cannot know, but they may have planted listening devices in the apartment and in the shop. They have done it before. Do not even discuss this with me. You must pretend that they hear everything we say, and then you will make no mistakes."

"I will remember, Uncle," promised Hsiang Yuen gravely. It was a game both to delight and to frighten him.

Fat Jow lay awake that night, studying the problem from all sides, planning each step and contingent move. Caution, caution; larger issues than himself, than Hsiang Yuen or Dunya Skarin, than the Sung Tusk, loomed before him. Betrayal of Dunya was not in him, whether Hsiang Yuen was taken from him or not. His happiness with the child would forever be a reproach to him if through him she were taken.

Yet he could not sit by. Once before he had permitted himself to be used by the Reds. Though simple fund-raising and not sabotage or espionage, it was undeniably work performed for the Reds, and this lingered upon his conscience. Dunya Skarin was here upon another mission; could he again be an accomplice, if only by doing nothing?

Why the boat? Previously, Dunya had occupied quarters in Chinatown, above the restaurant with the exterior staircase. The Reds would not have installed her in the very entrance to San Francisco Bay without a reason. She had ready water access, perhaps to a fishing trawler or submarine in international waters. His thinking impeded by the intricate convolutions of theory and fact, Fat Jow slipped exhausted into a restless sleep of eternal and incomplete tasks.

On his way across Nob Hill in the morning, he paused at a corner pharmacy to use the telephone booth among the shadows at the dusty rear. The number of Low Electronics he knew without consulting the tattered directory, for there worked First Son, the only heir of Moon Kai, former owner of the herb shop. Young and old had grown very close since the tragic death of Moon Kai.

"I need your assistance as liaison with the police," said Fat Jow.

"Are you in trouble, old man?"

"The less you know, the less you will be tempted to reveal. Call Detective Lieutenant Cogswell and warn him I have reason to suspect listening devices in my shop."

"Oh well, if you think the place is bugged, that's my specialty. I can check it out for you. . . ."

"Which is exactly what I do not want," said Fat Jow crisply. "It is essential that I seem unaware of the presence of such devices."

"Last time, you were mixed up with the Red Chinese."

"Please call Lieutenant Cogswell," begged Fat Jow. "Is it not burden enough for me that Hsiang Yuen's future is affected?"

"Okay, but I'd like to be more than a messenger boy."

"You are my only means of frank talk with the police. We shall work it out. If you will join me for lunch, you may tell me what the lieutenant said."

All through the morning Fat Jow worked against distraction, ever conscious of a possible unseen listener recording his every move, every word of conversation with occasional customer or visiting merchant within his shop walls.

Well before the time expected, First Son appeared in the shop doorway. "Lunch, old man," he sang out toward the loft at the rear. "Drop everything, time for lunch."

Fat Jow knew that his early arrival was the doing of the lieutenant. He came down the narrow loft stairs, touching his ear in a gesture of warning. "Can you not see I am busy?" he said curtly. "Do not think you can excuse your long silence so easily, neglect me for months, and then suddenly remember I exist, come without invitation and without warning, and lure me away from my work before it is midday."

First Son blinked his surprise, but recovered quickly, and followed his cue. "I was in the neighborhood, I hadn't seen you for a long time. And besides, I'm buying."

"That, of course, makes a difference," twinkled Fat Jow.

"I only have an hour and I can't spend it arguing with you."

"Very well." Fat Jow drew the "closed" shade, locked the door, and accompanied him up the hill.

They took luncheon at the corner of Powell Street, removed sufficiently from the pagoda façade of Grant Avenue that the small Chinese sign did not attract the tourist. They went down one flight, to a decor clean and utilitarian in white tile and yellow paint, where one saw only well-known faces. Both ordered the same dish, the long slim noodles with spiced sauce, which in previous centuries had been copied by the imitative Italians and called spaghetti.

"Cogswell wants to know who got to you," said First Son.

Fat Jow gave his attention to the food. "I am not at liberty to say."

"You and the boy can have police protection."

"It is no good. I have reason for what I do."

"But this is big, old man! Bigger than you know."

"How big?" asked Fat Jow uneasily, raising his eyes.

"The San Leandro police department just may have come up with something. A top-security nuclear scientist turned up missing this morning."

Fat Jow stiffened, stopped eating. "Who?"

"A refugee from Red China, On Leong-sa. Took graduate courses at Berkeley, went from there to the radiation lab at Livermore. Owns a house in San Leandro. Married an Oakland girl, couple of kids. He left for work at the usual time, but didn't check in at the lab. Then his car was found in downtown San Leandro, a few blocks from the house. Wherever he went from there, or was taken, it's anybody's guess."

Fat Jow had lost his appetite. "And the lieutenant relates this to the Sung Tusk?"

"Don't you? It's the kind of thing you told him to look for."

Fat Jow frowned unhappily. "Perhaps."

"Perhaps nothing! They've got to know who your contact is, who's going to smuggle him out of the country, and how."

Fat Jow felt that he knew both answers, but he could not bring himself to speak. "You have had cause to defer to my judgment in past. . . ." he began, but First Son cut in angrily.

"Look, you got me here, and I've told you what you wanted to know. Why are you playing coy now?"

"I must do things in my own way," said Fat Jow patiently. "Have you ever known me to act capriciously?"

First Son expelled a long breath. "Well, I sure as hell don't always know where you're heading, but you always seem to get there."

"You will answer me truly, I know. Are the police keeping me under surveillance?"

"I don't know, old man. Cogswell didn't say as much, but right now I'm beginning to think it's a good idea."

Fat Jow slid back his chair and stood up. "Will you help me and say nothing?"

"I ought to have a psychiatric evaluation . . . but sure. What?"

"Please drive me downtown, to the alley entrance of the Palace Hotel."

First Son opened his mouth, closed it again, then signaled the waiter for the check.

Even if he failed to keep his word, First Son could

have reported only that Fat Jow hurried from the car into the hotel, and that following traffic urged First Son to drive on.

Fat Jow wasted no time in the hotel lobby, but hurried through the long arcade which had once been a passage for horsedrawn vehicles, and out the New Montgomery Street door. "Taxi," he said officiously to the uniformed doorman who, assuming him to be a guest of the hotel, immediately whistled up a cruising cab. The driver twisted to open the rear door, and Fat Jow jumped in. "Marina Green," he said, "and hurry."

Seeing the *Celestial III* still at her mooring, he was greatly relieved, but no less tense. He directed the cab to stop at the west end of the green, and as he paid the driver, he saw Dunya on deck watching him, her hand shading her eyes; when he reached the breakwater, she was gone. The thought that he had been mistaken came to annoy him. He went directly below to the cabin, thinking to find her there. He did not, but as he turned back to the ladder, a shadow darkened the daylight flooding down the companionway.

"What are you doing here?" asked Dunya coldly, approaching no nearer than the foot of the ladder, and blocking his return to the deck. She had exchanged the silken pajamas for dungarees and a gray jersey: working garb. Her hair was plaited into twin braids, out of the way. The languorous female had become a commander.

Fat Jow now knew that he was not mistaken. Dunya was prepared to go somewhere, and he had arrived at an awkward moment. He said casually, "You seemed most interested in my taxicab. Why?"

Dunya looked sharply at him, but did not speak.

He continued, "You have been expecting someone else. Let me venture a guess—Mr. On has not yet arrived."

She gasped, but then a thin smile moved the corners of her mouth. "I continually underestimate you," she said begrudgingly. "Again you come alone, and not the police. Do they know?"

"I learn more from them than they from me. They

know of him, but not of you. They know only that he is gone and that his car was found abandoned. They now speculate upon his means of transportation from that point."

She leaned back lazily against the ladder. "And what do you hope to accomplish, now that you are here?"

"I am not sure. I knew I must come, somehow to dissuade you, although I do not expect the illegality of kidnapping to deter you."

She laughed with genuine amusement. "I am kidnapping no one! Let Mr. On tell you when he arrives. He is correcting an earlier error he made, in deserting his homeland. The diplomatic and propaganda strength of my mission is his voluntary return. It has been only a matter of communication. I assure you, I am quite alone."

"The importer has acted as your accomplice."

"The importer does only what he is told. He does not know the purpose of my mission, and he asks no questions."

"I must compliment you for your imagination in affixing a stamp of legitimacy to everything you do, but you cannot dispute that the Sung Tusk is stolen property."

"An interesting point of international law. Stolen from whom, by whom? The People's Republic faces a gigantic task in gathering from all parts of the world treasures looted from the people over centuries of exploitation."

"A commendable opinion," conceded Fat Jow. "And what of me? If you are to remain scrupulously legal, am I then to go my way freely in the city, knowing what I do, without coercion to accompany you, wherever it is you go?"

Dunya paused before replying. "That would be unwise, even if it is true that you have discussed your suspicion with no one."

"You may rely upon my continuing silence."

"I know that, but my superiors do not. Already I have much to answer for in my dealings with you. We shall say that I am inviting you for an ocean cruise. We were to have shipped the *Celestial III* back to the importer from

Vancouver, and similar arrangements can be made for you . . . although my superiors may have other plans after they meet you. It must be this way."

"I understand," said Fat Jow with stolid resignation. "My major anxiety is for the child, but I know my landlady will care for him until I return." He did not voice what both were thinking: *if* he returned.

"I shall have the importer notify her that you are delayed."

A slight rocking of the boat interrupted them. From above, a man called, "Hello, Miss Skarin?"

Dunya tilted her face toward the light. "Down here, Mr. On."

A slight well-dressed man in gray suit and black homburg appeared on the ladder, carrying a small satchel. Midway down, he stopped, surprised at sight of Fat Jow.

Dunya said lightly, "An unscheduled guest has joined the party at the last minute. You are late."

He descended the remaining steps. "I thought they might be watching for me on the Bay Bridge; I came by bus, the long way around the bay, through San Jose."

"Laudable caution," approved Dunya. She started up the ladder. "Please keep our friend company here while I get under way. Do not come on deck until I call you." She was gone, and the hatch cover slid shut with a bang.

The scientist remained at the ladder. Although lighter in weight than Fat Jow, he was also younger and stronger.

"She is indeed alone," marveled Fat Jow. "You come of your own accord."

"Did you believe otherwise?"

The engine caught with a throaty surge of power, and they felt the *Celestial III* slide smoothly into motion. Fat Jow moved his eyes about the cabin; the ports were all screened by heavy wire mesh and fastened with small padlocks. He looked back at On Leong-sa, said wistfully, "My original intent in coming here was to prevent her from taking you away; now I see that escape is not indicated."

"I am simply going home. No matter what their ideological leanings, all Chinese are secretly proud of China's new stature in the world. You yourself . . . do you deny it?"

"No," admitted Fat Jow. "As a native San Franciscan, I too know pride."

"Then how much more I, who came here only after the liberation of China from the grasp of the Kuomintang reactionaries? To be proud at last of being Chinese, it is a great thing. My homeland has now expressed its need for me, and I respond. I cannot refuse. Chairman Mao is a man with a message which the world would do well to hear."

"Beware the man with a message. Infallibility and arrogance are his constant companions. If his message is worth disseminating, let him live it instead of shouting it."

Dunya's voice floated down the companionway: "Come up. We are passing the bridge."

They came on deck to see the aerial roadway two hundred feet above their heads, linking the low Presidio banks of the city with the frowning Marin hills to the north. White fringes of surf edged tiny beaches along both sides of the mile-wide straits, and ahead lay the open sea, limited by a cotton-white curtain of fog waiting several miles offshore.

"Will the fog cause complications?" asked On Leong-sa.

Dunya nodded toward the instrument panel. "We have the latest in radar equipment. There need be little delay in making our rendezvous. My superiors have chosen coordinates well beyond the range of shore-based radar."

The scientist jammed his hands into his trouser pockets and shuffled aft. He stood staring astern, along the spreading white wake toward the East Bay hills. The Gate narrowed as they felt the swell of the sea beneath the counter. Dunya opened the throttle, and the *Celestial III* plunged forward, bow climbing up on the curling double wave.

Fat Jow stumbled down the slant of the deck to join On Leong-sa. "You look behind," he commented. When after a long moment the other did not answer, Fat Jow sighed. "Miss Skarin is a captivating woman, in more ways than one."

On Leong-sa sank upon the stern seat and looked up at him. "Do you think she personally influenced my decision?" he chided.

"Appearances may have various interpretations. May I gather that you retain your devotion for your wife?"

"Yes," said On Leong-sa in a low voice.

"Yet here you are. Is this not perhaps a decision which should have been made in the first years after you departed China, while you were yet alone? As with any major change of direction, can one be certain that he does not leave behind more than he goes to? I am curious about the inevitable questions which must now lurk within your mind. What of your wife and sons?"

"They will join me when I am established."

"Ah, then they too come from China?"

"You know they did not," snapped On Leong-sa. "I met my wife at the University."

"And do you do them a service by uprooting them from the homeland they know?"

"They must join me and be part of the new world which is building."

"What will their life be in China, hopelessly infected as they are with imperialist ideas? You, who would devote your life to serving the people, launch your new career by subjecting your family to pressures which you know must come."

"My wife and sons are free agents," growled On Leong-sa. "They will not be forced to join me."

"Then," said Fat Jow with a small shake of his head, "you will not see them again."

The scientist winced as if in pain. "My personal affairs are of minor importance beside the monumental and historical task of fashioning a socialist society. It is not easy, it is not kind."

"I judge you to be a rational and humane person; your own instincts will not permit you to sacrifice your American-born wife and sons for an ideal."

On Leong-sa twisted to peer glumly toward the receding shore. The *Celestial III* sliced into the fog bank, and at once the coastal mountains and the great red bridge were lost to view, washed from existence by a universal permeating gray. The circle of calm sea was now all the world.

Fat Jow knew what he was thinking. Placing an understanding hand upon the younger man's shoulder, he said, "Roots are not necessarily born in a person, Mr. On; they are sent down as he matures, tendril by tiny tendril, into a soil he knows. Roots are the small, the familiar: the market, the place of worship, the house of a friend, the bank, the park. My roots are in San Francisco, not because I was born there, but because I have lived my life there. Where, then, are your roots, and the roots of your wife and sons? If it was error for you as a single person to have uprooted yourself from China, is the error corrected by ripping up the roots of these three from California?"

On Leong-sa shrugged angrily away from him, glared toward Dunya at the wheel, then surged forward up the slope of the deck. Since they had entered the fog, her attention had been fixed upon the instruments, and she did not notice him until he said, close behind her, "Will you stop?"

Startled, she reduced power. The roar of the engine sank to a muted rumble, the cruiser settled into a level glide. "What?" she barked at him, while keeping her eyes directed ahead.

"Stop, please," said On Leong-sa. "I must talk to you."

Dunya switched off the engine, took both hands from the wheel, and looked wryly past him to Fat Jow. They coasted silently to a stop, rising and falling with the swells, wavelets slapping along the hull. "Well?"

"Is it still true that I come voluntarily, or has that changed since we left the harbor?"

"Persuasion was the essence of my mission. You saw."

"There are varying degrees of persuasion," observed On Leong-sa. "Let us suppose that your initial attempt failed."

"But it did not. Where are you?"

He looked out into the fog, his features like stone. "Would you now, if I asked, put about and return?"

"Do you so ask?"

"I find that I cannot continue."

"You have allowed this old man to weaken your will?" she scoffed.

"He has helped me to *know* my will, Miss Skarin. There is no need for further discussion. Self-examination has proved more effective than persuasion."

"But as you say, there are degrees. My orders are explicit; we have come this far, I cannot turn back now." She pulled a tiny automatic pistol from a pocket of her dungarees and leveled it at his middle. "You will both go below, and I will proceed without distractions to impair my navigation."

On Leong-sa recoiled, and began to edge around her toward the companionway.

"Wait," said Fat Jow suddenly. Both turned; he had not moved from his position by the stern seat. "Consider, Mr. On," went on Fat Jow in a reasonable tone, "can Miss Skarin risk damaging you? Where the propaganda coup then? And what value a gun which she cannot use? Stop where you are."

Dunya pointed the gun at him. "I am under no such restriction with you, however." She gestured with its muzzle toward the companionway. "Get below."

"I think not. Miss Skarin, you do disappoint me. Heroics are hardly your style. You have shown your talent to be of the mind and the tongue."

"At which talent I am your inferior. Therefore, I must rely upon a talent in which *you* are inferior. Please."

"Death holds few terrors for a man in his seventh decade," said Fat Jow. "A swift departure is a privilege. In ending my problems, you but compound yours. You may be an agent of a foreign power, but I cannot see you as a murderer."

"Put me to the test," she said softly.

"Let us see." Fat Jow took a slow step toward her. "You will perceive that you are now directly between

Mr. On and myself, and you can watch only one of us. While you have the gun upon me, Mr. On could move upon you and relieve you of the weapon, were he so inclined."

Nervously she backed toward the port rail, snapping her head first toward one man, and then the other. "I cannot fail!" she cried. "You will not. . . ."

"You have had no heart in this assignment from its beginning," pursued Fat Jow inexorably. "You have demonstrated that from your first words to me. It signifies that you are not confirmed in your direction."

"I am," she said as if to herself. "I am."

"Yes? Then why do you hesitate? Because within you the two worlds are at war. Do you not unnecessarily torment yourself with unresolved inner conflict, by setting them at incessant opposition? Failure in your mission is ordained. If you do not deliver Mr. On, you fail. If you harm him, you fail. If you intimidate him, you fail. If you thus cannot harm him, and he is no longer willing to go, how can you navigate this craft, whether I am here or not?"

She leaned back against the rail, keeping the gun on him. "We are warned that the enemy will disemble, distort the truth, and cloud our vision. We are to be ever on our guard."

"Am I the enemy, Dunya Skarin? Am I?"

Slowly the gun fell to her side, and she looked down, frowning at the deck. She did not reply.

"You must answer," said Fat Jow, "if only for yourself and clarity of thinking."

She lifted her eyes to him. "You do not cooperate; you have never matched my picture of the enemy."

"Because that picture, you now understand, is an inaccurate one. Inconsistencies, small in themselves, mount into one vast question. As Mr. On has requested, will you now return us to the city? I shall continue to say nothing about you to the authorities and I am sure that Mr. On will promise the same."

"Gladly," said On Leong-sa. "I shall have problem

enough explaining my absence today."

"This is impossible," moaned Dunya.

"What is your alternative?" asked Fat Jow. "How can you report to your superiors? But if you were to surrender to the authorities as a defector, their welcome would be lenient."

"You know I cannot."

"Is it better that you oblige us to overpower you? In your present state of indecision, I think we could, but force would be a poor weapon for me, the exponent of freedom of choice. Besides, I daresay you are well versed in karate or whatever other violence they teach agents today."

"I could wish," she said dully, "that someday I might hear you debate Party officials." She looked at the gun in her hand. "I presume that you will want this?"

"Oh no, unless Mr. On does. It is yours; I should not know what to do with it. Is not your choice the sounder if you are not weakened by being disarmed? It rests solely with you."

She hesitated an instant only, then with a small shrug, returned the pistol to her pocket. "You see, I *can* make a decision myself."

"And you will go to the authorities?" breathed Fat Jow in relief.

"One thing at a time."

"I shall respect your wish. And you, Mr. On?"

On Leong-sa nodded. "It is the least I can do."

"Thank you." Dunya covered her eyes, drew her fingers down her face. "I must become accustomed to this new experience of trusting people." She started the engine, spun the wheel, and the *Celestial III* sped round in a broad southward arc, making back for land.

When they emerged from the fog bank, it lay no more than a mile outside the Gate. The late-afternoon sun, still topping the fog layer, limned the red towers of the bridge, twin beacons setting the Gate apart from the deceptively uniform rampart of hills which the Coast Range presents to the sea.

The *Celestial III* nosed around the breakwater and into the inner basin; they were returning from an afternoon's pleasure cruise. Because it was the comradely gesture among the yachting company, people waved and they waved back.

Dunya steered skillfully into the berth, but she did not leave the wheel and she allowed the engine to idle.

His voice carrying no opinion, Fat Jow said, "You are not coming ashore."

"No," said Dunya.

"Where will you go?"

"I must go somewhere alone," she said emptily, "away from everyone, to do some sorting."

"Shall I see you again?"

She smiled. "When I return to San Francisco, old man, you are the person I shall call first. I would learn more about self-examination." She stepped to the companionway, turned. "I had almost forgotten. . . ." She went below, soon returned with an awkward long parcel wrapped in brown paper, handed it to Fat Jow. "Since I am not planning to make delivery. . . ."

He need not look under the wrappings to know that he held now the irreplaceable Sung Tusk.

From the floating dock the two men watched the *Celestial III* back out into the channel and head for the gap in the breakwater. They did not wave and Dunya did not look back. They climbed to the breakwater for a better view as the cruiser gained speed in open water.

"What *are* we to tell them?" asked On Leong-sa.

"As little as possible," said Fat Jow. "I shall take the tusk to police headquarters, so that the importer cannot deny its return. They will know only that the thief, frightened by the virus of the Sung curse, brought it to the herbalist in exchange for assistance and anonymity."

"And I?"

Fat Jow thought in silence. "You were on an errand in the city—an important errand which occupied the day. So that your wife will ask fewer questions, an impulse gift for her: something big and expensive."

"But what? I have no imagination in these matters."

"What else? A car, with much shiny metal, and a roof which folds down."

"I do not know that our budget can afford it," said On Leong-sa.

Fat Jow laughed softly. "What is your return home worth to you? You were about to give up much more than money; now you worry about the budget."

The *Celestial III* dwindled under the bridge and vanished into the fog. The two men turned and slowly walked back toward the world they knew.

ECHO OF A SAVAGE
Robert Edmond Alter

He was a lonely old man and he lived in a great swamp. Born and raised in Okefenokee, he had never seen a city or even a proper town and the first time he ever saw television was during the Kennedy-Nixon debates. He had thought they were both mighty fine-talking men.

"Yeah, but Jube," fat Joel Sutt, the storekeeper at Sutt's Landing, had asked, "which one you fixing to vote on?"

And Jube had smiled his mild one-cornered smile and made a half-hitch with his head, and said, "Neither, I reckon. I wouldn't want'a take and hurt one or t'other's feelings."

That was just the trouble with old Jube Wiggs, Joel always said to the trappers and hunters and gator grabbers and their wives when they came in to buy or look or just to stand around and gab. "You cain't never tell if he's serious and jest plain stupid, er if he's joshing you."

But most of the folk who knew old Jube figured he really was serious, though not necessarily stupid. He was a mighty mild man. He never wanted to hurt anyone in any way.

The truth was, Joel worried about Jube. He liked him, and he didn't think any man should live out in that swamp by himself the way Jube did, and the way Jube's daddy before him had done, and the way Jube's daddy's daddy had done before both of them, clear back to the time when that first tough old Wiggs had returned from the Civil War and said, "To hell with the world! I'm taking me whar I ain't goan see no more Yanks ner Rebs ner no damn body! Never, ever!"

"At least, Jube," Joel would argue, the few times Jube gave him the chance to, "at least your granddaddy and daddy kept a gun by 'em. By juckies, man, hit jest ain't safe! You way out thar with all them gators and cottonmouths and no gun. You'll end up panther-et is what!"

Then Jube would make that half-hitch with his head and say, "You got a gun handy and sooner er later you're bound to use it. My granddaddy kilt men in the war, and my daddy kilt the Boyds in the Crane Crick feud, and men kilt my boy in thet Tarawa place. All with guns. But me, I don't aim to hurt nobody. I couldn't face God's sunrise each day had I a killing on my heart."

God was fooling around with sunset when Jube turned off the black little Suwannee River and paddled up a tupelo-crowded creek. A joree went chirp at him from a log and a bear working a larvae stump raised his snout and gave Jube's scent a snorf. A floating cottonmouth zigzagged away from the oncoming skiff, making S-shapes on the tarnished surface.

The banks—where you could see them for the maiden cane and pindown thickets and log litters—were turning mucky now, and the titi and cypress were crowding out the tupelos. Then the witch-hobble jungle opened up like a stage set and Jube paddled into a cypressbound water prairie, a lake.

His home was a shabby old shantyboat moored to cypress knees. The bonnet-covered lake was his temporary estate. He relocated the shantyboat periodically, according to what creeks he was working with his traps. Moving the shanty was a chore because he had to tow it with the skiff. He'd never had enough money to get himself an outboard motor, and even if he'd had one he knew he'd never have enough cash to keep the blame thing in gas.

Jube was dissatisfied with his present location because the land going on around the lake was all gator ground. The mama gators were building their cone nests back in the hurrah bushes and they were a mighty rily bunch during and right after their gestation period. Still, the creeks were animal rich and he felt tradition-bound to work them until they played out.

Jube swung the skiff alongside the shanty and made the boat fast with a bit of line. He picked up his gunnysack of canned stuff and grunted himself up to the stern porch. The porch was his workshop, so to speak. He had his cutting table there and his racks for stretching hides. He walked down the port gangway.

A six-foot gator was tooling around in the pickerel-weed alongside the shanty, watching Jube with cold speculative eyes. They liked his garbage. This one unhinged its upper jaw, showing Jube its disorderly stoblike teeth and its great pink glob of tongue, and hissed wetly.

"Now," Jube said mildly, reprovingly. "I ain't bothering you none. You got no call to git fractious."

The gator whacked its tail and submerged. Amber twilight was on the land now, and the listless foliage seemed to close in possessively, as if with the intention of making the old shanty a permanent part of the bug-flittering swamp. Then a gang of night-feeding ducks came down and everything was as it should be.

Jube stepped into the kitchen room and struck a match, got his oil lantern going. The room was muggy and still and the lantern flame stood straight as a spike. He made his supper.

He didn't think anything when he heard a splash outside. Gators were always fooling around. But then he heard, felt it too, something knock against the side of the shantyboat—another skiff. He listened to the light tread of feet on the gangway.

The man, stranger, didn't bother to knock. He opened the door and looked in at Jube at his table and smiled.

"All right if we bother you?" the stranger asked.

"I'm Mr. Folly," he said. He had an ageless look, and his eyes bore a haunted expression.

Jube swallowed his mouthful of potato and remained silent.

Mr. Folly said, "Do you have any guns here?"

"I don't believe in 'em."

"Don't you really?" Mr. Folly seemed interested. "I'd think that living in a primordial morass would make a gun a necessity."

Jube said, "How's thet you called hit? Prime what?"

"It means the primitive state—out of the time of elemental savagery," Mr. Folly explained.

Mr. Folly stepped inside and away from the door. A second man came in, a lean, angular, hungry-eyed man with a look of tired swagger in his face.

"This is Jink Williams," Mr. Folly said. "And this—" the third man was a squat simian man with huge awkward hands. He shuffled, blinking, into the lights, "—is Sam."

Mr. Folly looked dubiously around at the cobwebby kitchen room, down-cornering his thin mouth, and stamped the floor with one foot, as if to test the strength of the aged boards. "Is this boat safe?" he wondered. "It looks older than the Ark."

"I took and built her myself," Jube said defensively. "Her bottom's still sound as a nut."

"I hope so," Mr. Folly said doubtfully. "I don't like water. I don't swim." He turned to Jink Williams. "You'd better scout around for any guns, just to be sure."

"Why can't Sam look?" Williams said. "I'm bushed."

"Because Sam will look for the wrong things," Mr. Folly said, his smile returning. "Sam will look for little valueless objects that he can stick in his pocket. Won't you, Sam?"

Sam grinned and looked away. He shuffled his feet.

Williams was holding a large square canvas bag, and he glanced around for a place to put it. He flopped it on the table in front of Jube's dish and cup.

"Keep an eye on that, huh, dad?" he said. He pointed at the closed door forward. "What's in there?"

"Sleeping room," Jube said.

Williams went away. Sam shuffled over to the cot which had belonged to the son who had died twenty years ago at the faraway place with the strange name, and sat on it, his empty clumsy hands between his legs. Mr. Folly sat down across the table from Jube. He seemed very amiable.

"You live here alone?"

Jube nodded.

"Many people live in this immediate vicinity?"

Jube shook his head, fairly certain he understood the question.

"I'll explain exactly what we want from you," Mr. Folly said. "Food, blankets, and directions. We want to get across the swamp."

"Need you a airplane then," Jube told him. "Hit's six hunnert miles acrost and ever' mile is kindly hell on earth."

"We'll worry about that end of it," Mr. Folly said pleasantly. "Because of this"—he tapped the canvas bag with a pale, slim forefinger—"we're in a bit of a hurry."

Jube stared at the canvas bag. "I reckon hit goes fer money, don't hit?" he said. "And I reckon hit's stolt from a bank or somesuch."

"I'm afraid it's more than a case of stealing, old man," Folly continued. "You see, there was some objection to the transfer of ownership."

"What he thinks he's telling you," Williams said to Jube with an air of weary patience, "is that Sam there doesn't know his own strength when he gets excited. You've known men like that. Somebody makes a pass at them, and they go all wild and grab on like a bulldog and everything upstairs goes blank. Sam's like that."

Jube looked over at Sam. The apelike man was sitting in the shadows staring down at his large empty hands.

"Had me an uncle like thet," Jube said. "He was a gator grabber—'til he got aholt on the wrong gator once."

"Why don't we lay up in this scow for a while?" Williams said to Mr. Folly. "I'm not any too excited about getting deeper into this gator slough."

"No. We're too close to the Suwannee. They run excursion boats along that river, and where an excursion boat can go, a police boat can go one better."

"Well, at least tonight," Williams insisted. "I'm bushed."

Mr. Folly agreed. "Just for tonight. We'll lock the old man in that front room."

"Why waste a double bed?" Williams wanted to know. "I can fix him up out in that slough. Sam and me can—"

"No. Some local just might come along. Then we'd

need the old man to act as a front."

That's hit then, Jube thought. *This here's my last night. Because they already done tolt me more than they kin let me live to tell on them.*

Williams reached for the canvas bag.

"Let's see how it divvies."

"I thought you were bushed, Jink?" Mr. Folly said idly.

Williams looked at him, a flat stare. "I'm thirty-five, pal. That's thirty-five years I been waiting for this haul. I ain't *that* tired I can't count out my share. You don't have any great urgent objection, do you? You don't really want it to stay in one lump, so that all some smart boy has to do is pick up the whole bag of boodle tonight and skip out while his pals are sleeping, do you?"

"Of course not, Jink—pal." Mr. Folly smiled at him. "By the way, I don't suppose you found a gun when you looked?"

"I didn't find one. You want to search me?"

"I take your word for it, Jink. Just the way I took your word when you told us you'd lost our only pistol on the river."

"Dammit, Folly, if you think I didn't, then—"

Mr. Folly held up his hand, smiling. "Forgive me, Jink. I was only ribbing you. I'm sorry."

Williams shouted, "Sam! C'mon over here. We're divvying!"

Jube got to his feet. "I'll say good night now. I'm almighty tard."

"Do that," Williams snapped. "Say night-night and get the—"

"Jink," Mr. Folly interposed. "Aren't there some windows in that other room that should be locked from the outside?"

Williams shoved back from the table in a rage and stamped on out the front door.

Mr. Folly walked toward the sleeping room with Jube. He glanced back at Sam who was now sitting at the table staring blankly at the canvas bag. Mr. Folly spoke in an undertone.

"Don't let Williams upset you. We're not going to kill you. We're going to need you to guide us across the swamp."

Jube nodded. "I already done figured thet one out fer myself, mister. I ain't worrit none."

Mr. Folly patted him on the back. "That's very smart of you, old fellow."

Then the door swung shut and Jube, standing alone in the dark, heard Mr. Folly nudge a chair under the knob, while Jink Williams shuttered the two windows from the outside.

No, Jube thought. *They won't go to kill me yit. Not til they git what they want out'n me.*

He stretched out on the double bed, on top of the patchwork quilt that his dead wife had made twenty-some years ago, and he looked up at the dark rafters overhead. For years now he'd thought that he didn't really have much to live for, that it didn't much matter whether he lived or died. Yet, now, when it came right down to the act of dying, he realized how wrong he'd been. Dying at his age was nothing. But living was poling up the shadow-dappled creeks with the ibises and wood ducks and squawk herons fluttering their gaudy plumage around him. It was watching the yellow jessamine and scarlet ivy trumpets and pink hurrah blossoms come to bloom in the spring. It was coming home after a hard day's toil and settling into his old chair with his pipe and coffee and his memories. Lots of memories.

There was a way out, of course—one that the three city fellas didn't know about, but he hated to take it because it was a mighty mean row to hoe. Seemed to him it would be easier to go along with the three of them and lose them in the swamp. That shouldn't take much doing. A city man stood less chance in a swamp than a snowball stood in hell.

What was it that Folly fella called it? Prime-or-dial? Well, Jube reckoned it was all of that and then some. Okefenokee was about as far removed from anything that smacked of civilization as hell was from a nursery rhyme.

It kept surprises in store for strangers, real abrupt violent surprises.

He drifted into a deep sleep.

It was a little after dawn when Jink Williams suddenly threw open the door and started yelling at Jube.

"Where's Sam? Wake up, you bleary old coot! Where's Sam?"

Jube sat up and felt a ripple of pain down his back. *Gitting old*, he thought. *Gitting almighty old and worn.*

"What?" he said.

"Dammit, I said where's Sam?"

Jube blinked stupidly around the shadowy room. "Ain't in here. Didn't he go to sleep out thar with y'all?"

"Sure he slept out here with *us all*. I want to know where he is now!"

Jube got up and went over to the door. Mr. Folly was sitting on the cot. He was fully dressed, and he was watching Williams.

Williams yelled, "Where *is* that bent brain?" He ran out of the kitchen and onto the front porch. Jube heard him clomping along the gangway. He glanced at Mr. Folly, who smiled at him but said nothing.

Williams reentered the room. He looked at Mr. Folly and he no longer seemed excited. Indeed, he appeared to be homicidally calm. "He's gone," he stated flatly. "The boodle too. His, yours, mine. All gone. But both the boats are still tied to this scow. That's funny. Ain't it funny, pal? Because Sam can't walk on water, and he ain't the type for suicide."

"Very funny," Mr. Folly agreed.

"Yeah," Williams said. He fished out a cigarette and put it in his mouth and found a match and struck the head with his thumbnail and held the little peak of flame to the cigarette.

"So you had to do it," he said tonelessly. "In the night when the poor saphead was asleep."

"Not asleep," Mr. Folly murmured, smiling, watching Williams.

"Not asleep, then," Williams agreed. "When me and

the old man was asleep. And when Sam was thinking we were all asleep, and he was up and busy rummaging around to see what little trinket he could find to put in his pocket. The poor simple nut never would have enough sense to think of walking off with the forty grand that was laying on that table, because dollar bills are mostly just paper to him. They ain't pretty like a ballpoint pen or a brass ring or a cheap watch."

Williams paused and blew smoke through his nose. "And you were laying there on that cot watching him and thinking to yourself how much easier it would be only to have to split two ways. Or better yet—no split at all. So you got up and you said something to him like, 'Hey, Sam, come out here on the porch and take a gander at this elk's tooth I found.' And he went. And then you put him over the side for those toothy garbage disposals to take care of. That was it, wasn't it?"

"Why be angry?" Mr. Folly asked. "You were thinking about it yourself. It was as plain as print on your face. But that's the difference between us. You think while I act. That's why at thirty-five you'll never see the extra twenty years I already have on you."

"I won't, huh?" Williams drew a switchblade knife from his pocket and pressed the spring button. The five-inch blade went *ssst* into place. He grinned at Mr. Folly. "Sorry, pal. I forgot to tell you about this little item."

Mr. Folly chuckled and drew a snubnosed .32 from his jacket. "Makes us even, uh—pal. I neglected to mention this."

Williams spat out his cigarette. "You filthy. . . ."

"Out on the porch, Jink!" Mr. Folly motioned with the pistol. He was no longer a wistfully smiling man. He was all business. Williams shrugged and went to the door.

The distant shaggy-headed cabbage palms stood starkly against a rose dawn. Mr. Folly and Williams faced each other on the porch. Jube stayed just inside the doorway.

"Get into the water," Mr. Folly ordered.

Williams balked. "Let me take one of the boats, Folly. It's thirty yards to shore. You can keep the cash, but at least give me a boat!"

"I'm letting you keep your knife. What more can you ask? Go on—overboard."

"NO! There's gators out there!"

"Listen to me, *pal*," Mr. Folly said. "The alligators are peacefully sleeping behind those thickets. But if I have to fire this gun, they'll panic and take to the water. Then you and they can have a swimming match. I'm giving you a break, *pal*. A far better break than I gave Simple Sam. I'm turning you loose in this place on foot. If you keep your wits, and if you're lucky, you might make it. All right. Over! I'm tired of this."

Williams stalled at the edge.

Mr. Folly cocked the hammer on the .32.

"Wait!" Williams cried. "Now wait, dammit!" He wet his lips and faced the water. Nothing moved in the pickerelweed or the maiden cane. The cypress-ribbed body of brackish water was dead still, deserted. He hunkered down and eased himself over the side and started dog-paddling toward the nearest shore.

"He's goan at gator ground, mister," Jube said.

Mr. Folly glanced back at Jube, smiling mildly. "Well, Jink never was too bright."

Folly aimed the pistol toward the swimming man. "Jink! You're going too slow. You need a little prompting!" He fired and the bullet struck a yard behind the swimmer.

Williams cast a frantic look around as the shot caromed across the water and a gang of limpkins and bitterns splattered into the sky. Mr. Folly fired again.

Jube looked at the distant mudbank. A couple of coffee bushes had started to tremble on the semisolid earth. All at once a wild charge of spooked gators burst from their thicket tunnels and lumbered pellmell down the bank, crashing again and again into the churned water, all around the treading, screaming man.

Jube stepped back. He turned and hurried into the sleeping room and closed the door, picked up a chair and put the back under the knob and tried the knob. Good. The trick worked either way.

KA-POW! Splinters flew from the center of the door

panel as a hard-nosed .32 slug came plowing through. Jube stepped to one side.

Mr. Folly called from the other room, "You're being foolish, old man. You might have stood a chance if I'd let you take me into the swamp. That's what you were thinking of all the time, wasn't it? To get me out there and lose me? But I can do without you, you know. I'm quite self-sufficient. Even in this primeval hangover."

Jube said nothing. He listened for the telltale sounds in the other room. The trod of feet, pause, a scuffle, a bump, feet going away. Yeah. Mr. Folly was gathering up canned food, blankets, anything he thought he would need in order to cross the swamp. That would keep him occupied for a while.

So—it was time to hoe the mean row.

Because he ain't about to jest walk off and leave me here alive, Jube thought. *He'll think a something. He's got to.*

He tossed aside a braid throw rug, uncovering a small square trapdoor. He raised the lid and looked into the well. Dark scummy water was waiting one yard below the floorboards.

A shiver ran through Jube's scrawny frame like icewater. He hated getting down in there and swimming under the flat bottom of the shantyboat. Hated it like poison. Especially now, with gators in the lake. One thing though, most of them would be almighty busy with Williams' corpse....

Gingerly Jube lowered himself into the cool black water. He winced as he felt it inch up around his body. Then he had to let go and he slipped straight down, clawing at the splintery sides to keep his head above water. Then he smelled smoke.

Thet's hit then, he thought. *He finally figgered hit out —what to do about me.*

Jube heard Mr. Folly's muted voice calling from the kitchen, "At the risk of using a tired cliché, old man— dead men, you know, tell no tales!" Then he laughed.

The laugh did something to Jube—clinging there in the

dark, wet, cramped well. It shattered some of his old convictions, illusions. It was the voiced embodiment of all the evil that thrived in the mud and muck and decay of a world that was still elementally savage. Some men needed killing.

Jube stopped treading, sucked his breath and sank. The totally opaque blackness of covered swamp water rushed over him, and he started kicking, feeling his way along the scummy bottom of the shantyboat. His lungs swelled like balloons and he shoved up in a panic, but still the bottom of the boat was above him and he couldn't seem to go anywhere at all. Then he went a little mad—thrashing and crying bubbles and clawing across the slimy boards; and all the time he could vividly see in his mind those awful gator jaws rising under him, opening. . . .

And then the water turned from black to brownish-green to olive, and Jube broke the surface. His own skiff was only a few feet away. He swam to it, looking up at his looming shantyboat.

Black smoke, eagerly licked by tongues of orange flame, coiled from the kitchen windows. Jube didn't think about it. He grabbed the stern of his skiff and climbed aboard.

He untied the skiff's line and stepped over to the other boat. Mr. Folly had already dumped in a gunnysack of canned food, a pile of blankets, and the canvas bag that had caused the death of three men.

Jube cast off from the shantyboat, gave his skiff a good shove into the lake, then hunkered down with the paddle to get away from the other boat.

He was maybe sixty feet into the lake when he saw Mr. Folly come out on the front porch. Smoke followed him and he turned back for one last look.

Mr. Folly smiled and started along the gangway. He stopped altogether, staring at the place where the two boats should have been. His head snapped around and he spotted Jube rowing for the creek. He whipped out the .32 revolver.

Jube flinched as the bullets splashed in the water

around him, but he didn't stop paddling. He glanced back. Mr. Folly had started along the gangway again, only to reel back as from a physical blow as a belch of smoke gasped from one of the windows. For a moment Jube couldn't see the man for smoke.

"Come back! Old man, don't leave me here! I can't swim! I've thrown my gun away! Come back!"

Jube stalled, raised his paddle to stroke, and stalled again. He looked back. A curtain of brownish smoke closed between the blazing shantyboat and himself. He winced and looked around at the swamp like a man who is lost and searching for signpost. "What should I do?" he muttered. "What's right?"

A crossback fox slipped through the palmettos and peered out at the conflagration. It whipped about with a furry show of its tail and disappeared. Then three gators went thrashing across the lake in a welter of white water, and a pair of egrets winged over the moss-strung cypresses. Every living thing seemed to be fleeing from a place of contamination.

Jube let out his breath and brought down the paddle.

All the way along the creek he concentrated on the remembered sound of Mr. Folly's laugh. And after a while the distant dwindling screams became no more than that to old Jube. An echo of a savage laugh.

THE NONCONFORMIST
William R. Coons

For years I endured with patience and with fortitude slights and indignities from Robert Cressy.

Endured, not tolerated. Fortitude came from the knowledge that one day I would kill him. Patience was born of necessity. I had to find the perfect method. It is to the quality of patience in my character that I attribute my success.

Know Thine Enemy, the Good Book says. I had every reason to know mine.

I had known Robert Cressy since he was a very small and very obnoxious boy. Precisely the obnoxious sort of boy you would expect to grow into an obnoxious sort of man, granting Nature was left to develop its mistake. Nature was. It was left to me to correct the error.

At seven, Robert Cressy looked like any normal child, only more normal than most. Granting that the norm is a rarity. Even then, normality was his most outstanding characteristic. He *reeked* normality, from his well-scrubbed cheeks and vaselined hair to his polished brown oxfords. In this age of the Organization Man, I have been called many things, including a "Beatnik." This because I refuse to shave twice a day and because I refuse to pay the outrageous sum of a dollar and fifty cents biweekly for a haircut. I cut my own, when it needs it. I am sure no one ever thought of accusing Robert of belonging to such a confraternity of self-styled oddballs. Quite the contrary. It was he who first applied the derogatory epithet to my person.

"Look at you," he said, walking uninvited into my sign-painting shop: "You're becoming a middle-aged Beatnik!"

It took restraint for me not to throttle him then and there. How I loathed the man! Rage choked me.

Conformity is the curse of our society, and a man like Robert Cressy is a symbol of conformity. But was Robert Cressy a man? He seemed to me more like a machine. For as long as I knew him he lived his life with the precision of clockwork. In school he was always punctual, while I was constantly being called to account by teachers and principals for being tardy. How he smirked at the punishments I received! *He* was never late; not once—a fact which he never tired of reminding me of. Well, I disliked him heartily enough in school, but my hatred of him was a mature emotion ripened over a period of years. For some reason I never seemed to be able to escape from a world dominated by the Robert Cressys.

I often tried to guess his secret. That he had one I was sure; I remember having dreams, violent dreams, in which Robert would be laughing at me and I would deal him a powerful blow with my fist, and then he would be lying at my feet, his head split open, revealing not blood and brains but a series of tiny wheels and springs and cogs oozing oil, all functioning smoothly like a Swiss watch. He would still be laughing and I would start to scream, and then I would wake up.

A person's character can be read in his basic habits. There is nothing more revealing, for instance, than how and what a person eats. Robert's daily routine and menu, on paper, would look more like a train schedule than the daily history of a man. But it would *be* Robert. It would look something like this:

Breakfast: 7:15 (two eggs, poached, on toast; black coffee)
Leave home: 8:00 (bus to work)
Office: 8:30 (International Data Processing Center)
Lunch: 12:00 noon (bowl of soup, tunafish sandwich, apple)
Office: 1:00
Leave work: 5:30 (bus home)

Supper: 6:00 (meat, vegetable, potato, no dessert)
Bed: 9:30

And there you have it. The complete Robert Cressy. Mine Enemy. In the evening, he might take a walk or go to a movie. No other activities. Work, eat, sleep, work, eat, sleep. He was a modern-day cipher.

Why kill a cipher?

Because he was a living, walking refutation of everything I was and everything I believed in: freedom from monotonous routine; overindulgence when it is enjoyable to overindulge; responsibility to no one but myself; a carefree life lived fully.

But I couldn't live fully with Robert Cressy around. He was always there to remind me of my failures when I failed; to belittle my achievements when I achieved anything. And when I fell flat on my face, he was there, grinning, to inform me that the position exactly suited my behaviour pattern.

He was there when Laura left me.

I had been drunk for a week. For an entire week I lived on nothing but the contents of bottles, and the little shop where I tried to make enough money as a hack sign painter to support my attempts at something greater, in the name of Art, was strewn with bottles of all shapes and sizes, when Robert found me lying in a stupor on the filthy cot in my office.

He lectured me.

Yes, this is what you *would* do, isn't it, Bradley? Drink yourself silly, instead of getting up and admitting to yourself what a stupid fool you've been and what a waste you've made of your life.

"Did you really think you deserved a girl like Laura? Did you really think she'd stay with you once she found you out for the shiftless, irresponsible, disorganized person you are?

"Let this be a lesson to you, Bradley—if you are still capable of learning anything. Get up and get yourself *organized*. Get rid of those half-baked notions about being an artistic genius and start setting your life in *order*.

A man is a success only if he creates a *pattern to follow*."

I said nothing. I had heard it all before. I listened to him rant, and thought about Laura, whom I loved and who was Robert's friend.

I knew the time had come to kill him.

It took me a few days to sober up. I wanted to be perfectly sober for what I was going to do.

I was going to kill him. I was going to kill him in a way that would humiliate him and everything he stood for.

After three days, I could hold a razor in my hand without fear of cutting my face to pieces. I shaved. Then I took a long bath and after that I went out and had a haircut and bought a new suit of clothes. Afterward I stared at myself in the mirror, mockingly, denying the lie I saw before me, or any relation between it and the real me.

That evening, I invited Robert over.

He was amazed at the change in me. It was almost worth it just to see the expression on his face as he looked first at me and then around the shop, which was swept and cleaned and set in order.

I laughed. "You shouldn't look so surprised, Robert. After all, this is all your doing. You see, I decided to take your sage advice—you see before you a new man; a man created by your superior judgment and wisdom."

Awe was replaced by a look of smug self-satisfaction on his face. For that look alone I could have killed him then and there. But I remembered my vow of patience and stuck to my subtle plan.

"How about a drink on it, Robert?" I dropped the question as casually as I dared. It was a crucial step. Robert seldom took a drink, and when he did, it was only one. Never more. But one was all I wanted him to take.

"Well . . . very well, Bradley. This *is* an occasion. Only one, though."

I mixed him a Bourbon and water. He watched me closely, making sure I didn't sneak in an extra shot. We clinked our glasses.

"To a new man."

"To a new man."

We drank in silence. Robert drank his quickly, as if drinking were merely a social task to be got over with as quickly as possible. When he had swallowed his one drink, I beckoned him over to a corner of the room where an easel stood with a cloth draped over it. He would have a last view of my work as an artist.

"We profit even from our mistakes," I said, watching him closely. "This is my latest work." I ripped away the cloth.

"Why, it's Laura!"

"Yes," I said. "Take a good look at her. It's your last." And then I sapped him neatly behind the ear with an old sock filled with sand. He folded like a leaky bag of water and sank to the floor unconscious before her picture.

I worked fast. He would be out for a good while, but I didn't want to chance someone dropping by. I removed his left shoe and sock. Then I took a large hypodermic needle from the drawer and filled it with Bourbon.

When I finished working and had his sock and shoe back on, there was enough whiskey in his veins to kill him. The mark of the hypodermic would hardly show at all on his heel.

I called the police.

By the time they arrived, I had drunk just enough Bourbon to appear slightly drunk. But I still knew what I was doing.

"He just keeled over," I told the officer nervously. "We had a bet. I bet he couldn't drink a whole fifth of liquor and he bet he could. He grabbed the bottle and drank the whole thing down without stopping, and then keeled over. I . . . I didn't think he'd really do it. . . ."

I hate order and regularity as much as ever. More. Meals served at the exact time, people coming and going according to a clock, everything neat and clean and on schedule—the very thought of it all makes me want to scratch where I don't itch. I feel as though my skin doesn't fit me any more. Maybe I'm wearing somebody else's skin?

The trial was all over with one statement from the prosecuting attorney: "Did you really expect us to believe, sir, that a man who has led the strict life of a diabetic since childhood would bet his life away on a bottle of whiskey?"

It's the bars. All those regularly shaped and spaced bars here in Murderer's Row that are driving me out of my mind. . . .

THE SAPPHIRE THAT DISAPPEARED
James Holding

"Señor, the principals of a famous firm of private detectives... Landis & Landis."

Laurie was clowning when she said it; she was therefore very surprised at Quesada's reaction. He unpinned his glasses from the bridge of his nose, slapped the top of the counter enthusiastically with his hand, and beamed at them. "What!" he exclaimed. "The detectives who recovered the stolen jewels of Caresse Carter, the cinema star?"

Jeff stared at him. "Yes," he said, "we're Landis & Landis, all right. But how do you know about us? And Caresse Carter's jewels?"

"We have newspapers in Buenos Aires, you know," said Quesada blandly. "And that theft was played up here. Partly because some of Miss Carter's jewels were bought in this very shop." Quesada raised his voice. "Maria! Come down! Maria is my wife," he explained. "Also my partner. She would be honored to meet Landis & Landis. You do not mind?"

"Not at all," Jeff said.

"Milagroso!" Quesada returned his pince-nez to his nose and looked at Laurie. "And you, señora, are a detective? You? So much a lady and so beautiful?"

"Well, of course." Laurie was pleased. She flashed Quesada a dazzling smile. "I'm the brains of Landis & Landis. He's the brawn." She jerked a thumb at Jeff, who obligingly made a muscle and grinned. Being on vacation was responsible for their behaving in this lighthearted way.

Maria Quesada, a petite black-eyed woman, descended a circular staircase from the shop's upper regions. She was introduced, proclaimed herself enchanted to meet the great detectives Landis & Landis, then quietly withdrew after congratulating them upon their recovery of Miss Carter's famous jewels. Before she disappeared, however, she suggested to her husband, "Luis, why do you not ask the gentleman and his lady about the incident of last night? Perhaps they can solve our puzzle."

"What puzzle is that?" Jeff asked.

Quesada shrugged. "A lost sapphire," he said. "But fully insured." He offered another charm for Laurie's inspection, a tiny golden reproduction of a maté cup and *bombilla*. "Twenty-four-carat gold, also," he said. "And very typical, the maté cup of a *gaucho*. Only six thousand pesos. No tax."

"Seventy-five clams," Jeff converted gloomily, "for something no bigger than a pea!"

Quesada launched into a eulogy of the precision craftsmanship required to produce such exquisite miniatures. Laurie listened with shining eyes to this sales talk. To stem it, Jeff said hurriedly, "What about this sapphire you lost? Something mysterious about it?"

"Very mysterious," Quesada admitted. "In a way. Now, Mrs. Landis, may I point out that this *cuchillo*, this *gaucho*'s knife, is only fifty-five hundred pesos?"

"And no tax," Jeff said. "Yes. But what about your lost sapphire?"

Laurie said to Quesada, "Go on, Señor Quesada, tell us your mystery. My husband will sulk all day if you don't. He is a compulsive mystery-solver, by inclination as well as trade. I'll be looking at the charms as you talk."

"We stayed open after our usual closing time last night," Quesada said, "to serve the members of your Sudair Tour. We knew your plane would get here about five. Do you know a Mrs. Thompson?" They nodded. "She came in about nine . . . our first customer after the dinner hour. She bought a beautiful set of aquamarines. It was while she was here that we lost our sapphire."

Jeff said, "You don't think she took it, do you? She's perfectly honest. And rich enough to buy anything she fancies. We've gotten to know her pretty well on this trip."

"Oh, no, señor!" Quesada was distressed. "You misunderstand. I do not suspect Mrs. Thompson. I know she did not take the sapphire."

"You know? How can you be sure?" This was Laurie.

"She was searched."

"Searched!" They breathed the word simultaneously, picturing the dignified Mrs. Thompson submitting to a search of her person.

"At her own request," Quesada hastened to explain. He waved an arm around him at his shop. "It is difficult to understand how a sapphire could become lost in here, eh?" he said. The room was round. Beige carpeting covered the floor to within an inch of the circular walls. There were no corners. The glass-railed staircase down which Señora Quesada had appeared led upward to the silverware department on the floor above, and downward to the vaults on the floor below. Except for the semicircle of glass display cases, set on slender pedestals around half the room's perimeter, and the leather stools that fronted them, the room was monastically bare. "All in one little minute," Quesada said in bewilderment, "the sapphire is gone."

He gave them details. It seemed that while Mrs. Thompson was looking at aquamarine necklaces, attended by Quesada, an Argentine gentleman named Ortega had come into the shop to inquire about a gift for his wife. He asked to see some unset stones. And it was while one of Quesada's clerks was bearing a tray of such stones from the vault to Señora Quesada, who was waiting on Señor Ortega, that the accident occurred.

The clerk, approaching the counter at which Ortega sat, and carrying the tray of gems before him in both hands, suddenly tripped or stumbled, and in attempting to recover his balance, dropped the tray and its contents to the floor.

Muttering apologies, the clerk immediately went to his knees and began to pick up the scattered gems. Señora Quesada came around from behind her counter and squatted gracefully to help him. Señor Quesada temporarily deserted Mrs. Thompson at the next counter and joined the retrievers. And even Mrs. Thompson, insidiously affected by the sight of half a million dollars' worth of gems lying about on the rug like glass beads from a broken string, finally left her stool and also stooped to help recover the treasures.

Only Señor Ortega held himself aloof from the excitement. When the clerk stumbled and spilled the tray almost at his feet, Ortega got up from his stool with startled alacrity, but stood calmly beside it, looking on as the others scrabbled on all fours about him on the rug.

In less than a minute, Quesada estimated, the scattered jewels were returned to their tray. All but one. There was one missing. Quesada identified it as a ten-carat Ceylonese sapphire of pure cornflower-blue color whose asking price would have been in the neighborhood of eight hundred thousand pesos.

Followed then a painstaking search of the entire room without result. The upshot was that before Señor Ortega left the shop, he asked as a favor to him that Quesada should have him searched, since some taint of suspicion, however faint, might cling to him if he went off to his hotel while the sapphire was still missing. Quesada protested. When Mrs. Thompson added her voice to Ortega's, however, and also begged to be searched, he yielded.

One of the clerks, thereupon, with Quesada looking on, made a thorough search of Ortega's clothing and person in the gentlemen's room belowstairs, Ortega removing his outer garments for the purpose. No sapphire came to light.

And Señora Quesada performed a like service, albeit unwillingly, for Mrs. Thompson in the ladies' retiring room abovestairs. No sapphire. And that was the way it ended. Both Ortega and Mrs. Thompson left their names and addresses with Quesada and departed.

"So where," Quesada finished, "can my sapphire have gone? Neither Mrs. Thompson nor Señor Ortega took the stone. I would trust my clerks with my life. Maria is above suspicion. And so, I assume, am I. Yet the sapphire, that was merely dropped on the rug, can nowhere be found. What, then, is the explanation?"

"A good question," Laurie said.

"A baffler," Jeff agreed, with unmistakable relish in his tone. "Let us think it over for a bit, Señor Quesada, will you? If we get any ideas, we'll let you know."

"A thousand thanks," said Quesada. "I shall be waiting in the certain knowledge that Landis & Landis will succeed where I have failed." He bowed to Laurie. "Shall I wrap up this *boleadora* charm?" he asked.

"I think we'll wait until my husband and I solve your great mystery, Señor Quesada," said Laurie with a madonna smile, "and then perhaps you'll give us a little discount on the charm."

Gallantly, Quesada rose to the occasion. "For brains, no discount is needed," he said. "As for beauty, my dear lady, will your husband permit me to say that you already possess more than your fair share of charms?"

Laurie clapped her hands in delight. They rose to leave. Jeff said, "We'll see you later, perhaps. But one question first. Did your search of the showroom last night yield anything at all?"

Quesada shook his head. "Nothing." Then he suddenly grinned and reached into his pocket. "Unless you count this. I found it at the edge of the rug there." He held out to Jeff a tiny ball of paper.

Jeff smoothed it out between his fingers.

It consisted of two wrappers from sticks of Wrigley's Spearmint Gum.

They decided to have luncheon at one of Buenos Aires' famous restaurants, La Cabaña, and caught a taxicab in the Plaza San Martin just outside Quesada's shop. Riding through the broad avenues of a city so reminiscent of Paris, past parks and gardens gay with the crimson blossoms of "drunk" trees and the blue of jacaranda, they held hands like romantic teen-agers and avoided the subject of Quesada's sapphire by mutual consent.

But once La Cabaña received them into its savory comfort and they sat with their preluncheon gimlets at the bar, while the three-inch steaks they had ordered sputtered on an open grill nearby, they began to chatter about the case.

"This one I don't believe we can handle," began Laurie with a gamine grin at Jeff. "If you'll forgive a vulgarism, darling, this one is for the birds."

"Why?" asked Jeff.

"Why? Because there are just too many things that could have happened to that crazy sapphire, that's why. I could name you a dozen different ways it could have disappeared."

"Name me just a couple," Jeff invited.

Laurie said, "It could have dropped into the trouser cuff of one of those clerks and still be there. *They* weren't searched."

"Didn't you notice? Those boys had on cutaways with striped pants. No cuffs on the trousers. Sorry."

"Well, Ortega must have had cuffs on *his* pants."

"Searched," Jeff reminded her. " 'Thoroughly searched' was Quesada's phrase, I think. Both clothing and person."

"Person!" Laurie was deprecating. "That's another thing. How thorough a search do you think they could make? And what if one of them swallowed the sapphire?"

"Not likely. A ten-carat sapphire is no aspirin tablet, honey. You'd at least need a drink of water to wash it down, I should think. If it didn't choke you outright."

Laurie said, "Maybe Ortega was the man in the Hathaway shirt. He had an eyepatch on. And he suddenly clapped the sapphire into his eyesocket under the patch when nobody was looking."

This was greeted by several seconds of silence.

"Okay," Laurie said defensively, "think of a better one, then."

"That I can easily do," Jeff began. But Laurie interrupted him.

"Wait," she said. "What do we know the most about in this case? The people. How many of them, who they are, what they did and et cetera. So let us start with them, my dear Sherlock. If the sapphire was pinched, somebody must have pinched it. Who?"

"Ortega," said Jeff without hesitation.

"I don't see why."

"I'll tell you why. Quesada's two clerks are out on his sayso. Old retainers. Right?"

"It was one of them that precipitated the whole thing by stumbling," Laurie pointed out.

"Correct. But let's believe Quesada. If he trusts those clerks so implicitly, the stumble must have been an accident. So cross them off. Cross off Maria and Quesada, too. They owned the sapphire already. Why should they steal it? And we come up with only two other possibilities. Mrs. Thompson and Ortega."

"Mrs. Thompson! That's silly. She's a Philadelphia Quaker so honest she won't even dye her hair! And besides, you said yourself she's loaded. She could buy Quesada's whole setup with one year's interest from her tax-free bonds." Laurie giggled. "Wasn't Señor Quesada a riot with his 'no tax' routine? And he wanted seventy-five dollars for a simple little charm!"

"Darling," Jeff brought her back, "please. If we cross off Mrs. Thompson, who's left?"

"Ortega."

"So for purposes of a hook to hang a theory on, let's agree that if anybody swiped the sapphire, it was Ortega."

"Ortega it is. *If* the sapphire was stolen."

"Where else could it go? A cornflower-blue sapphire would show up against that ice cream rug of Quesada's like blue ink on a snowdrift!"

"I guess you're right. There simply wasn't any place for the sapphire to go without human help. They'd have found it in a second."

"Unless," said Jeff, flattening the two chewing gum wrappers on the table and setting his drink on them, "these two pieces of paper have some significance. They're our only clues."

"Some clues! Quesada said his rug had been vacuumed at seven last night, during the dinner hour."

"And Mrs. Thompson was their first customer thereafter. Does she chew gum?"

"I never knew her to. She smokes a lot, though."

"You're no help." Jeff mused a moment. "The American make of gum means nothing, I'm sure. You can get it here in Buenos Aires easily enough. However, suppose one of our suspects *did* drop these wrappers on Quesada's floor. Makes you think, doesn't it?"

"Not me. Why should it?"

"Chewing gum," Jeff said. "Chewing gum. Don't you get it, Laurie? It's sticky stuff. And sticky chewing gum could pick up a sapphire off the floor, darling."

"You're mad," Laurie laughed. "Chewing gum! Whoever picked up the sapphire could do it with his fingers. Why chewing gum?"

"For concealment. A wad of chewing gum stuck between the heel and sole of a man's shoe, for example, would readily pick up any small hard object that the man stepped on just right."

"I've heard of gumshoe detectives," Laurie said, "but this is ridiculous!"

Jeff ignored her. "In which case," he pointed out, "the chewing gum *and* the sapphire that was sticking to it would have been discovered immediately when Ortega's clothes and person were searched."

"I suppose so."

"But I like the chewing gum idea." Jeff brightened. "We can check whether they *did* find any chewing gum. Excuse me a minute." He stood up and left the bar abruptly.

In five minutes he was back. "Guess what?" he said. "The telephone operator could speak English!" He sipped his drink. "I talked to Quesada on the phone. Neither of the clerks and neither of the Quesadas *ever* chews gum. Further, no chewing gum has been found anywhere in the shop, chewed or unchewed. Not on Ortega. Not on Mrs. Thompson. Not on the rug or the floor. Not in any wastebasket or ashtray." Jeff grinned at his wife. "Isn't that lovely? No chewing gum."

Laurie said, "Ortega was probably still chewing it when he was searched."

Jeff shook his head. "No. The guard made him open up and say 'a-a-ah.' "

"Swallowed it in his agitation, then."

"Not likely."

Laurie drained the last few drops of her cocktail. "But didn't Quesada realize that the place to look for used chewing gum is under the stools at the counters?"

"He went and looked there at my suggestion," Jeff laughed. "No chewing gum."

"Wait a minute." Laurie sobered. "The clerks. One of them stepped on the gum when Ortega threw it away. It stuck to his shoe. And he picked up the sapphire unknowingly by stepping on it when they were all scurrying around retrieving the jewels. Call Quesada again, darling, and tell him the sapphire is on the bottom of one of his clerk's shoes. Or his own. Or Mrs. Quesada's."

"I don't want to sound smug," Jeff said. "But I thought of that, too. No good."

Laurie sighed. "Well, let's have lunch. Those steaks are about done."

After luncheon, they returned to their hotel for a brief *siesta,* a pleasant habit they had acquired on this trip to South America. But on this occasion, Jeff didn't sleep. He left Laurie napping in their room and seized the opportunity to hunt up their fellow tourist, Mrs. Thompson. In the lobby of the hotel, the Sudair Tour Director told him she might possibly still be in the portrait photographer's salon on the hotel's mezzanine floor, having her picture taken dressed as a *gaucho.* Jeff found the shop, barged in, and sure enough, there was Mrs. Thompson. He struggled to keep from smiling at the spectacle of the dignified gray-haired widow posing in the flat cowboy hat and striped poncho of the *pampas.* After greeting her warmly, he quizzed her, between shots, about her experience at Quesada's shop the evening before.

Half an hour later, he woke Laurie. He reported his chat with Mrs. Thompson while Laurie listened closely. "Mrs. Thompson looked on last night's incident as a very exciting adventure," he said. "She describes Ortega as tall, handsome, suave, with a slight romantic limp, impeccably dressed, the perfect Latin gentleman of means, certainly not the type to go around pinching people's sapphires, in her opinion."

"What about the search?" Laurie asked.

"Mrs. Thompson says the search to which she was subjected by Señora Quesada, although unwillingly undertaken, was a very good thorough search, all the same."

"Good. Then it is reasonable to assume that Ortega got the same thorough treatment. Or more so."

"Right. Now, her next answer. Mrs. Thompson doesn't ever chew gum. Nor would she even carry it."

"Ortega." Laurie said. "He's our boy."

"It seems so." Jeff made a face at her, the gimlet-eyed squint of the fictional private eye. "Mrs. Thompson happened to raise her eyes from her aquamarines at one point last night, and saw Ortega slip a stick of gum into his mouth so casually as to almost seem surreptitious."

"Oho!" cried Laurie.

"You may well say 'oho!' She remembers the gum because it wrecked her initial image of Ortega as a man of breeding."

"So where are we?" Laurie summed up. "Ortega took the sapphire. He used sticky chewing gum in the process, some way, presumably to make the sapphire adhere to it. But where, and I repeat where, did he conceal the chewing gum *and* the sapphire while he was being given such a thorough stem-to-stern search?"

They sat in silence for several minutes. "I believe," Jeff said at length, "you have put your pinkie on what, for lack of a better term, we shall call the crux. And to mix a metaphor, our whole theory founders on that crux. Without an answer to your question, we're still out in left field." He sighed and stood up. "Let's go take a ride on the Buenos Aires *subterráneo*," he proposed, "before Quesada telephones to say he has found his sapphire in his hip pocket with his Diner's Club card. They tell me the B.A. subways are cleaner, faster, and less crowded than ours."

They left the hotel.

Afterward Jeff claimed it was the subway ride that should be credited with the solution of Quesada's puzzle. Laurie claimed it was just dumb luck.

Whatever it was, the light broke over them when they left the subway at the Diagonal Norte station and ascended to the surface. Emerging from the subway exit, they almost collided with a blind man tapping his way along the sidewalk. Jeff muttered "sorry" and stepped back, jostling Laurie in the process.

"Be careful," Laurie said. Then she added, "And now you're blocking traffic."

But Jeff didn't hear her. He was staring at the cause of their collision. She followed his eyes. Then she got it, too. They turned together back into the subway entrance, moved by a common impulse.

"To the Plaza San Martin," said Jeff with definite cavalry charge overtones.

"Back to Quesada's," Laurie said.

Ten minutes later, in the silverware department of Quesada's, the portly bespectacled proprietor was answering their questions.

"Mrs. Thompson says Ortega had a limp," Jeff began. "Did he?"

"Yes."

"And did he, therefore, carry a cane to help him walk?"

"But of course, Señor Landis."

Jeff and Laurie looked at each other and smiled. Laurie said, "Was it a slender cane, a thick one, what kind, do you remember?"

"Thick. A Malacca stick, very sturdy."

"How thick at the tip, would you say?"

Quesada shrugged. "Two centimeters, perhaps one and a half. I paid no attention. Furthermore, there was a rubber cap over the stick's tip, I believe."

"Better and better," Jeff said with satisfaction. "Think carefully now. When you took Señor Ortega down to the washroom to search him last night, did he take his stick with him?"

Quesada nodded.

"Very good. And when you began to search him, when he removed his clothes for your inspection, where was the stick?"

"He leaned it against the wall of the washroom."

"Ah." Laurie took over. "And you did not examine the stick itself when you were searching Ortega for the sapphire?"

"I did not. To what purpose? Can a smooth stick of solid wood hide a ten-carat sapphire?"

Jeff gave him an engaging smile. "It could," he said.

"Fasten your seatbelts!" Laurie crowed, "here we go!"

Quesada ventured, "Something about Ortega's cane?"

"His cane indeed," Jeff said. "He used it three times last night. Once to trip up your clerk who was carrying the tray of stones. Once to pick up the sapphire from the floor without even stooping over. And once to conceal the gem from your search."

"I do not follow," Quesada said. But his eyes were shining behind their glasses.

"Ortega chewed up some chewing gum," Jeff said, "after entering your shop last night. And he made his only mistake when, without thinking, he threw the crumpled wrappers away on your floor. He sat at your counter with his cane across his lap. And when your clerk went to get unset stones for his inspection, Ortega slipped the rubber cap off his cane tip, and put the freshly chewed gum from his mouth into the end of the stick, which had been carefully hollowed out beforehand to receive it."

Quesada started to say something, but Laurie anticipated his question. "Your wife, who was waiting on Ortega, couldn't see this from behind her counter. Neither would anybody who was not looking carefully at Ortega in that split second. And nobody was. When your clerk came back from the vault with the tray of stones, Ortega skillfully tripped him up with his cane. And when he stood beside his stool, while the rest of you were picking up jewels from the rug, Ortega merely placed the tip of his stick firmly over the jewel nearest his feet . . . which

happened to be your Ceylonese sapphire. He pressed
down with the stick; the chewing gum swallowed up the
sapphire, holding it fast in the hollow of the stick's end.
And then, when Ortega sat down again, when the excitement was over and you were all looking at the empty
space on the jewel tray, Ortega slipped the rubber cap
over the end of his stick again. The deed was done. The
sapphire had disappeared. And the cane stood innocently
against the washroom wall while Ortega was searched at
his own clever request. Wasn't that beautifully simple?"

Quesada listened in astonishment. At the end he jerked
his pince-nez from his nose, slapped the counter resoundingly, and turning to Laurie, clearly revealed an unsuspected knowledge of American western stories.

"*Díos!*" was what he said, quite reverently. "Landis &
Landis ride again!"

Fifteen minutes before their Sudair Tour was due to
leave the hotel for the airport, whence they would fly
across the Plata estuary to Montevideo, a tiny package
was delivered to their room as they were closing their
bags for imminent departure. Jeff ripped it open to find a
brief note and a small item wrapped in tissue paper. The
note read:

> An hour ago, the police at my request located Señor
> Ortega at the address he so brazenly left with me.
> They examined his stick. And the sapphire was still
> there, exactly as you said, stuck in a wad of chewing gum under the rubber cap. What better hiding
> place could he have found? Maria and I salute
> Landis & Landis. And we beg, on behalf of our insurance company, that your lady will graciously accept the enclosed *boleadora* charm for her bracelet
> at 100% discount from the quoted price. *Adios*.
>   Luis Quesada

P.S. No tax!

Presenting Dell's
Alfred Hitchcock series
for those who dare to read them!

- ☐ MURDERER'S ROW $1.95 (16036-7)
- ☐ DON'T LOOK A GIFT SHARK IN THE MOUTH ...$1.95 (13620-8)
- ☐ BREAKING THE SCREAM B'ARRIER $1.95 (14627-0)
- ☐ DEATH ON ARRIVAL $1.75 (11839-5)
- ☐ NOOSE REPORT $1.50 (16455-9)
- ☐ MURDERS ON THE HALF SKULL $1.50 (16093-6)
- ☐ BEHIND THE DEATH BALL $1.50 (13497-8)
- ☐ WITCHES' BREW $1.25 (19613-2)
- ☐ A HANGMAN'S DOZEN $1.25 (13428-5)
- ☐ SCREAM ALONG WITH ME $1.25 (13633-4)
- ☐ HAPPINESS IS A WARM CORPSE $1.50 (13438-2)
- ☐ KILLERS AT LARGE $1.50 (14443-4)
- ☐ MURDER GO ROUND $1.50 (15607-6)
- ☐ SLAY RIDE $1.50 (13641-5)
- ☐ THIS ONE WILL KILL YOU $1.50 (18808-3)
- ☐ 12 STORIES FOR LATE AT NIGHT $1.50 (19178-5)
- ☐ STORIES MY MOTHER NEVER TOLD ME $1.25 (18290-5)
- ☐ 13 MORE THEY WOULDN'T LET ME DO ON TV $1.50 (13640-7)
- ☐ STORIES TO BE READ WITH THE LIGHTS ON $1.50 (14949-5)
- ☐ SIXTEEN SKELETONS FROM MY CLOSET $1.25 (18011-2)
- ☐ 14 OF MY FAVORITES IN SUSPENSE $1.50 (13630-X)

At your local bookstore or use this handy coupon for ordering:

Dell | **DELL BOOKS**
P.O. BOX 1000, PINEBROOK, N.J. 07058

Please send me the books I have checked above. I am enclosing $_____
(please add 75¢ per copy to cover postage and handling). Send check or money order—no cash or C.O.D.'s. Please allow up to 8 weeks for shipment.

Mr/Mrs/Miss _____

Address _____

City _____ State/Zip _____